POPULAR PUBLICATIONS  FACSIMILE EDITIONS

Dime Detective Magazine #3 (January 1932)

Dime Detective magazine was the flagship detective pulp in the Popular Publications stable, running for almost 300 issues over twenty years. The third issue contains stories by Madeleine Sharps Buchanan, Frederick Nebel, Carroll John Daly, and Oscar Schisgall, and includes another appearance by Nebel's long-running series character, Cardigan as well as Carroll John Daly's character, Vee "Crime Machine" Brown.

Authors:

Madeleine Sharps Buchanan, Robert H. Rohde, Frederick Nebel, Carroll John Daly, Oscar Schisgall, Norman H. White, Jr.

Illustrators:

William Reusswig, Amos Sewell, John Fleming Gould

10¢ DIME DETECTIVE MAGAZINE

Every Story Complete   *Every Story New*

Vol. 1   CONTENTS for JANUARY, 1932   No. 3

Watch for the February Issue   **On the Newsstands Jan. 20th**

Published every month by Popular Publications, Inc., North Broadway, Albany, New York. Editorial and executive offices 205 East 42nd Street, New York City. Harry Steeger, President and Secretary, Harold S. Goldsmith, Vice President and Treasurer. Application for second class entry pending at the Post Office at Albany, New York, under the Act of Congress, March 3, 1879. Title registration pending at U. S. Patent Office. Copyrighted 1932 by Popular Publications, Inc. Single copy price 10c. Yearly subscriptions in U. S. A. $1.00. For advertising rates address H. D. Cushing, 67 West 44th Street, New York, N. Y. When submitting manuscripts, kindly enclose sufficient postage for their return if found unavailable. The publishers cannot accept responsibility for return of unsolicited manuscripts, although all care will be exercised in handling them.

BIG PAY JOBS
open
for the Radio Trained Man

Scores of jobs are open to the Trained Man—jobs as Designer, Inspector and Tester—as Radio Salesman and in Service and Installation work—as Operator, Mechanic or Manager of a Broadcasting station—as Wireless Operator on a Ship or Airplane—jobs with Talking Picture Theatres and Manufacturers of Sound Equipment—with Television Laboratories and Studios—fascinating jobs, offering unlimited opportunities to the Trained Man!

Ten Weeks of Shop Training
AT COYNE IN CHICAGO

COME TO COYNE IN CHICAGO AND PREPARE FOR THESE JOBS THE QUICK AND PRACTICAL WAY, NOT BY CORRESPONDENCE, BUT BY ACTUAL SHOP WORK ON ACTUAL RADIO EQUIPMENT. Some students finish the entire course in 8 weeks. The average time is only 10 weeks. But you can stay as long as you please, AT NO EXTRA COST TO YOU. No previous experience necessary.

TELEVISION *and* TALKING PICTURES

In addition to the most modern Radio equipment, we have installed in our shops a complete model Broadcasting Station, with sound-proof Studio and modern Transmitter with 1,000 watt tubes—the Jenkins Television Transmitter with dozens of home-type Television receiving sets—and a complete Talking Picture installation for both "sound on film" and "sound on disk." We have spared no expense in our effort to make your training as COMPLETE and PRACTICAL as possible.

FREE Employment Service To Students

After you have finished the course, we will do all we can to help you find the job you want. We employ three men on a full time basis whose sole job is to help our students in finding positions. And should you be a little short of funds, we'll gladly help you in finding part-time work while at school. Some of our students pay a large part of their living expenses in this way.

COYNE IS 32 YEARS OLD

Coyne has been located right here in Chicago since 1899. Coyne Training is tested—proven by hundreds of successful graduates. You can get all the facts—FREE. JUST MAIL THE COUPON FOR A FREE COPY OF OUR BIG RADIO AND TELEVISION BOOK, telling all about jobs ... salaries ... opportunities. This does not obligate you. JUST MAIL THE COUPON!

H. C. Lewis, Pres. RADIO DIVISION Founded 1899
COYNE ELECTRICAL SCHOOL
500 S. Paulina St.   Dept. 12-5E   Chicago, Ill.

H. C. LEWIS, President
Radio Division, Coyne Electrical School
500 S. Paulina St., Dept. 12-5E, Chicago, Ill.

Send me your Big Free Radio, Television and Talking Picture Book. This does not obligate me in any way.

Name ....

Address ....

City .... State ....

9

4

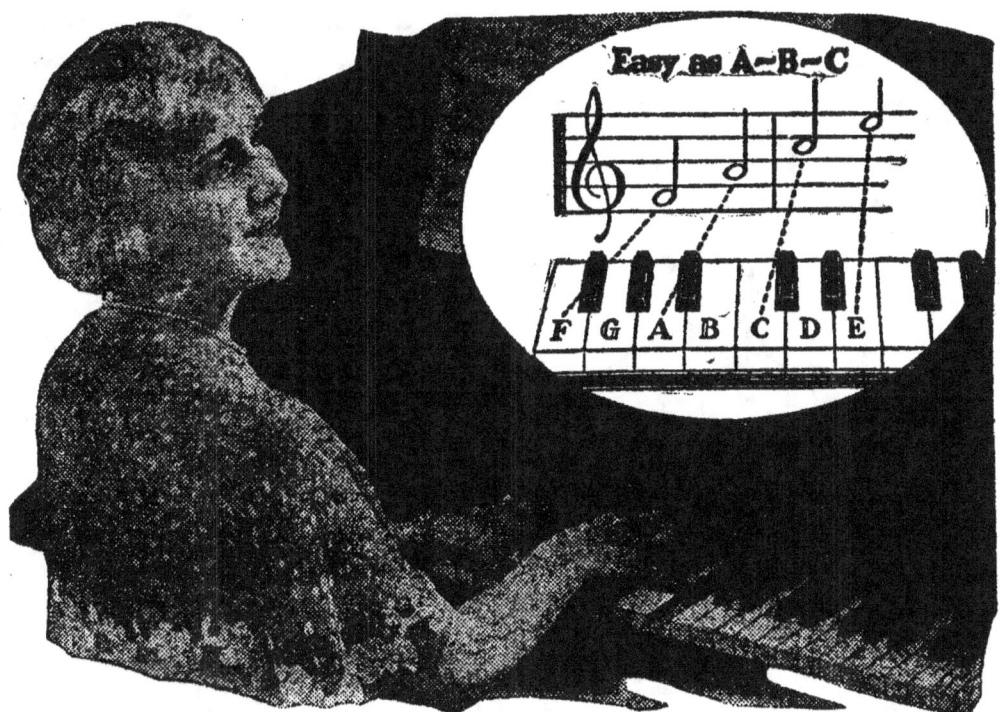

Easy as A~B~C

F G A B C D E

Too Old to Learn Music?

Hardly. Not after thousands of men and women between the ages of 30 and 50 have enrolled with the famous U. S. School of Music and have learned to play their favorite instruments without the slightest difficulty or waste of time!

WHAT has your age got to do with learning music when you now have a method at your disposal that has done away with compulsory practice—tabooed monotonous scales—that has slashed expensive fees—that makes *you* the boss instead of requiring a personal teacher?

If hundreds of children, scarcely in their "teens," learn to read notes and play a musical instrument with only our printed instructions and illustrated diagrams, think how simple it must be for older people to follow, benefit, and progress rapidly in this home-study manner.

Always Fascinating

You'll never lose patience. You *want* to study — you'll actually look forward to the "next lesson" when you study music the U. S. School way.

And no wonder. You spend a little time each day in your own home hearing your musical dreams come true. There's no personal teacher — no intricate explanations to baffle you — no trust-to-luck tactics. For right with you at all times are our concise print and picture instructions keeping you on the right

track—telling you what to play and showing you how to play it. Each new lesson contains a new thrill. For the entire course from the very beginning to the end is brimful of cheerful, tuneful selections which you eagerly learn to play *by note.*

And, regardless of which instrument you select, the cost of learning will average only a few cents a day.

Music Will Be An Unfailing Friend

The older you get, the more you need the solace and pleasure that self-made music affords. Anyone can tune in on a radio —play a record or get music out of a player piano. But what empty satisfaction compared to making music *yourself!*

The ability to play offers you a definite escape from monotony —gives you the opportunity to do something real—to meet people—to make friends. And there's nothing like good music to help you forget your troubles.

Every child, too, who can play a musical instrument enjoys an accomplishment that attracts, entertains and holds chums—that replaces bashfulness with confidence and poise—

that assures a social and profitable "standby" for their later years.

Think of the satisfaction of being able to play what and when you want. Forget your age. And bear in mind, you don't have to know one note from another to start your lessons from the U. S. School of Music.

Write Us First

Are you sincerely interested enough in music to want to find out all about this easy as A-B-C method of learning? Then send at once for our free 64-page booklet, "Music Lessons in Your Own Home" explaining this famous method in detail. With it will be sent a Free Demonstration Lesson, which proves how delightfully quick and easy—how thorough —this modern method is.

If you really want to learn to play—without a teacher—in one-half the usual time—and at one-third the usual cost—send for the Free Booklet and Free Demonstration Lesson TO-DAY. No obligation. (Instrument supplied if desired—cash or credit.) U. S. School of Music, 861 Brunswick Bldg., New York City.

Thirty-fourth Year (Established 1898)

PICK YOUR INSTRUMENT

Piano	Violin
Organ	Clarinet
Ukulele	Flute
Cornet	Saxophone
Trombone	Harp
Piccolo	Mandolin
Guitar	'Cello

Hawaiian Steel Guitar
Sight Singing
Voice and Speech Culture
Harmony and Composition
Drums and Traps
Automatic Finger Control
Banjo (Plectrum, 5-String or Tenor)
Piano Accordion
Italian and German Accordion
Juniors' Piano Course

Get a Grip of--
STEEL

Send Only 25c for My Double Strength
Krusher Grip

INCREASE the size and strength of your arm without further delay. A strong grip is the barometer of your personality. With each *KRUSHER GRIP* I will give

FREE

a beautiful illustrated booklet filled with handsome pictures. It tells you how you can possess a manly figure packed with energy and power. How to put inches on your chest, neck, arms, and legs and get a body as shapely as Sandow.

Fill in the coupon, mail it with 25c and get this *FREE BOOKLET* and my Double Strength *KRUSHER GRIP*—the finest thing you've ever seen for building up the hands, wrists and forearms.

This *KRUSHER GRIP* can give you a grip of steel. I guarantee it. Your money back if it fails.

THE JOWETT INSTITUTE OF PHYSICAL CULTURE

422 Poplar St.   Scranton, Pa.

45-Ab

Dear Mr. Jowett:

Enclosed is 25 cents for your double strength Krusher Grip, with which I am to receive your illustrated booklet FREE.

Name ....

Address ....

....Age..........

Follow This Man

Secret Service Operator No. 38 is on the Job!

FOLLOW him through all the excitement of his chase of the counterfeit gang. See how a crafty operator works. Tell-tale finger prints on the lamp stand in the murdered girl's room! The detective's cigarette case is handled by the unsuspecting gangster, and a great mystery is solved. Better than fiction. It's true, every word of it. No obligation.

FREE The Confidential Reports No. 38 Made to His Chief

And the best part of it all is this. It may open your eyes to the great future for YOU as a highly paid Finger Print Expert. More men are needed right now. This school has taken men just like you and trained them for high official positions. This is the kind of work you would like. Days full of excitement. Big salaries. Rewards. **WRITE** and I'll send the Free Reports—also a wonderful illustrated book telling of the future awaiting you as a Finger Print Expert. Literature will NOT be sent to boys under 17 years of age.

Institute of Applied Science, 1920 Sunnyside Avenue, Dept. 68-71 Chicago, Ill.

BE A RAILWAY TRAFFIC INSPECTOR

WRITE TODAY

Railways and Bus — Steady Pay Plus Expenses ACTIVE MEN — 19 to 55 — needed at once in Railway and Bus Passenger Traffic Inspection. Recent graduates earn up to $250 per month plus expenses. Many S. B. T. I. men have gone on to executive positions. Interesting, outdoor work—travel or remain near home. We'll train you for this uncrowded profession and on completion of a few weeks' home study place you in a position paying from $120 to $150 per month up (plus expenses) to start, or refund tuition. Free Booklet tells about this assured opportunity in the field of Transportation. Write today. STANDARD BUSINESS TRAINING INSTITUTE, Div. 511, Buffalo, N. Y.

He Stopped Whiskey!

Wonderful Treatment Helped Faithful Wife to Save Husband When All Else Failed

The Happy Reunion

Try it FREE

Wives, mothers, sisters, it is you that the man who drinks Whiskey, Wine or Beer to excess must depend upon to help save him from a ruined life and a drunkard's grave. Take heed from the thousands of men going to ruin daily through vile bootlegger's Whiskey, and the horrible stuff called home brew from private stills. Once he gets it in his system he finds it difficult to stop—but you can help him. What it has done for others is an example of what it should do for you. All you have to do is to send your name and address and we will send absolutely FREE, in plain wrapper, a trial package of GOLDEN TREATMENT. You will be thankful as long as you live that you did it. Address

DR. J. W. HAINES CO.

316 Glenn Building   Cincinnati, Ohio

FREE Sample SAVASOLE

Amazing "Plastic Leather" Invention Revolutionizes Shoe Repairs!

See For Yourself How It Puts On New Soles for as low as 9¢ A PAIR

Send No Money!

Brings You as high as $42. Daily Profit!

SAVASOLE
The Original Perfected "Plastic Leather"

BEFORE—Here is an old shoe worn down, ready to be sent to the shoemaker, who would charge $1.00 to $1.75.

AFTER—Here is the same shoe repaired with SAVASOLE. No hammer, nails, or pegs. All the cracks and breaks are filled in and covered up with a hard, smooth, waterproof, non-skid surface. SAVASOLE repairs shoes for one-tenth shoemaker's cost.

Sent by Return Mail Postpaid!

I am determined to put a FREE SAMPLE OF SAVASOLE in the hands of every man and woman who is ambitious to share in Savasole's success! I want you to test for yourself this amazing discovery of mine—without a penny of cost. See how Savasole builds smooth, waterproof, leatherlike new soles on any old shoes for as little as 9c a pair! You will then know why city workers, farmers, housewives, everybody snaps up this perfected product which is such a blessing in hard times—why you can make so much money. Just mail the above coupon—send no money—get your FREE SAMPLE!

Builds up Leather or Rubber Heels

What SAVASOLE Is—What It Does

Savasole is a scientific "plastic leather" invention that does away forever with costly shoe repair bills. It puts new soles on old worn out shoes. It spreads on easily with an old knife and fills in all holes, cracks and worn spots. Let it dry over night and in the morning you have a brand new sole that is smooth, thick and waterproof; that looks and wears like leather. Rebuilds run down heels, too, and is good for repairing 1001 other articles.

I'll Help You Start

I give you unlimited cooperation. You can become my District Manager and have sub-agents of your own. And besides your liberal daily cash commissions, you can share big bonuses and extra awards! Remember, SAVASOLE is never sold in stores. Folks can buy it only from you. Only Savasole can use the genuine Bollman Double-action Cement process, on which patents have been applied for. And genuine, perfected Savasole is unconditionally guaranteed. People order and re-order it for shoes, boots, harness, rubbers, cuts in auto tires—1001 uses. Beware of imitations.

Exclusive Rights!

I'll show you how to start as my representative and immediately—without experience—earn money like Miller of Ohio. Read his story opposite. He is only one of hundreds who are making real money with SAVASOLE I expect a flood of answers to this offer. Somebody in your town is going to get my FREE SAMPLE—start taking those big cash profits—"sew up" the exclusive selling rights! You can be that lucky representative if you act PROMPTLY. Clip, fill in and rush back the above coupon for your FREE SAMPLE and lifetime opportunity TODAY! Address me personally. R. R. Bollman, Pres.

$135 a Week

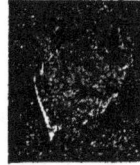

I gave up my former connection where I ranged in earnings from $315 to $386 per month. I started out with three gross of Savasole. Since that time, my earnings have netted me over $135 per week and I am sure that I will soon hit $200 per week. Savasole has solved my financial problems, and you are the whitest bunch of people to work for I ever saw. G. C. Miller.

THE PERFECT MANUFACTURING COMPANY
A-57 Daylight Bldg.   Cincinnati, Ohio

The White Diver of Death

by

Madeleine Sharps Buchanan

The body lay prone in a patch of moonlight as Donovan searched the logs.

Night after night—a corpse-white silhouette against a gibbous moon—that ghostly form dived from the rock and stroked its silent way to shore. Now, with dreadful dripping hands, it came to Mary Ford's bungalow—and murder followed in its wake!

CHAPTER ONE

Mystery Lake

THERE was the lake at last. Frank Donovan got out of his car to look at it in the hot moonlight. It was delightful looking—small and picturesque and romantic. But it was colored with crime and stained with what he believed to be murder.

As for phantoms and ghostly divers, well— He believed in no such nonsense and he'd come to Cullen's Point to convince a few people of that.

Walking a short distance along a wooded path which completely surrounded the lake, he came out upon a cleared space and stood looking across at the huge rock from which, it was said, the white form which haunted the lake dove into the water.

Frank Donovan was young and strong and of a very practical turn of mind. His lip curled as he stood looking at the rock in the breathless moonlight, but he confessed to a healthy curiosity regarding the phantom diver. He had learned that there was a reason for everything and he was sure there was a reason for that. He knew the diver existed because Helen had told him so. It was because of Helen—and poor old Jack—that he was there.

Retracing his steps, he paused beside a pile of logs to the right of which loomed a vast accumulation of enormous rocks, which graduated down to the edge of the quiet water. It was there they had found Jack Ford, two weeks ago.

Jack was the best friend he had. He was almost certain that big Jack Ford had never in all his adventurous life had heart trouble, and yet that is what they said had caused his death. Right there by that haunted lake it was sup-

posed to have caught him. He had been on his way to spend the rest of the summer at his uncle's cottage at Cullen's Point, where his sister Helen had been staying for a few weeks already.

Donovan's face grew dark as he stood there staring at the ground. It had not been heart trouble. But what had it been? He was going to find out. There was a rowboat there, drawn up on the shore. Donovan climbed in and pulled out toward the rock. He rowed clear around it but could see nothing. Obviously there was no one there. He rowed back to shore and beached the boat then thrusting his hand in his pocket to make sure that a certain paper was safe there, he turned toward his car.

He could not say afterward what made him look back over his shoulder at the rock from which the ghostly diver was said to take off now and then; but he did turn—and was just in time to see a misty white form drop into the lake; to note that the water was scarcely disturbed; to follow with startled eyes a white something that swam away from him into the velvet shadows— that swam without a sound in the breathless heat of the night! Why had he not seen it? Where could it have hidden—

A choked exclamation behind him brought him sharply about to confront a man who had approached without his knowledge. The man was dressed in golfing clothes and was a fine-looking chap of possibly thirty-five or so. Donovan did not know him.

"Heaven! Did you see it?" the stranger asked Donovan in a low tone. "I never believed that cursed yarn before."

"I saw somebody dive off that rock, yes," said Donovan coldly. "How did you happen to get here, brother?"

"I've been here every night since

Ford's death," said the other man, still staring at the placid bosom of the moonlit lake. "I don't put much credence in ghosts, you see. I've never seen the phantom until this moment."

"You knew Ford?" asked Donovan, regarding the man curiously.

"I should say so," was the quick reply. "I'm staying at his uncle's cottage up yonder."

"I am going there," said Donovan quietly. "I'm Frank Donovan. You probably know that they expect me. I was away at the time of poor Jack's death."

"Oh, Donovan? Surely. Yes. How do you do?" The other put out his hand. "My name is Leslie—Tom Leslie. I'm just a friend. Come up here every summer with the Porters. Horrible thing, Ford going out like that."

"Yes," said Donovan quietly. "Tell me about it."

"Nothing at all to tell," said Leslie, still looking across the lake. "Our man at the cottage, Ed Giles, cuts through here every morning to get milk and eggs from a farm. He found him. Doc up here, said it was heart disease. No marks of violence on him at all and no sign of robbery. Awful shock for Helen—his sister."

Donovan nodded grimly. His hand again caressed the paper in his pocket. "And where does this phantom come in?" he asked.

"Oh, that!" Leslie laughed nervously. "You see, that's about a hundred years old or more. Woman threw herself off that rock once, I believe, and drowned. Result—a haunted rock. This summer the phantom has taken real shape and several people have seen it, as you and I did just now. Since poor Ford's death I've wondered—a bit. Just curiosity. Nothing to back it up. And I've come down here every

night around midnight. By the way, you know it's after midnight now. Aren't you rather late getting in?"

"Yes," said Donovan curtly. "I got off the road. But when did the phantom come to life this summer? Before Jack died?"

"Lord, yes. It was seen several times about a month before he was found here."

"I see. And didn't it strike any of you as strange that he should get out of his car, for I believe it was found parked on the road yonder where mine is, and walk to this spot on the edge of the lake?"

"It struck me as rather strange," nodded Leslie. "But what could be wrong about it? There was no evidence of anything. And you should see the doctor and the chief of police in this neck of the woods!"

"I can fancy them," nodded Donovan in reply. "Well, let's be getting to the cottage. Did you drive?"

"No. The cottage is not far from the lake, you know, just up that hill on the other side."

"Oh, it is? Same side as the haunted rock, eh?"

"Well, yes. But the rock is quite a way around the lake, as you'll find. It's in a most desolate spot. I've examined it."

DONOVAN said no more until both men were seated in the roadster. Then he asked as he negotiated a steep little hill: "The same people still at the cottage?"

"Yes," replied Leslie. "We come every summer. Several of us went to town with Helen and the body, but we brought her back here as her uncle and aunt thought this the best place for her after such a shock. They were all pretty well broken up by it."

"Believe this, do you?" snapped

Donovan, a grim look about his mouth.

"What?" Startled, Leslie turned toward him.

"This phantom rubbish."

Leslie gave a short laugh. "I believe what I saw just now," he replied carefully. "But there is only one kind of spirit I put any faith in. Perhaps you'll join me?"

He produced a pocket flask but Donovan shook his head.

"Never touch it, thanks."

"Poor Ford did," said Leslie as he helped himself generously from the flask. "He had some on his hip when they found him and the doc said he might have been intoxicated and got out of his car and wandered about."

"Ford?" Donovan turned in contemptuous amazement. "What nonsense! He took a drink now and then but he was not a drinking man."

He lapsed into silence then until the car drew up before a picturesque log bungalow from which the lake could be seen plainly. A few warm-looking lights still burned in the living room.

"Mr. Porter and Helen are waiting for you, I know," said Leslie as he jumped from the car. "No garage here. We just leave our cars under that shed yonder. They rather rough it up here, you know."

Donovan did not reply as he drove toward the shed which loomed up at the left of the charming-looking cottage. He felt an odd chill crawling along his spine, and the sensation that hostile eyes were watching him grew as he put the car away and lifted his bag from the luggage carrier.

As Donovan reached the steps of the porch a slight white figure rose from a couch swing around the corner and ran toward him.

"Frank!" cried a sweet voice which was choked with tears. "I am so glad to see you! I've needed you! The others gave you up and went to bed, but I waited. I knew you'd come."

Donovan held her close, his face against her rose-leaf cheek.

"Helen, I must talk to you alone, immediately," he whispered. "You know how I feel about being away when all this happened. But I'm here now and I shan't leave again. Where can we go where we will not be overheard?"

"That is a difficult thing to answer," said Helen with a shiver. "I feel of late that everything I do is watched and all I say is noted. I have a little sitting room off my bedroom. We can go there."

Walking softly through the lighted living room Helen showed Donovan the room assigned to him. She waited until he placed his bag inside it, and then with a finger on her lip, she led him to her own apartments.

All the sleeping rooms led off the enormous living room and Donovan noted that each door was firmly closed. The place had a strange atmosphere which he could not deny or explain. It seemed like some dormant peril was biding its time.

Helen Ford's little sitting room was a delightful place of gay cretonnes and easy chairs. Pushing Donovan into one of these she locked the door and brought him cigarettes, matches, an ash receiver.

"Leslie is about here, somewhere," said Donovan as she came and sat on a stool at his feet, arms about her knees, charming face lifted to his. "He was down at the lake. I brought him up. Did you see him?"

"Yes. He told me you were putting the car up and went on into his room."

"What sort of chap is he?"

"Oh, nice enough. Everyone is nice. But do you feel it, Frank? Is it my nerves?"

"Feel what, darling?" He bent to kiss her again.

"The menace of this place, the horror in it." She shuddered. "I seemed to feel it gathering before that dreadful thing happened to Jack."

Donovan frowned. Then he did not imagine his strange sensations! The story of the phantom, however, might account for it.

"It is natural for you to be nervous," he said soothingly. "But snap out of it. I am here now. Tell me about Jack."

The story, as Helen told it, was exactly what he had obtained from Leslie and from her letters. But now there were a few questions he wished to ask.

"Leslie said Jack had a pocket flask on him, Helen?"

"Yes. It was half full."

"Have you got it?"

"Why, of course! I have all his things."

"Here?"

"Yes. In my trunk. They found two hundred dollars in his wallet and his watch and ring and pin were not touched. There wasn't a sign of violence on him, Frank. Oh, I can't believe it!"

Donovan gathered her tenderly into his arms. "Now, listen, Helen, you and I must keep our heads," he said quietly. "I do not for one moment believe that Jack had heart trouble. And neither do you."

HORROR leaped into the girl's eyes, a horror she had been trying to keep down. "There was nothing taken from him," she whispered.

"Wasn't there?" Donovan's voice grew suddenly stern and he took from his pocket the paper he had felt now and then to make sure it was there.

"Didn't they find anything else on Jack's body, Helen?"

"Anything else?" breathed the girl.

"Anything like—a small, black, jewel box full of unset pearls?" asked Donovan bending toward her. "Because Jack Ford had that box with him and he was bringing it to you. He was giving it to you as an engagement gift. He had collected them for years. I was the only one who knew he had them, and just before he came here to spend the summer with you he sent me this letter. It was this letter and the fact that you told me nothing about the pearls, and that the papers did not mention them, that brought me here immediately. Of course, I would have come to you anyway, Helen—you know that. But a fear that Jack Ford was murdered and murdered for this fortune in pearls which was intended for you, lent wings to my feet."

"Why—I knew nothing about any pearls, ever!" whispered Helen Ford, her lovely face a chalk white. "Are you sure he had them with him?"

"Have you looked in his safe-deposit box?"

"Yes. It was in both our names."

"And no pearls there?"

"Of course not. Just the insurance papers he carried for me."

Donovan nodded grimly. "Read this," he told her and placed a letter in her hands.

With dazed eyes Helen Ford skimmed through the letter written by the brother she loved to her future husband. Near the end Ford had written:

I am taking that black box of unset pearls from my safe-deposit box down to Helen. I want to give it to her as an engagement gift. The pearls are worth a hundred thousand. I want her to have it from me before your engagement is made public. I collected them for her. She's wise enough to keep them, or sell them and invest the money. Try to cut your vacation short and come to

Cullen's Point for a short time with us, old man. I'm looking forward to it. I never felt better in my life. Give you some good golf.

"Frank!" Helen dropped the letter and flung herself in Donovan's arms, her voice breaking in sobs. "He was murdered! Beside that awful lake! I think I've known it all along. What shall we do?"

"You see it was a clever trick not to touch his money or his jewelry," said Donovan as he held her close. "Somebody beside myself knew about those pearls, and Jack always said no one knew he had them. It shall be my job to find out who else was in on that. Have you got a small bottle, Helen?"

"Why, yes."

"Then pour some of the contents of Jack's flask into it and give it to me. I want to send it up to a friend of mine to have it analyzed."

"You think—poison?" The girl's eyes widened with alarm.

"Well, there were no marks of violence on him," said Donovan grimly. "We must at least consider the poison theory."

"I'll get the bottle at once," whispered Helen, looking pale and frightened. "Oh, I've been so afraid here! I can't say why. I think I must have known."

"Who is here now, Helen? Tell me again," requested Donovan as she moved toward her bedroom.

"My uncle and aunt, of course—the cook, Sukey, a dear old soul whom they have had for years—Ed Giles, a man of all work—Tom Leslie, Mary Trask and Halsey Burns. These same people come up here every year and I've known them for a long time."

"You like them?"

"I don't exactly know." Helen shivered slightly. "Lately I've suspected everyone, of—of I did not know what! I had no reason to think Jack

had been killed. He had no enemies."

"But he carried a fortune, the trusting young fool," muttered Donovan rising and pacing up and down the room. "Up here into this jumping-off place, through those lonely pine forests! I don't believe he even had a gun."

"But he did!" said Helen startled. "I have it. It is a thirty-two caliber revolver and it had not been discharged!"

"That looks strange, doesn't it?" asked Donovan, frowning. "Well, we shall have to be as secret about our investigation as possible, Helen. Don't let anyone know that we suspect there was anything wrong about Jack's death. Not even your aunt and uncle."

"I wouldn't trust them." Helen curled her lip. "Uncle Lou would do almost anything for money. And Aunt Bert would back him up. I've never cared for them or trusted them. Although this—" As she spoke she went close to her lover and laid her hand on his arm. "Frank," she whispered, "have you heard about the thing at the lake? The phantom diver? The swimmer?"

"Yes," he said quietly. "I saw it tonight. That is, I saw someone in white dive off that rock."

"You were down there?"

"Yes. I stopped at the spot where they found poor Jack."

"And—"

"And I saw someone, as I said." He shook her shoulders slightly. "Snap out of that trance of fear, Helen. You were always a clever well-balanced girl. Get back to yourself. You aren't believing in ghostly swimmers, are you, at a summer resort?"

"I don't know," she tried to smile. "You haven't been here long. The atmosphere hasn't gotten you as it has me. I tell you it is a horrible place, that crawls slowly up on you and envelops you in a cold sort of fear, of something—you don't know what—before you are aware of it! I can't stand it here any longer, Frank! The nights are dreadful! Take me away. If I told you about what happens in the nights—"

As she spoke the shrill scream of a woman in mortal terror tore through the peaceful hush of the bungalow.

CHAPTER TWO

The Hand At the Window

AS Donovan darted to the door Helen was at his side.

"That was Mary," she cried, "Mary Trask! Her room is just across the hall! Oh, perhaps it has gotten in at last!"

"Gotten in?" demanded Donovan as he ran across the wide living room. "What has gotten in?"

"I don't know," shuddered Helen. "Here—here is the door."

Turning the knob of the door before him, Donovan, followed by Helen, entered a dimly lighted, charmingly furnished bedroom where a girl in a lacey robe crouched in the middle of a wide bed, and stared at the window which was nearest to her.

"It tried again, Helen!" she screamed at sight of the other girl. "It almost got in this time!"

As she fell prone upon the bed in what looked like a bad case of hysterics, Donovan crossed to the screened window she had indicated. One side of the screen had been torn out and he was examining it carefully, when a pompous voice at the door drew him about.

Lucien Porter, Helen's uncle, stood there in purple pajamas and a thin bathrobe. He was a portly jovial man of fifty odd, whose shrewd little eyes alone would warn people not to trust him too far.

"What's this, what's this?" he wanted to know. "I declare, you girls had better be getting back to town! This is the third night one or the other of you has wakened us! What is it now, Mary?"

"It almost got in this time!" said Helen Ford faintly. "Just look at that screen. No wonder she screamed."

"What almost got in?" demanded Donovan.

"Oh, that you, Donovan?" Mr. Porter came forward with outstretched hand. "Sorry we didn't wait up. Gave you up tonight. What got in? We cannot tell you. Since poor Jack's death these girls have been mighty jumpy. The story about the lake phantom and Jack being found down there near it, I fancy, is responsible for these nerves. Perhaps now you have come Helen will be better. Now, Mary, tell us what frightened you."

Mary Trask lifted her head from the pillows and Donovan saw that she was a pretty woman of possibly thirty years or so, as dark as Helen was fair. Just then her face was a mask of fear.

"I was not asleep," she whispered. "I was lying here thinking. It was bright moonlight and hot. And suddenly I heard that screen tear, with a horrible ripping sound, and a dreadful hand reached into the room and felt for the handle of the window. The hand was white and—and wet. I could see it glisten. It seemed to drip water. I got the impression that it was the thing from the lake—the diver."

Helen put her arms soothingly about the girl as she sank again with a shudder into her pillows.

Donovan caught a glimpse of Mrs. Porter and Leslie crossing the living-room and stepped quickly to the French windows where the screen had been torn. Stooping to the floor he scooped into a twisted bit of paper some of the water which lay in two puddles on the waxed floor just under the window. Holding this carefully in his hand, he examined again, with a grim smile, the torn screen.

He was no detective—only a very successful young lawyer. But there were some things that—

"Merciful heaven, is that water on the floor?" cried the shrill voice of Mrs. Porter, and Donovan was aware of her kimono-clad figure at his side. "How did that get there?"

"It dripped off the hands of the thing which broke my screen," moaned Mary Trask. "I tell you I saw the water! I saw the hands, long and white and unhealthy looking! As though they'd been drowned a long, long time!"

"Mary, hush!" said Porter's voice sternly. "Your imagination is running away with you. Nothing that is drowned reaches in through screens that it has just torn out. Get your senses back, girl. Donovan, Leslie, what shall we do with these women?"

"I suggest bed," smiled Donovan as he stepped to the door. "Here, just a moment if you please, Helen."

As the girl reached his side he dropped his voice to a whisper. "Get me two bottles, Helen, instead of one, and right away," he requested. "Bring one into the living room to me. I'm not anxious for any of these people to see what I am going to put into it."

A door far down the living room opened and Helen glanced toward it. "That will be Halsey Burns," she whispered. "Goodness, everyone is up! All right, Frank. Just wait a minute. Stand behind this screen and no one will see you."

"I must talk with you, too, before you retire, Helen," said Donovan as he

obeyed her and disappeared behind a tall fire screen which stood at one side of the spacious fireplace. Logs were still smoldering there, filling the picturesque room with their pine fragrance.

Helen, however, followed him for a fleeting moment. "You discovered something in there," she breathed. "Tell me! I know you did. What was it, dear?"

"Keep your eye on the Trask woman," said Donovan curtly. "And your mind off ghostly visitants who roam at night. That screen in her room. You saw it?"

"Of course." Helen shivered. "It was torn almost completely out—"

"Yes, from the inside," said Donovan grimly. "The strands of wire all pointed outward, Helen. I've an idea the story of the ghastly white hand dripping water was manufactured by Miss Trask, and it is going to be my business to find out why."

WAITING behind the screen for Helen to return, Donovan was conscious of a feverish excitement. The first shock of finding that something criminal had been and was still going on at Cullen's Point, had worn off and he was aware of a keen eagerness to uncover the plot and get at the criminals.

The hideous aspect of that ghostly diver in the lake, at the spot where Jack Ford had strangely died, and the story of the pallid visitant to the bungalow, lent a pleasing tang to the affair in Donovan's opinion. He felt oddly interested in specters! And he had to admit that the behavior of the one he had seen drop into the untroubled waters of the lake a short time since was quite what it should have been. A very clever phantom, that! But why a phantom at all?

In the morning, he decided, he

would look up the chief of police and this doctor who had been so instant in his verdict of heart failure.

Meanwhile, Mr. Halsey Burns had emerged from his room and as he advanced down the living room, Donovan saw that he was a slight young man with smooth, shiny dark hair, high cheek bones, and a small waxed mustache. He had not the attractive appearance that Leslie had, but Donovan took small stock in attractive appearances. He had seen in his day some very handsome criminals in the dock.

To one of these people Jack Ford had confided his intention of bringing the pearls to the bungalow. And one of these people had those pearls at that moment—Helen's pearls. Donovan's face darkened.

Mr. Burns was unaware that there was anyone in the living room with him. He acted in a peculiar manner. Walking stealthily to the front door he opened it and listened intently. Closing it softly he walked in turn to each of the windows in the living room and tried their catches, while Donovan watched with growing interest.

Why did not the man go instantly to the room from which the scream had issued and ask the cause of the excitement? Possibly because he knew the cause?

Advancing to a door on the opposite side of the room Burns went inside, listened, tried the door, opened it and glanced inside the room. For a moment he hesitated, looking around the living room and paying no attention to the voices which came from Mary Trask's apartment. With a stealthy movement he slipped inside the room, and just as he did so, Helen emerged from her door and crossed to Donovan's side.

"I've brought you several little bottles," she whispered, pressing them into his pocket. "I don't know what you're up to, but I have a tremendous amount of faith in you. If you say there is no ghost, I know there isn't one."

Her faint brave smile told him how sorely her nerves had been tried since her brother's tragic death.

"Helen," whispered Donovan, his lips close to her ear, "whose door is that one that is partly ajar?"

"That?" She glanced across the room. "Why, Tom Leslie's."

"Well Burns is in there sneaking about."

Helen frowned wearily. "You'll find that's how it is," she nodded. "You don't know whom to trust and on the surface they are all so—so likeable. I've gone nearly mad."

"Well, I'm here now," grinned Donovan. "I suggest that you go over there and knock and call Leslie. I want to see how Burns behaves."

Without a word Helen crossed the living room on light feet and knocked softly on the door of Leslie's bedroom. "Ed!" she called. "Ed, I would like to speak to you."

For a tense moment there was no word, no sound from within the room and then Burns sauntered out, closing the door softly.

Donovan did not like his cock-sure manner or the smile with which he regarded Helen.

"I was looking for a book I lent Ed," he said. "Don't know where he is."

"He is probably in Mary's room," said Helen dryly. "Didn't you hear her scream? Everyone else did."

"Lord, no! What was she screaming about?" Burns looked startled.

"She can tell you," shrugged Helen. "Go and ask her. And it was only last night you told me what a light sleeper you were. Besides, that story about hunting a book in the early hours of the morning won't wash. It is completely worn out."

Burns grinned. He glanced back over his shoulder as, hands in the pockets of his dressing gown, he sauntered to the door of Mary Trask's room. "It is as good as any other that is told around here," he said. "There have been some whoppers."

Helen was after him like a flash, her tense fingers catching his thin muscular arm. "What do you mean?" she demanded.

"Do you believe in ghosts?" He still grinned amiably as he released her hand and stepped into Mary Trask's room.

Donovan, as Helen returned to his side, pondered two questions. Why had Leslie gone to the lake to investigate the ghostly diver, and why had Burns seized the moment when he knew that Mary Trask had called everyone to her room by her shrieks, to examine Leslie's room?

"I have a few things to ask you, Helen," he said when the girl had joined him. "Let us go back to your sitting room for a moment."

ONCE inside her apartment Donovan left the door open and took a seat which let him have a good view of Mary Trask's room and of the living room.

"When you ran across to that woman's room you said something about something having gotten in at last. Tell me what you meant."

"Last night," replied Helen, twisting her hands nervously together, "I was awakened by something scratching at the screen of my window. I was nervous and wakeful anyhow and it frightened me. I crept out of bed and stole to the window and peered out just in time to see a white figure vanish

around the corner of the porch. I screamed and wakened them all."

"But that isn't all," persisted Donovan gently. "Porter said tonight that this is the third time they've been wakened."

"Yes, two nights ago Mary got us up," whispered Helen. "She insisted that something tried to break in the screen of one of her windows and that she saw a tall white figure. When we looked, sure enough, the screen was torn a little. But you said just now——"

"Yes, that it was torn from the inside," said Donovan grimly. "And so it was. Whoever ripped that wire from its frame tonight, Helen, did so from inside Mary Trask's room. What do you make of that?"

"I don't know," said Helen wretchedly. "Oh, Frank, these people are old friends of mine! They are well-bred, likeable, our kind of people. You've never met them because they travel a lot and so do you. Somehow, it has just happened that way. But I know Burns and Leslie and Mary well—and so did Jack. And of course, our aunt and uncle are——"

"Just so," nodded Donovan sternly. "Did Jack know any one of them well enough to tell him, or her, he was bringing those pearls to this jumping-off place with him? That is all that interests me."

"I don't believe he would do that," said Helen slowly, her face very white. "But this was not the first summer Jack came to Cullen's Point you know."

"I know that he was up here last year for a time."

"Yes. Well, everyone liked Jack. He made lots of friends."

Donovan put his hands on the girl's shoulders and swung her about until he could look deep into her frightened eyes. "Out with it," he said softly. "Who is the person you are thinking of—outside this cottage?"

"I have no reason to think, none at all," said Helen helplessly. "But the doctor who saw Jack after his death was a good friend of his. They fished together last summer and hiked. They played golf together at the club a few miles away. Jack only met him last summer. He has a city practice and comes here during the warm months every year."

"Who is this doctor?"

"His name is Fernly, Roger Fernly, and he is a very nice fellow, Frank. I have no reason in the world to suspect him."

"He lives at Cullen's Point?"

"Yes, in the village three miles from here. Rents a summer cottage. Oh, he is very popular and successful!"

"All right," nodded Donovan gravely. "But he said instantly that Jack died of heart failure, didn't he?"

"Why—yes."

"And you say he had fished and hiked and golfed with him? And this bird is a physician? I'll call on him tomorrow."

Helen regarded her lover with tragic eyes. In them he read stark fear, but not of any certain thing. It was more than that; it was fear of herself.

"Frank, am I going mad?" she whispered. "I have the wildest thoughts that perhaps—perhaps—"

"Yes? Perhaps what?" he smiled reassuringly.

"The ghost, the thing that has tried to get in here at night, the phantom diver in the lake, killed Jack," whispered the girl.

"Now, look here, Helen," said Donovan sternly. "I have only been here a short time and yet I can see one thing that should be apparent to a girl as bright as you are."

"What is it?"

"That the idea you have is exactly what someone wants you to have. And just get it out of your head that there is any phantom diver or any ghostly visitant. There is a very neat plot and I intend to uncover it."

"It has been so dreadful until you came," sobbed Helen collapsing in her chair. "I've been so awfully afraid! You'll get the atmosphere of this place tomorrow. You haven't been here long enough."

"It's been fairly interesting, though, since I came," said Donovan. "Now, I am going to get a sample of the spring water used in this house—I believe you wrote me about the pure spring water—and a sample of the lake water, and send them with this bit I got off the floor of Miss Trask's room, to a friend of mine in the city who is very skilful at this sort of thing. And at the same time I will let him have a look at the contents of Jack's flask. If that proves all right and this water off the Mary Trask's floor is spring water, as I suspect, I must insist upon something immediately for which I will have to have your consent."

"You know you have my consent, Frank, no matter what it is."

"What I shall ask you is to permit us to have an autopsy performed upon Jack's body," said Donovan gently.

CHAPTER THREE

"Evil in the Air—"

WHEN Donovan entered his own room after he left Helen Ford he did not deceive himself for a moment regarding the very serious danger in which he stood. Until his arrival that night the criminal or criminals had had things very much their own way. His every move had, of course, been noted. Either by eyes inside the Porter cottage or by eyes outside. He was not prepared to say as yet where those eyes had been. He must not, for Helen's sake, take any unnecessary risks. He must guard his own safety as he would guard hers and yet he must expose this plot!

When Donovan thought of Jack Ford his eyes narrowed and his jaw tightened with pain. Good old trusting Jack, killed for a box of pearls! There was no doubt now in Donovan's mind that the pearls had formed the motive for the crime. They might possibly stand between the murderer and ruin of some sort, and the money they would bring was needed desperately probably. For, as Helen had said, they dealt with well-bred people, people like themselves—not bandits or racketeers.

But why the night diver? Why that white phantom on the edge of the lake and the ghostly caller at the Porter cottage? He could not see yet where that came in.

Donovan was up before anyone else was astir in the cottage the next morning, and as noiselessly as possible he got his car from under the shed and drove toward the lake.

The early morning air was fresh and invigorating and it was a glorious sunlit day. Donovan found it hard to believe that the ominous occurrences of the previous night had been real, but his face grew stern as he approached the mysterious lake, dimpling and gleaming in its girdle of rich green.

Leaving his car he stopped beside the water for a moment to fill the tiny bottle he held in his hand, corked the bottle and placed it with several others in his pocket. The rock from which the phantom diver had dropped the night before looked just like any other rock in the morning sunshine, save that it was flat and of enormous size, jutting out high above the lake on the opposite bank. Donovan felt an instant desire

to examine it closely, but decided that the first thing to do was to get the bottles off to his friend in the city.

There by that mountain lake where his friend had died, the silent menace of the Porter house was not experienced at all. He felt cheerful and capable and vastly determined to get to the bottom of the crooked game somehow and get back those pearls for the girl he loved. In the cottage he had been unspeakably depressed and conscious of a danger he could not define. Therefore, he argued, as he drove toward the village of Cullen's Point, it was in the Porter house that the horror had its root.

The chief of police, one Emanuel Spratt by name, received Donovan in his cluttered little office at police headquarters, a frame building close by the post office where Donovan had mailed those small bottles to his friend in the city.

Early as it was, the chief was immaculately dressed in a pongee suit, and his round red face had been freshly shaved.

Donovan was delighted to find a man of such evident intelligence, but decided to say nothing about the bottles which he had just mailed. The chief looked like a man who would not permit interference.

The moment Donovan told him his name and where he was stopping he became slightly aggressive.

"If you are calling about the Ford matter, Mr. Donovan," he said pompously, "there is nothing I can tell you. A plain case of heart."

Donovan regarded the chief keenly. Was it possible that the man believed that? Did he stand in with this Doctor Fernly?

"I have reason to know, chief, that my friend never had had heart trouble," he said gravely. "Ford was a strong young chap. Never sick in his life. I know he did not die of heart disease."

"How do you know that?" The chief grew faintly purple.

"Because he carried with him at the time of his death almost a hundred thousand dollars' worth of unset pearls which he had collected for his sister, and they were stolen from him!" snapped Donovan and laid the letter he had received from Ford on the desk before Spratt.

Without further words the chief read the letter carefully and Donovan watched his bushy brows draw together. "This is the only thing which makes you think Ford did not die of heart trouble?" asked Spratt as he handed back the letter.

"No, indeed. This only clinches it," replied Donovan. "I know that my friend had nothing wrong with his heart and so does this Doctor Fernly if he is any kind of a doctor. He played around with Jack all last summer."

Spratt held in his temper with evident difficulty. "Anything else, young man?" he roared.

"Yes," said Donovan boldly, "the phantom diver at the lake where you found Jack's body!"

"What!"

"Exactly," Donovan nodded. "Ghosts. Specters which roam about at night trying windows. White forms which drop into that cursed lake without a sound!"

"Young man, you are——" The chief sputtered but Donovan held up his hand.

"Just give me a moment," he interrupted. "This is a mighty serious matter, chief. Murder has been committed right under your nose and you've swallowed it. A fortune has been taken from the sister of the murdered man. Nobody knew that but myself and one other—the killer. Now, I know that we cannot afford to waste

any more time, and that we cannot afford any more to overlook the ghost of that lake out there!"

"You believe, then, in ghosts?" The chief was painfully polite.

Donovan grinned. 'I believe in this one," he nodded. "I've seen it."

"Get along and tell me."

RELIEVED to see that although the chief of police was seriously perturbed by his call and probably had been greatly upset already by the Ford affair, he was going to listen to him, Donovan swung into his story, omitting nothing, not even the torn screen in Mary Trask's room or the bottles he had just mailed. The result was all that he could have desired. Chief Spratt rose and walked nervously about the office.

"There was no sign of violence upon the body, none whatever," he muttered. "No sign of the presence of anyone else near the body. We went over the ground carefully. All the valuables were upon the body when we found him."

"There may have been poison and remember the pearls were gone," reminded Donovan. "Besides, a ghost leaves no sign of its presence."

"The gun in his pocket had not been discharged," went on the chief as though Donovan had not spoken. "And he looked like a young man capable of defending himself."

Something caught at Donovan's throat. His eyes misted. "Jack never knew that death crept up on him," he said. "Do you know what I thought as I stood last night in the spot where you found him?"

"What did you think?" The chief glared from worried eyes.

"I thought that Jack had gotten out of his car to look at the ghostly diver on the rock," said Donovan. "And it —got him."

"That ghost, young man, is about five hundred years old!" snapped Spratt impatiently, dropping heavily into his chair. "But I agree with you that we must do something about it. The pearls—I knew nothing about the pearls. Motive seemed to be lacking, and according to the people at the Porter bungalow—"

"Ah, yes, according to them!" Donovan shook his head. "Well, I'd be happy if I didn't have to spend another night in that place, chief. And it is nothing from outside that I fear."

"We've never paid any attention to that story of the spirit diver from the rock," frowned Spratt. "These things grow, I don't know how. Tourists are always delighted with that stuff. I never saw any phantom swimmer myself."

"I did," nodded Donovan. "Last night. And I give you my word it was uncanny. I never saw such an eerie performance. Jack would have been immensely interested. He wasn't afraid of the devil himself."

"This ghost story came to life a few weeks before your friend died," said the chief musingly. "Several people reported seeing the diver. Now, why should that be connected with the death of Mr. Ford?"

"That is what I am here to find out," said Donovan grimly. "And I intend to find it out before I leave. If I can't get back those pearls for Helen Ford I will send her brother's killer to the electric chair at least."

The chief looked seriously worried. "I can't get any sense out of it," he said. "Why these nightly visits to the Porter place? And the screen torn from the inside of the room—"

"Chief, is it possible for you to place someone at the lake to catch this diving ghost?" asked Donovan seriously. "It is my opinion that the case did not end with Jack's murder. For some reason it still goes on. We've got to get that phantom, somehow!"

"Why, yes, I have several good men who would enjoy nothing better," said Spratt. "I'll send Melcher out tonight. He is a great oaf of a man who shoots straight and isn't afraid of anything. I'll tell him to lie low near the rock and bring the ghost in to headquarters. If —if you are right about this affair being murder, young man, it is going to hurt me very much. I never suspected—Doctor Fernly is—"

Donovan glanced at the stout comfortable body of the chief and nodded. Spratt was only too delighted to have a mysterious murder dubbed a normal death and taken from his hands. Meaning no harm, he probably knew his own limitations.

"That is all I wish just now, chief," said Donovan as he rose. "Just that you understand the matter and will cooperate with me and that someone will be on guard by the lake every night until this ghost is caught. I may be needed at the bungalow. I don't dare stay away all night since these things have been frightening Miss Ford to death. There's evil in the air of that house somehow."

"It is quite possible," said Spratt heavily as he set a fat finger on a button on his desk, "that the criminal is doing all in his power to scare people away from the lake. Has it occurred to you that the case may be still going on because he did not get the pearls?"

"Yes," said Donovan grimly. "But it has also occurred to me that this criminal may be smart enough to want us to figure just this way. If we did, we naturally would pay little attention to the lake and the ghost would have it to himself."

"Well, I'll send Melcher tonight and there will be a man there every night until we get to the bottom of this," nodded Spratt heavily. "I can't have the lake haunted, anyway, you know. I don't see, however, what else I can do at present—"

"Nothing, chief, and thank you," grinned Donovan as he left the office leaving behind him a much perturbed and perspiring official.

DONOVAN found the little cottage which Doctor Fernly occupied during the summer, and he even penetrated to the doctor's private living room before the maid told him that Fernly had gone out to the Porter bungalow to see Mr. Porter who had had an "attack."

"An attack of what?" asked Donovan in surprise.

"I don't know, sir," replied the woman. "He often sends for the doctor. I think the heat gets too much for him. He's awful careful of himself."

So Porter who looked the picture of jovial health had attacks of some kind and Fernly was in the habit of treating him. Helen had not told him that.

Donovan walked out of the cottage with the picture in his mind of several handsomely framed photographs of lovely women which had stood and hung about the small living room. Were they the doctor's or did they belong to the person from whom he rented the cottage? If the doctor's, then a young man who had so many friends among the fair sex probably was often in need of a great deal of money. He might have asked the maid about those pictures. But he did not wish Fernly to know that he had any interest in him.

Conscious of an overwhelming desire to look at the haunted rock by sane daylight, Donovan drove to the side of the lake, left his car and climbed toward the spot where he had seen the ghostly diver in the hot moonlight.

If this man Melcher had nerve and ingenuity the mystery might be solved that very night and Helen's pearls be in her hands. That the solution lay with this uncanny swimmer in the quiet lake, Donovan felt sure.

The lovely little lake lay rippling in the warm morning sunshine. Salamanders and water snakes darted about beneath its quiet surface, and here and there in a secluded nook, waxen water lilies floated serenely.

As Donovan climbed to the rock, perspiring profusely, and stood upon it, a strange sensation swept him. He had a sense of daring, as though he had done something very bold and fearless. This was, after all, a weird spot to stand, ghost or no ghost! It was a place used for some criminal purpose and it was without a doubt in some way entangled with poor Jack Ford's death.

From the rock Donovan could see plainly the place where Jack's body had been found. The theory that he had left his car to look at the misty white form on the rock was probable. But had he? Jack had not been dragged from the car. Had anyone laid hands on him or even held him up with a gun there would have been evidence enough of the fact, Donovan felt sure, knowing Jack. He would never have submitted tamely to anything, and certainly not to death! What, then, was the doom that lurked about this delightful little mountain lake?

On the rock where he stood there was no evidence whatever of any ghostly diver. And although Donovan spent some time looking carefully about it on all sides, and for some distance from it, he found no trace of the presence of anyone beside himself. It was not difficult to understand that everyone at Cullen's Point avoided this one spot.

How to find out all he wished to know regarding the people at the Porter bungalow, Donovan could not figure, he had to admit frankly. Once the guilty party or parties became aware that he was doing his best to get at the truth of Jack's death, the game might be up.

But Mary Trask interested him especially. And Burns, with his sneaking behavior, and his cool defiance. Shut up there in the mountains with them, inside four walls, Donovan felt unbearably hampered. The very fact that he had stood that morning on the diver's rock at the edge of the lake might spell his death warrant. And yet there were certain things he must do. The chief might provide brawn, but what was needed was brain. And Spratt was not overburdened with that.

Returning to the place where Jack had been found, Donovan looked about at the thick woodland nearby, the vast pile of rocks, the accumulation of logs. Plenty of places there for an assailant to hide. But Jack had not been assailed!

He had said nothing to the chief about an autopsy. It had, however, been in Spratt's mind, he knew. And it was the last thing the chief desired.

The sound of a car approaching from the direction of the Porter house took Donovan hastily into the shadow of the trees.

A sport roadster of a violent yellow color emerged from a cloud of dust and to Donovan's surprise, stopped beside his own parked car. The driver appeared to be alone in the roadster and after a moment he got down and walked to Donovan's car while Donovan, from the shadows, watched him curiously. The young man, who was tall and stockily built, wore no hat and had rather reddish hair. That it was Doctor Fernly returning from his call on Porter, Donovan felt somehow sure, and he was anxious to see what could interest a stranger in his own machine.

Several sharp glances the young man flung toward the spot where Donovan stood concealed, as he went on with his brief inspection of Donovan's car. Having peered inside it for the second time he turned on his heel and walked briskly toward Donovan. Not seeing him, however, in the shadow of the trees, he paused near the spot where Ford's body had been found and stood looking across the lake at the diver's rock.

DONOVAN watched him as he stood there, biting his lips and rattling coins and keys in his trousers pockets. He was not a bad-looking chap, but Donovan's distrust of him grew. He looked too keen a fellow to announce that Ford had died of heart disease.

When at last the young man swung about and started back toward his car Donovan stepped out of concealment and confronted him.

"How do you do?" he said pleasantly. "You seem interested in my machine."

"Yes," said the other briefly, looking not at all startled or confused. "I wondered why anyone should park just here."

"Why not here?"

The young man shrugged. Then he lifted smiling eyes which Donovan had to admit were attractive. "Haunted," he said. "The lake is haunted. By ghosts. By spirits that swim, by phantom things which dive at midnight off yon rock."

"Rubbish!" said Donovan impatiently. "Am I right in believing that you are Doctor Fernly?"

"Right," smiled the other. "And

you're Frank Donovan, poor Ford's old pal."

Both men shook hands briefly.

"I knew you were Donovan, of course, because of your car and the fact that I found it—here. And because of Miss Ford's constant talk of you," went on Fernly gently. "She is worried about you—you've had no breakfast. She has a horror of this lake and rightly, too."

"Rightly?"

"Of course. Her brother was found —just here."

Donovan grew slightly impatient. "Yes. You found him, doctor?"

"No. Ed Giles found him."

"Then they came for you?"

"Of course. Lord, I was broken up! I knew Jack. Liked him. Hiked and swam and golfed with him."

"Yet you said he had died of heart failure?"

"Why, yes, there was no indication of anything else whatever." Fernly was frowning now, looking at Donovan with narrowed eyes. What was Donovan trying to stir up, his eyes asked.

"I gather that you are a good doctor," said Donovan. "And so you cannot believe that Jack died of heart failure."

"Of course I believe it." Fernly flushed angrily. "There was nothing else to believe. The man was not even robbed."

"No." Donovan looked across at the sunlit rock. "Of course not. Why did you say Jack might have been drunk and wandered away from his car? Jack was not a drinking man."

'I tried to figure the thing out," said Fernly impatiently. "He had a half-empty flask on his hip. He'd had a drink of the stuff. I knew that—I could smell it. How much, of course— What else was I to say?"

"I don't know," said Donovan slowly. "It's hard to tell. I'm laying my cards on the table. I know damn well Jack didn't die of heart disease."

"All right," said Fernly wearily. "Prove it. Do what you wish about it. Heard about the phantom?"

"Of course. Where does it come in?"

"It goes in, at midnight now and then, I believe. In the lake."

"What time had Jack died, could you tell?" Donovan was still staring at the rock.

"Around midnight as nearly as we could say, hours before Giles found him," said Fernly uneasily. "Look here, I am not comfortable about this, for it might have been suicide, I don't know. An autopsy is the only—"

"Perhaps," said Donovan briefly. "But when one dies by phantom hands, does an autopsy show up anything?"

"What are you talking about?" Fernly laughed shortly. "Let me assure you that I did all I could in the matter without harming or worrying Miss Ford. I had no grounds at all on which to start any proceedings."

As he turned away Donovan followed him to the brilliant yellow roadster. Gay sport car and pictures of lovely women, many of them—was that an index to the doctor's character? If so—

Had good old Jack told this chap about the pearls he had collected for his adored sister? The two had fished, hiked and swam together. Jack could grow confidential.

"What's wrong with Porter?" asked Donovan abruptly.

His foot on the step of his car, Fernly threw him a suddenly boyish grin.

"Too much food and heat and no exercise," he said. "He gets bad attacks of indigestion. Always sends for me. Nothing alarming. Likes to be pampered. He's got plenty of money and so I pamper him. I always need money."

With a nod Fernly sent his yellow car spinning down the hill and Donovan stood looking after the flurry of dust it raised.

Had that last statement been cunningly frank? About needing money? The doctor was certainly a likeable enough fellow. Jack might easily have liked him too well. He'd never, however, mentioned Fernly in any of his letters to Donovan.

CHAPTER FOUR

The Wrecked Roadster

HELEN FORD came to meet Donovan after he had run his car under the shed.

"I've been so worried about you, and uncle had another spell," she said. "Doctor Fernly was just here. Did you see him?"

"I met him, yes, down the road." Donovan smiled into her anxious eyes. "I am now going to interview Giles, if I can find him."

"But you've had no breakfast," worried Helen. "I've some waiting for you."

"Let it wait until I've seen Giles," said Donovan. "Is he about?"

"Yes, he is out by the kitchen somewhere. Frank, did you send them?"

"The bottles? Yes. And I saw the chief. He is going to place a man at the lake each night until the phantom is captured."

"I shall feel better," shuddered the girl, who looked white and worn in the morning light. "And there is something I've been thinking of ever since last night. It may not be likely that there will be poison found in

Jack's flask even if he died of poison. The stuff may be in someone else's flask, someone who met him, maybe, on the road or by the lake or even further away than that and asked him to take a drink."

"Yes, that is true," said Donovan gravely. "And who else has a flask?"

"They all have," whispered Helen looking about. "Uncle and Burns and Leslie. I think Mary Trask has one, too."

"But by now it will have been emptied and cleaned."

"Of course. It was just a thought." She looked very weary as she spoke. "And I've been thinking, too, of a few other things. If the poison is found in Jack's flask, they could say it was suicide."

"Yes."

"But it would not be, with Jack, Frank! Not Jack!"

"You bet it wouldn't and you hang fast to that," said Donovan with sudden force. "Jack was all for living. That won't stop us, darling, if we do find it."

"And if we don't?"

"I shall insist upon an autopsy anyhow. Just give us one more night beside this cursed lake."

"There is something else," said Helen, deadly pale now but vastly determined. "The evening I expected Jack everyone in this house was out for some time at different times! I've gone over and over that."

"That's important," said Donovan looking at her intently. "Tell me about that."

"Mary and Tom Leslie went for a drive in his car," said Helen slowly. "They were gone a long time. Got back about ten o'clock. Uncle drove down to Cullen's Point to a roadhouse there where he gets good beer. He came in about nine-thirty or so. And Burns was out almost all night. I don't know where he went. He has a girl, we think, at a summer hotel beyond the point. Of course, I waited in for Jack. And all the while he was— was—"

Donovan put his arm about her. "And where was Fernly?" he asked.

"I don't know. He wasn't here that day or night."

"And Giles?"

Helen looked startled. "I never thought of Giles. He had nothing to do with it. He is honest and good, Frank. Go back now and see him and I'll see to your breakfast."

"Your aunt remained with you that night?"

"She was in her room, reading. We have not much in common."

"You didn't see anything of the phantom, then?" Donovan smiled.

"Oh, no. It never—never came here until after Jack's death."

"But it was seen on the lake."

"Yes. I always laughed at it."

Donovan nodded briefly and patted her arm. "I'll be right in after I see Giles," he told her. "And then we'll go away for the day in my car and forget all this for a few hours. I heard of a great place where they serve lobster high up on a mountain top."

But as he walked around the corner of the sprawling log bungalow his face grew grave again and he seemed to realize even more fully the enormity of the task he had set himself.

Ed Giles was seated beside a creek which ran behind the house. He was whittling a stick and whistling softly. Donovan saw that he was a pleasant-faced, honest-looking man of possibly fifty-five years or so, a good type of backwoodsman.

Seating himself beside him he handed Giles a cigar.

"I'm Donovan," he said quietly, as the man looked startled. "Jack Ford's best friend. Engaged to Miss Ford. I want to hear all about it—everything. Get along to it, Giles."

FOR a moment Giles looked as though he might cut and run, then evidently thought better of it and accepted the cigar. His rugged face paled a little.

"That was sure an awful experience," he said presently. "But there ain't nothing to tell you. I go to the Butler farm for eggs and butter and milk every morning. I cut through past the lake just where Mr. Ford was layin'. I seen him. And that's all. Of course I raced back to the house here and Mr. Porter telephoned for the doctor and the doc brought the chief of police along with him."

"Tell me about it."

"He was just layin' there, and no sign of anything that could have happened to him," said Giles unhappily. "It gives me a bad turn. I knew Miss Ford had looked for her brother all night and when I seen that good-looking car of his parked in the road I knew it was him. That's all."

"Where is his car now?" asked Donovan sharply. He had forgotten Jack's car.

"In the shed behind my house yonder." Giles nodded his head toward a distant building at the edge of a wooded slope. "Miss Ford didn't want it so close to the house in among all the other cars like, and so we put it there. Ain't nothing wrong with it. Chief Spratt looked it over. The poor chap died of heart disease all right. Wasn't nothing took off him nor nothing done to him."

Donovan looked over the mountains for a moment, his lips pursed.

"You believe in ghosts, Giles?" he asked.

"Ghosts? Me?" Giles gave a great laugh. "I guess not."

"How about this phantom diver in the lake?"

"That? Some smarty trying to scare folks," sneered the man. "Working on that old yarn about the rock."

"You never saw this swimmer?"

"I never did. If I do, I'll catch him," was the caustic reply.

"Haven't you any suspicion who might try a trick like this?"

"Nope. But there's a lot of good-for-nothing boys in the town and at the point."

Donovan rose, his hand on Giles' shoulder. "All right. Thank you, Giles. Now, will you show me Mr. Ford's car?"

"Sure. Just come along this path."

Donovan followed his guide along a narrow little path which led through trees to the edge of a steep incline where a crude cabin and a cruder shed had been built.

"I live here the year round," said Giles as he passed the cabin and pushed back the door of the shed. "I like it. Born here. I been—" His mouth fell open and his startled eyes fled to Donovan's face. "Christmas! Where's Mr. Ford's car?" he gasped, for the little shed was empty of everything but a few rusty tools.

Donovan felt that he could answer almost without tracing the deep tire tracks through the dust to the edge of the steep ravine, but when he reached there, Giles was at his side.

Below them, far below, caught amid bushes and boulders, lay a twisted mass of wreckage which had once been a dark blue roadster.

Giles was sputtering at Donovan's side, his face gaunt with shock, his eyes bulging.

"That there car was safe last night when I went to bed, because I looked in on her," he told Donovan whose eyes had taken on an oddly triumphant glitter. "I can swear that, Mr. Donovan. I never so much as touched her. I went to bed at ten, or somewhere around ten, and the car was all right in that shed there. Who could —why, who would want to—"

Donovan turned and looked the man in the eyes for a moment and Giles seemed to crumple up with horror, his hand creeping up to stroke his shaking chin.

"Christmas, Mr. Donovan, you mean it was—you mean it wasn't heart trouble?" he gasped.

"It was murder," said Donovan curtly. "And right here, Giles, the murderer made a bad play."

"Murder!" Giles jaw seemed entirely out of control. "Why—why, ain't nobody breathed such a thing! How'd this here car get out of here without me knowing it? I was—"

"Nonsense," said Donovan sharply. "Easy enough to push the machine to the edge of that ravine."

"But the chief went all over the car, he did!" protested Giles, stroking his trembling chin.

"Well, I didn't," said Donovan with a short ugly laugh. "The killer fears me, Giles, and with damn good cause! I'm after him and I'll get him!"

As he spoke the thought of Doctor Fernly flashed through his mind, Doctor Fernly driving his yellow sport car madly down the hill such a short time ago! Had Porter really had an attack of illness which necessitated sending for him to tell him that Donovan, a menace to their crime, had just arrived? Plenty of men like Porter had been in desperate need of money before this and would be again.

Giles had got his chin under control and was staring at Donovan with stark terror. "Murder!" he was gasping. "Never has there been a murder at Cullen's Point. But there wasn't a mark on him nor a thing taken off him."

Donovan did not reply. He was looking down at the wreck of Jack Ford's car. "Is there any way I can get down there?" he asked, tight-lipped.

"A long way around and a mighty big risk," nodded Giles. "You'll likely break your neck. I wouldn't—"

"All right. I'm going in for a bite of breakfast, Giles, and you wait for me here," snapped Donovan. "I'm going to examine that car—what there is left of it!"

HELEN was waiting for him in the dining room, a delightful sunlit apartment off the huge living room at the rear, and as he entered it, Mary Trask crossed the living room in scarlet lounging pajamas. Donovan saw that she was very lovely, but he did not like her slanting dark eyes.

"Did I meet you last night?" she asked, smiling at Donovan radiantly.

"Hardly, but I invaded your room with the others after you screamed," he said. "I'm Frank Donovan."

"Oh, yes. Of course you know I am Mary Trask. This is a horrible place, Mr. Donovan."

"Is it? I think it very beautiful." He looked at her pleasantly as she lighted a cigarette, every move she made filled with sinuous grace.

"Lots of horrible things are beautiful," shrugged the girl and passed on to the porch where she dropped languidly into a couch swing.

"Helen, there is a woman I neither like nor trust," said Donovan as he sat down at the small breakfast table.

"I've always liked Mary," said Helen

Ford wearily. "But as I told you, of late I do not trust any of them."

"Where are the two men?"

"Off somewhere fishing."

"Together?"

Helen smiled mirthlessly. "They are not very good friends. They wouldn't be together."

"A strange house party," observed Donovan as he drank his excellent coffee.

"A dreadful one," shivered Helen. "I'm afraid for you, Frank. Promise me you will not go near that wretched lake at night."

"The lake!" A healthy grin touched Donovan's lips. "There is nothing wrong with the lake!"

"The thing is there that killed Jack," whispered Helen.

"Then it cannot be here, in this house. You talk at cross purposes."

"Yes," said the girl very low, "it is here, too. I cannot explain it. It is all connected somehow. Yet I dare not go away until I know what happened to Jack."

"Where are your aunt and uncle?" asked Donovan.

"In their room. Uncle is still in bed."

"Helen, do you know where that doctor was all the while he was up here?"

"Why, yes. He was with Uncle Lou."

"Sure? All the time?"

"Yes. Why do you ask?"

"Because someone, since last night, pushed Jack's car over the precipice behind the shed where Ed Giles stored it."

"But why would they do that?" Her eyes opened wide in horror.

"So that I could not examine it, perhaps."

"But the police examined it."

"Lord help us!" Donovan laughed unwillingly. "The police! Well, perhaps there is something, or the criminal fears there is something, which I will discover, having a few more brains and a trifle more energy than the law in this section of the country."

"Doctor Fernly did not push the car over, I feel almost sure," said Helen. "I can't be sure, for I wasn't interested in him. But I was on the porch all the while he was here and he went directly in to uncle and came out of the house through the living room. He was not here long."

"Which really doesn't prove much," sighed Donovan. "However, I think the car was disposed of in the night. That would seem the best time to get rid of it with the least danger. And now, before we start on our day together, I am going to examine it."

"But can you reach it?"

"Giles will show me how."

"But——"

"Helen, the way you can help in this is to keep an eye on these people in the house. Watch every move they make and note everything they say. And don't take any lonely walks or go away from here at all when I am not with you."

Helen was looking at him strangely and as he pushed his chair from the table she spoke in almost a whisper, looking behind her as though she expected someone to be standing there.

"I've been doing something myself while you were talking with Giles," she smiled faintly. "I've been in Burns' room. I had the chance and I took it. I am absolutely certain that his flask is gone."

"Gone!"

"Yes. I saw him on his way to the lake in his bathing suit with his bathrobe over his shoulders and I ran into his room and searched. The flask is not there now, but he had one—a beauty. I've often seen it. He wouldn't carry it to the lake in his bathrobe pocket, would he?"

"Men do strange things," smiled Donovan. "Perhaps he did."

"I'm sure he didn't," said Helen earnestly, "because he waved to Mary Trask on his way. She was lounging on the porch in her pajamas and I could not hear what she said but he said, 'All right. I'll join you in a drink when I come back.' He would have offered her one, then, if he had had his flask with him, wouldn't he?"

"If he is a good fellow, he would have," grinned Donovan. "I think it unlikely that he would carry his flask when he went for a dip in the lake. You think Burns gave Jack a poisoned drink from it on his way here that night, and that he has since disposed of the entire flask?"

"If his flask is gone, and if Jack died of poison, I think that—yes," nodded Helen firmly. "The flask is destroyed as the car is destroyed."

Donovan's face grew dark as he visioned one of his uncle's guests meeting Jack Ford on his way to the bungalow, chatting with him, offering him a drink, going on his way—the other way, leaving Jack to—— The callousness of the killer who could do that and later dog the footsteps of his victim, approach the body and rob it of the unset pearls!

"I'm afraid of another night," shivered Helen. "But I can stand it if you are here."

"Put in your time finding out if the flasks of everyone else seem to be in their usual places," said Donovan cheerfully. "We'll trap Burns with his if the others are O.K. But don't let any of them get onto what you are doing. I'll be back very soon."

CHAPTER FIVE

The Missing Flasks

THE descent to the spot where Jack Ford's wrecked car lay was more difficult than Donovan had fancied it would be. Guided by the reluctant and horrified Giles, he slipped and slid, crawled and jumped to a position where, by grasping the branches of a huge tree he could worm himself along to a flat stone, from which he managed a fairly good look at the ruins of what had been an expensive roadster.

Donovan did not expect to find out anything by examining Ford's car, but he wanted to tell the man who had pushed it over into the ravine that he was not to be stopped by a little thing like that.

Yet as he contemplated the wreckage he found himself wishing desperately that it could talk to him. That car knew the truth. What had stopped it on its glad rush to the side of the sister its driver loved? What had halted it near that cursed lake? And above all, what had caused Jack Ford to leave it?

"Can't make nothin' of that pile of junk," observed Ed Giles from his perch in the big tree.

"You never can tell," replied Donovan tersely.

But although after strenuous effort, he succeeded in landing beside the remains of the car, he knew that he could make nothing of it. It had evidently turned over and over in its fall, striking on something each time, and parts of it lay scattered all about. Donovan examined what he could of it, and paused beside what once had been the rear of the roadster. There the man who had pushed it over the edge of the precipice had stood. In so doing he had told Donovan that Jack Ford had been murdered. He must have been sure that

very soon other things would tell Donovan so, or he would not have bothered with the car. The destruction of the roadster was certainly proof that its owner had not died of heart disease.

Now Ed Giles was pointing at something, his hand shaking ever so little.

"Look at what's caught on that there tire holder, Mr. Donovan!" he said. "That was the rear of her, wasn't it? Well, sir, what is that long green trailing thing? See it? To the left of you. Be careful how you step."

Donovan saw it, and a strange icy sensation of which he felt ashamed crawled along his spine. Caught in the wrecked tire holder was a long string of green slimy grass such as one end of the lake was filled with! Donovan had seen it floating on the water only that morning as he stood on the diver's rock. Dry now, it had once been wet and clinging and rather horrible.

There was, perhaps, some excuse for Donovan seeing for an instant a picture of the phantom swimmer pushing that car off the precipice! The swimmer with dripping hands, slimy green lake grass clinging to him!

Ed Giles' matter-of-fact voice brought him back with a jerk. "Now, that's a darn queer thing to find on that there car, ain't it?" he wanted to know. "Looks like somebody is playin' up that divin' ghost down to the lake." Giles chuckled dryly as he spoke and spat into space.

Donovan felt oddly bucked up. "It sure does," he said disgustedly. "And we'll go back now, Giles. Just act wise if the subject of this car comes up and don't tell anybody what we found. See?"

He thrust a five-dollar bill into Giles' horny hand as he spoke.

"Reckon you found a lot," observed the woodsman as both men began the tortuous ascent. "Found out some-.

body is scared to death of you. I'd keep away from the lake if I was you, Mr. Donovan."

"Ghosts, Giles?" grinned Donovan as he crawled at Giles' heels.

"They's worse things than ghosts," observed the other grimly and said no more.

Helen had been unable to find out anything about the flasks of the other members of the household, and for the few hours which she spent with Donovan in his car as they drove over the mountain to the lobster inn he had spoken of, they said no more about Jack or the strange occurrences at the Porter bungalow. As they drove up to the house at twilight, however, Helen glanced about with a long deep breath.

"I dread coming back," she whispered. "I have the feeling that something is waiting here, ready to pounce!"

"Or run," grinned Donovan. "I'll have it on the run before long."

Mary Trask, Mrs. Porter, Leslie and Burns were all lounging about the porch as Donovan and Helen ascended the broad log steps. Their greetings were cheery and natural with an edge of good-natured teasing to which Donovan replied as best he could.

Porter came to the door of the living room and stood looking out on the porch.

"That you, Donovan?" he called. "You're wanted on the phone. Cullen's Point calling you."

With a faint shock of surprise Donovan walked to the telephone which stood on a desk table at the other end of the room.

THE voice of Chief Spratt spoke to him. "Mr. Donovan? This is Spratt. Didn't tell your folks up there I was police calling. Remember I told you I had a good man, Melcher, I was going to plant at the lake tonight?"

"Why, yes," replied Donovan.

"Well, he's got a lot of curiosity, has Melcher," chuckled the chief. "He got a notion of crime in his head and he went out there this afternoon and snooped around a bit, mostly near the place where we found your friend. He accumulated the notion that Ford had done some moving around before he dropped dead where we found him. Says he moved over toward the pile of rocks and then toward the logs, but Melcher aims to be a great detective and he's had no experience. We can't take his word for all that. Fact that we've had no rain since Ford died helps a bit in his favor, but I'm not taking that seriously. I'm just giving you the dope. One thing we do know is that Ford wasn't wearing anything that was red silk when we found him."

"Red silk?" asked Donovan, puzzled, but tensely interested.

"Yes. Melcher found two bits of red silk caught in that great pile of rocks near where we found Ford," ran on the slow voice of the chief. "He says somebody besides himself has the notion Ford moved around a bit before he died. Anybody up to your house wearing red silk? I'm just giving you a tip."

Donovan saw in his mind's eye Mary Trask's scarlet silk lounging pajamas, but he knew that the girl would hardly crawl over that great mass of rocks in such a garb. And anyhow, he was seeing something else. Halsey Burns stealing out of his room the night before while he himself waited for Helen behind the fire screen. Halsey Burns had worn a red silk bathrobe over his pajamas. And he was accustomed to wearing his bathrobe to the lake to bathe, according to Helen!

Another thing, too, popped into Donovan's mind in the flash of a second. Could Jack have known possibly that death was upon him and might he not have hidden those pearls in the few moments he had had before utter collapse? The criminal, finding him, not finding the pearls, had possibly searched and searched—was still searching! The phantom diver frightening people from the vicinity of the lake?

"By golly!" exploded Donovan into the telephone.

"What?" barked the chief. "You still there?"

"I'll say I am!" exulted Donovan, lowering his voice and keeping an eye on the people on the porch who seemed not at all interested in his telephone conversation. "And chief, I've got a line on that right now. Also, I wish to report a wreck. Ford's car was pushed off a precipice near the shed where it was stored, last night or this morning. It's a total ruin."

"I guess you're in for it now," came back the chief's reply after a moment. "We've got to act fast, Mr. Donovan. I've got a lot to make up for. Hope you'll give me credit for being onto the fact that it might be murder for some time, and conducting a quiet investigation."

"Oh, sure," chuckled Donovan, fired with the hope that Helen's pearls might yet be safe and that the mystery was close to solution.

"It's my opinion the pearls are hid somewhere about the lake," went on Spratt heavily. "And if we get this phantom we'll know plenty. Melcher is one of my best men. He'll get him. He's got the character of a bull dog. Just keep an eye on 'Red Silk.' "

"I will, thanks," promised Donovan and hung up.

Leslie curious about the lake phantom, hanging about the lake. Burns searching his room for fear he might have come across the pearls. Burns' flask destroyed along with Ford's car.

With that flask Burns had met Ford far down the road in his car—that wrecked car. Jack had taken a drink from Burns' poisoned flask.

All this flashed through Donovan's mind as he rose from the telephone, his lips grim and his eyes strangely bright.

He hoped Melcher was a good shot. And he knew that he could not keep away from that lake all night! It wasn't going to be humanly possible. But Helen wouldn't have to know.

Even on the way across the living room to the door of the porch, however, the exultation, the sense of triumph, left Donovan. As he approached the chatting group of well-bred folk on the porch it faded away and an indefinable oppression took its place. It was a horrible, heavy feeling of evil, of imminent danger.

He was dressing for dinner when someone knocked softly on his door.

"It's Helen," said a faint voice as he crossed the room. "May I come in?"

AS the girl stepped into the apartment and closed the door behind her, Donovan saw that her eyes were very bright and that her cheeks had a feverish color.

"Frank, we're on the right track, I know," she whispered. "It is not only Burns' flask which has disappeared, but Jack's has been taken also! It isn't in my room anywhere."

"Are you sure of that?" With a sensation of triumph Donovan thought of the little bottles he had sent to his friend in the city.

"Certain. I've looked everywhere. After you took that sample from the flask I didn't lock my trunk. Just put the flask under a lot of things in the bottom of it. But it's gone."

"You all leave your doors unlocked, of course."

"Oh, yes. No one thinks of locking anything up here."

"Well, it seems more dangerous than gangland's happy hunting grounds to me," said Donovan grimly. "However, I think I beat the guilty party to that trick. We should have a report on those bottles tomorrow. Morris works fast when I ask him to. And then I'll take up this matter of an autopsy with the chief."

"And in the meantime the beast who killed my brother is here with us!" shuddered the girl.

"Perhaps," said Donovan musingly. "And at any rate, that is the best place for him to be! Or her—I am not saying which sex is to blame for the killing of poor Jack. Pearls in one way seem to indicate a woman. A luxurious lovely woman like Mary Trask."

"You're thinking of that window screen," said Helen.

"Rather," admitted Donovan laconically.

Halsey Burns electrified them at dinner by announcing in no pleasant accents that his silver flask had been stolen from his room.

"It was an antique," he said, glaring about the candle-lighted table. "If you took it, Leslie, as a smart trick, I wish you'd hand it back at once. I paid an enormous sum for it years ago."

Donovan did not look at Helen during the discussion which followed the announcement. He proceeded with his excellent fish, but his mind was working rapidly. Was this thing straight that Burns had just said? Certainly the man looked sincere enough. He was hopping mad if one judged from his appearance. On the other hand, was it a bit of clever acting on his part? The public admission of the loss of something he had himself destroyed, and which he knew Helen Ford had discovered was missing? It was a very clever criminal.

of course, who had done away with Jack Ford. Donovan must expect him to continue to be clever. For a sickening moment he felt unable to cope with the case.

Porter was roaring with anger, sipping the broth which was all Doctor Fernly had permitted him to have that day.

"What has come over this place?" he was demanding. "It has always been the most restful spot in the world. Honest and peaceful and quiet. Now here we have ghosts that haunt the lake, ghosts that try to break into my windows at night and whiskey flasks that are stolen from guests' rooms! Are you accusing one of us, Halsey of being a thief?"

Mrs. Porter's cold eyes rested upon her husband disapprovingly. "Lou, you'll be sick again," she warned.

"I'm doing nothing but stating a fact," said Burns. "I liked that flask a lot, was damn fond of it. And it's gone."

"I don't get it, though, why you accuse me of taking it," said Leslie disgustedly. "I've got one of my own."

"Are you sure about it?" sneered Burns.

For a moment both men stared into each other's eyes and Donovan could almost fancy he heard steel clash. They most emphatically did not like each other.

And Donovan was thinking of something else. If Burns were guilty, and had taken Jack's flask from Helen's trunk, would he do anything that would cause the girl to look for it and find it missing?

"Sure I'm sure," grinned Leslie and produced a handsome little pocket flask. "It travels with me all the time. We're never separated."

And why, Donovan was asking himself while they talked, would Jack's flask be taken at all? Why, unless to put the poison in it which had not been in it when the police took it from Ford's body? That must be it. Suicide. A deadly dose of something in the contents of the dead man's flask. Yes, but he had a sample of those contents, or rather Morris had, and Morris was clever as the devil at work like that. He had been one step ahead of the killer. And then, too, there was the damning wreck of the roadster in which Ford had been riding.

"Donovan isn't saying much," said Leslie with a glance across the table. "He thinks there are some mighty queer things doing up here. I found him down by the lake all alone last night. I think he feels that there was something not quite so simple about poor Jack's death."

"What!" Porter swung about and stared at Donovan, his face turning red with anger. "Are you trying to stir up trouble, Donovan?"

"How?" asked Donovan gravely.

"Darned if I know," growled Porter. "But I've felt that somebody was. Since Jack's death this bungalow has had an air about it not conducive to rest and peace. Out with it, Donovan. Do you believe Jack died of heart trouble? Or are you concocting some mystery with it?"

"I am not concocting any mystery," said Donovan pleasantly as he glanced about the table. "But I do not believe he died of heart disease and if your doctor knew anything he would never have signed a certificate of death from that cause. Jack never had heart trouble and he was one of the fittest chaps I ever knew."

A COOL breeze had come with the evening and now it whipped saucily about the bungalow in the brief silence which followed Donovan's dar-

ing speech. Awnings flapped and papers rustled and somewhere a screen banged. A white moon peered curiously in at the wide plate-glass windows which gave glorious view of mountain and lake.

Helen Ford, white-lipped, stared across the table at her fiancé.

"That's a pretty serious thing to say, young man," said Porter. Then, his trembling hand setting down his cup of broth with a little crash, "Got any proofs of it?"

"Oh, none whatever," shrugged Donovan. "That is just my own private opinion."

The relief around that dainty table could almost be felt.

"Well, let it alone, then," advised Porter heavily. "Helen and Mrs. Porter and I are satisfied, and so is Fernly and so are the police. That ought to be enough. Nobody on this earth would wish to harm Jack Ford. Everybody liked him. These things happen. The boy wasn't even robbed."

Donovan said no more and presently the women spoke of something else and the meal came to a close.

But while Donovan stood on the porch smoking, a few minutes later, his eyes fixed on the vast moonlight distances, Leslie joined him.

"Just what do you think was the motive for Ford's murder?" he asked quietly.

Donovan actually jumped, turning to stare at the young man's pleasant inquiring face. "You think, then, that it was murder?" he asked.

"Why , yes," shrugged Leslie. "I have from the start. That's why you saw me at the lake last night. The whole thing has me going. Can't get head or tail of it. I haven't a leg to stand on but I—well, I don't like the idea of finding Ford dead like that so close to the place where this ghostly diver is seen. I'm modern enough but it gives me the creeps."

"I'm interested in the ghostly swimmer myself," said Donovan dryly.

"And there is something else," went on Leslie steadily. "Jack's car was stored away in a little shed not far from Giles' cabin. It's been pushed over into the ravine. I saw it myself today. That looks devilish queer, doesn't it? As though someone might be afraid of you or of—evidence. And what does this flask business mean?"

For a space Donovan did not reply. The muscles around his jaw tensed. Here was Burns informing them all of the missing flask and now Leslie telling him of the wrecked car! Somebody was taking him for a fool! One of them would come to him with the evidence of that screen in the Trask woman's room, next!

He did not like this. It savored of the methods of a cat with a mouse and it was distinctly colored with a sort of amused fearlessness. If good old Jack had hidden those pearls—

"Yes, I saw the car," nodded Donovan. "I climbed down and looked at it. It told me quite as much as though it had remained in the shed."

"Then you have started definitely to make investigations?" asked Burns' voice out of the shadows behind the men. "Are you moving for an autopsy, Mr. Donovan?"

"Oh, yes," said Donovan quietly. "Of course. Helen has consented to that."

As he spoke he felt a mad desire to drag his opponent into the open, to declare war, to force him to move. This blind sparring was a thing Donovan felt he could not endure another day, cooped up with these people.

It was possible, however, that Fernly was the man after all. That both these chaps were innocent. But what about the Trask woman? And the white phantom? He could not see either Leslie or Burns playing the part of the lake ghost.

The women came out to the porch at this moment and there was no opportunity to say anything more on the subject.

CHAPTER SIX

Pearls—And a Body

AT eleven-thirty Donovan left Helen Ford at her door, with strict instructions not to open it to anyone and to bar her windows.

"If anything ghostly comes snooping along let it tear the screen if it likes," he grinned. "But you keep your windows closed. A little patience and nerve, Helen, and this affair will be in our hands—the pearls, too."

Helen clung to him, her eyes wide and fearful. "Stay away from that lake, Frank!" she begged. "Don't go there tonight! Let that policeman watch it. If anything happened to you—"

"Nothing will," he promised. "You go in there and get some sleep. No matter what goes on in this cursed house, stay in there. I want to feel that you are safe tonight."

He lingered until he heard her bolt the door and then sought his own room.

Everyone had retired. There was little else to do in that neck of the woods unless one motored to Cullen's Point or to some roadhouse in the mountains. Donovan wondered why people wanted to spend a summer in such a place. Of course, if he could have fished and hiked and golfed with Jack, it would have been worth while. At thought of Jack his throat tightened and he made sure his automatic was in his pocket.

It was tedious business waiting until he could feel sure that he could leave the bungalow without anyone seeing him. He managed it, however, sitting by his window listening for any suspicious sound. He watched the pallid moonlight and wished heartily that the ghostly visitant would call while he was on guard. Finally when everything seemed quiet he stole out of the house.

He did not chance taking his car but took the short cut to the lake—the one Helen had told him Giles used every morning.

The whole world seemed to be sleeping and only the gurgle of a little stream somewhere disturbed the utter quiet. Strive as he might it seemed as though Donovan could not make his going soundless, but at last he reached the lake and stood upon the place where Ford's body had been found.

Of the policeman on guard there was no sign and Donovan had no way of knowing where he was. He was conscious, however, of eyes upon him but set it down to Melcher's observant gaze or a trick of his imagination.

For the moment he was Jack Ford, staggering from his car possibly, in an illness he knew to be his last. Ford, eager only to hide the pearls, aware that he had been poisoned, using his last few precious moments to best his murderer. If he had been Ford, where would he have hidden those pearls?

To the right of the spot where the body had lain the vast accumulation of rocks led down to the water's edge, and to the left, a short distance away was the pile of logs. Had Jack had time to hide those pearls? And if he had, had their hiding place been discovered already by the murderer?

Using his flashlight carefully, Donovan began an exhaustive examination of the rocks where Melcher had found the bits of red silk. Into the crevices

he sent the ray of light, shielding it as best he could with his hat, and listening carefully for any sound which might indicate that he was not alone.

The silence of the night pressed about him. An occasional twig snapped under the feet of some passing wild creature, but nothing occurred to disturb Donovan in his wearing search for something which might not be there. The thought, however, that he was doing as Ford would wish him to do, bucked him immensely as he went on. If Jack had hidden the pearls it had been in the expectation that Donovan would guess as much and hunt for them.

It was during one of the moments when he stood erect, stretched his arms and drew a long breath, that he saw the flash of white across the lake and heard the faint splash that told him the phantom had slipped into the water. Too far for his flash to illumine it, something was swimming, and swimming almost noiselessly. The effect was horrible. No wonder people called this expert midnight swimmer a ghost! It was about as clever a performance as one could witness.

The swimmer had gone away from Donovan. The thought of Melcher on guard soothed him and he turned again to his search. He might never get another chance such as this. And anyhow, it was best to use every moment. If the diver went on up to the bungalow, Helen was safely locked in. His best bet was to keep on looking.

If he had been Ford, and had hoped desperately in his last living moments that his friend Donovan, who was going to marry his sister, would guess that he had hidden the pearls he was taking to her, where would he hide them? In a mass of rocks where they might never be recovered? And then as he stood there, Donovan remembered. Remembered a trick of Ford's when, as lads together, they stole away from school and party to fish! Jack had kept his fishing tackle and his can for worms in a hollow log by the water. A hollow log!

A silent moment Donovan stood there, feeling as though his friend had spoken to him, beside that haunted lake. And then, "All right, Jack, old son," he muttered, and turned to the pile of logs near which the body had lain.

He never knew afterward how long he searched before he found the hollow log, and reaching in his arm with a slight shudder, touched a thing like a box!

And then, as he slowly drew it out, Donovan kept his gun in his other hand and a sharp look about him.

THE thing to do was to act fast. He was in deadly danger and he knew it. At any moment he might be killed. For he felt certain that what he held was the box of pearls. He dared not look into the box after he found it, but keeping his eyes busy about him, he unclasped the lid and thrust in his fingers. Under wads of cotton they touched cool smooth globes, many of them. The precious pearls!

Still watching and listening and pretending to keep up his search, Donovan rolled the gems in the cotton and thrust it into his pocket, replacing the box in the hollow log. It was possibly better not to remove the box, he thought. It might serve as bait if luck were with him.

Jack Ford must have had quite a bit of strength when he stopped his car and reached that pile of logs. His brain was working clearly, so clearly that he knew he could drive the car no further, that death was upon him, that he had been poisoned and that he must hide Helen's pearls from his killer! It had taken him some desperate moments to find that hollow log. It must have. Poor old Jack. But he had trusted Donovan. He had thought Donovan would remember.

Donovan's eyes were wet as he stole from the place where Ford had been found and started toward the bungalow. He dared not look for Melcher. The thing to do now was to get those gems to the bungalow and hide them in some fashion, so that he would know they were safe until this killer was behind bars.

The problem of the phantom diver faded away as he moved noiselessly around the side of the lake toward the Porter place. His nerves were throbbing with triumph, and the sense of awe which had overwhelmed him by the logs when he remembered the old fishing habits of his dead pal, was still upon him. So that, when he came unexpectedly upon the body of Melcher prone in a patch of moonlight near the water of that accursed lake, he was on the edge of screaming like a frightened woman.

That it was Melcher he knew by the uniform, and the badge, and the size of the man. An "oaf" the chief had called him. And now Melcher lay as Jack had lain.

After the first palsied moment, Donovan acted. Stooping over the man he made sure that he was dead, that he had not been dead very long. And there was no sign of violence upon him! He had evidently not been aware of his approaching doom, for his automatic, fully loaded, reposed in his belt. He had been lying there, dead, staring at the moon, while Donovan, across the lake, searched the rocks and the pile of logs. Dead when that white form slipped into the water and moved soundlessly toward the place where his body lay!

"Heaven!" muttered Donovan in shuddering horror.

Knowing well that he dared not linger there, where death stalked silently and struck without a trace, Donovan yet gave a quick glance about before he hurried on his way. And the brazen moon showed him something that glittered not far from the body. Picking it up Donovan saw that it was a thermos bottle, and that beside it lay a paper napkin with the half of a sandwich upon it.

Sick with horror Donovan thrust the thermos in the pocket that did not hold the pearls and with a hasty glance about gun in hand, resumed his journey up the hill to the Porter bungalow.

The thing to do was to get his car and drive to Cullen's Point to the police headquarters. Not only must he report this crime at once, but he must put those pearls in a place of safety. He could not risk going about with them on his person. Prying eyes might have seen him take them from the log. And he might not be able to withstand the doom that loitered on the shores of that pretty but sinister mountain lake.

The bungalow was wrapped in darkness when Donovan reached it. He moved as silently as possible to the shed where his roadster stood. Backing it out with as little noise as he could manage, he turned the car toward the town, thinking with an unpleasant chill that he was walking in Jack Ford's footsteps, driving alone past that cursed lake with Helen's pearls in his pocket!

No one attempted to stop him, however, and apparently his movements did not rouse the sleeping occupants of the bungalow. He dared not stop to wonder if all were right in that strange household and, as he neared the lake, Donovan stepped on the gas.

It was a lonely way to Cullen's Point, beautiful by day, but desolate at night and especially when one rode with such thoughts as were Donovan's just then.

However, nothing happened. And the fact that nothing did, drew little furrows of anxiety in his forehead as he drove through the quiet streets of the little town, and stopped before the door of the unimposing frame building that housed police headquarters.

A single lamp burned dimly in the office and Donovan surprised a sleeping sergeant with his feet on the desk.

"I must see the chief at once," announced Donovan. "Where is he?"

The sergeant, whose name was Mulligan, set his feet on the floor and blinked at the caller.

"Why, he—he's in bed, I guess," he stammered. "What's wrong?"

"Plenty," snapped Donovan. "Your man, Melcher, has been killed out beside that lake. He's dead, anyhow. I just saw his body. And I've got to see Spratt at once."

"Melcher!" The color left Mulligan's face. "Are you sober?"

"Certainly I'm sober!" Donovan flushed angrily. "Tell me where I can find the chief."

As the sergeant lifted a telephone receiver and held it to his ear he was still dazed with Donovan's news. "Why, Melcher was a crack shot and afraid of nothing!" he was saying. "Everybody liked Melcher. Who would—"

Donovan walked about the grimy little office while Sergeant Mulligan got the chief of police on the wire and gave him Donovan's message.

"He'll be right down," he told Donovan, turning from the telephone. "Gosh, that breaks me all up! Melcher! Why, we ain't never had a killing here before! This here is a peaceful community."

DONOVAN said no more until Spratt entered, looking as though he had flung his clothes upon his large indolent body, his face quivering with agitation.

"What is this you tell me, Mr. Donovan?" he cried. "Poor Melcher dead? The man was in perfect health, perfect. What—"

"So was Jack Ford," reminded Donovan dryly, and took the pearls in their cotton bed from his pocket. "I have here, chief, positive proof that my friend was killed and possibly just as your officer was killed. These are the pearls Jack was bringing to his sister. I found them in a hollow log near where his body lay. I brought them here to place in your safe, if it is a secure one."

Spratt seemed momentarily deprived of the use of his limbs. Dropping into a nearby chair he stared at Donovan with sagging jaw. "Good Lord— good Lord!" he muttered. "We've got plenty to do now, haven't we?"

"Is there a safe?" asked Donovan patiently and Spratt roused himself a bit.

"Mulligan, take Mr. Donovan back to our safe," he nodded. "Let him put his valuables in it. Sure, it is a good safe. One of the best. Nobody but myself knows the combination. The man I leave here at night never knows it. I'll write it down for you so you can open it."

Handing Donovan a slip of paper the chief turned to the telephone and, as Donovan followed the sergeant into a rear room which was windowless and almost filled with the bulk of an enormous safe, he heard Spratt asking for Doctor Lee.

"Lee will be here soon," the chief told Donovan when the latter joined him a moment later. "He's coroner, you know. I won't disturb Fernly—this time. Mulligan, you send a couple of men out after us with Doc Lee."

"We can use my roadster," said Donovan as Spratt hurried from the of-fice. "No need to rush, anyhow. You will find exactly the same conditions prevailing in this case that you found in the Ford case. I've got his thermos in my pocket and I want to send a sample of its contents up to my friend in the city if you don't object."

"What can this round of mysteries mean, Mr. Donovan?" asked the wretched chief. "Poor Melcher—"

"It means the fortune I left in your safe," said Donovan grimly. "A great many men would do a lot for a hundred thousand dollars. It would save a number of them from disgrace, even from jail. A desperate man, to whom pearls meant safety, honor, happiness or health, killed and tried to rob Ford. The motive was exceedingly desperate. It must have been. There was nowhere else for this man or woman to get the money. I say woman, too, because poison seems a woman's weapon and pearls a woman's lure."

Beside the narrow mountain road the trees pressed close, and the thick pine dust made their progress soundless. Spratt's hand held a gun in his lap, while beside him, at his right thigh, lay Donovan's, ready for use.

The chief was silent for a moment and then he turned to Donovan quietly. "You've got this case pretty well tied up, Mr. Donovan," he asked.

"Pretty well. I'm fairly sure that the guilty man or woman, or both, will be found in the Porter bungalow."

"Could you force a finish to the affair tonight?"

Donovan hesitated, but his pulses began to pound with eagerness. The night was still young. It was some hours before dawn. Why permit another night of horror to creep upon them with this hideous mystery unsolved? And into his mind flashed the thought of Jack Ford's little black box which he had thrust back into the hollow log.

"Perhaps," he said. "If I could get my friend in the city on long distance. I want his verdict regarding the bottles I sent him. He has had time, and if I know him well, he will work all night on them. He liked Ford."

"But to do it quietly——" Spratt frowned while the car dipped into a damp little valley and crossed a wooden bridge.

"I shan't do it quietly," said Donovan. "If you want this affair cleaned up before your failure with Ford hurts you, chief, which is, I figure, your object, we must work apparently in the open. Now that the pearls are safe, I'll take a risk and pretend to find them in that box in the log. I'll carry the box on my person. And if you'll play along with me I'll force our criminal to show his hand before morning."

"Good," nodded Spratt. "And if you succeed, I don't want all the glory. Just give me credit for ordinary brains, which I admit I didn't seem to have with the Ford case."

"Get Fernly up to the bungalow," said Donovan as they drew near the lake. "I haven't eliminated him. Tell him to come and look at Melcher."

At the spot where Ford's car had once been parked Donovan stopped the roadster and slipped out.

"You drive on around, chief," he whispered. "I've told you just where Melcher lies. I am going to pretend to continue the search for the pearls. When I find them, then I'll join you."

Spratt nodded, slid into the driver's seat, fumbled a moment with gears, and drove silently away over the narrow road toward Melcher's body.

And Donovan, left alone, began what might have been taken for a hurried and furtive search of the rocks and the logs. There was a chance that when he really found the pearls, dangerous eyes had

watched him, and that no one saw him now, but he went through with the little farce, finding the box at last and stowing it carefully in his pocket. Either his first search had not been witnessed and the little box had been left undiscovered, or else the box had been examined, found empty and put back in the log.

Hoping that the efforts he had made to have those small bottles reach Morris in the city in as few hours as possible had been successful, and that his friend had obeyed his note and gotten at the work at once, Donovan hurried along the road in the direction in which Spratt had driven his roadster.

CHAPTER SEVEN

The Trail of The Phantom

FIFTEEN minutes later, Donovan, having come to a complete understanding with the chief and leaving him with the coroner and two of his men beside poor Melcher's body, made his way on foot, as silently as possible, toward the Porter bungalow.

It was his intention to use the telephone to call long distance, the telephone in the living room which, no matter how softly he spoke, was close enough to any of the bedrooms to be heard by anyone who was wakeful.

The moon had gone behind a cloud when he came out on the top of a hill and drew nearer to the bungalow, and a sighing wind moved the leaves of the trees together.

Unnerved as he was, and keyed to a high pitch, Donovan knew it was not his imagination when, in the shadowy bushes to the left of the house, he saw a flutter of white. It would be luck he had not hoped for if he caught this elusive phantom after poor Melcher's tragic failure!

Slipping behind a nearby tree he made for the place where the fluttering thing had stood. And there ahead of him, in the darkness of closely bunched trees, he caught another glimpse of it.

Running now, as silently as possible, dodging around and behind bushes and trees, but keeping that pale form in sight, Donovan felt a sort of savage joy. Whatever the part this ghostly creature played in poor Ford's death, he would know it now!

And then, suddenly, he realized that a miracle had happened! The fluttering white thing he followed had doubled on its tracks and was making back toward the bungalow! Now, why would that be unless only at the bungalow was shelter and security for the phantom? That, at any rate, was what Donovan believed and he redoubled his efforts to cut off the specter's escape.

Rounding a tree suddenly he came into close contact with the thing, and for an awful instant knew the terror of the touch of it, firm, and white and wet—wet, so that his hands slid off it. He was conscious of it only for a second—faceless, pallid, swathed in something he could make nothing of, drowned eyes staring at him blackly from the place where a face should be. And then, holding fast to his horrified senses, Donovan dashed forward, his hands clutching and slipping on the white slimy surface of the creature, when—bang! He crashed head on into the trunk of a tree and for a short space staggered dazedly. It was long enough. Brushing his hands over his eyes and looking about, his head ringing, he saw that there was no longer a flutter of white. He had that section of the forest which hemmed in the haunted Porter bungalow, to himself.

"Damn!" muttered Donovan as he plunged toward the house. "What the devil was it?"

And yet he knew. Knew what it had been, even with the sickening terror of it still rocking his nerves, and with jaw set grimly he kept on to the porch of the bungalow.

There Doctor Fernly met him. "Heavens, I thought you were some wild creature coming out of the forest!" said the doctor with obvious relief. "You gave me a start. Something chasing you?"

"No," said Donovan staring at the physician fixedly. "I was chasing something. There is a difference. I almost caught our phantom, our ghost."

"Oh, come now!" Fernly laughed shortly. "I can't get this thing at all, you know. Ghost!"

"And isn't this a strange hour for a doctor to be calling?" asked Donovan curtly.

"Yes, but I was sent for," grinned Fernly. "Mr. Porter called me to come to his wife. The ghost, it appears, paid her a visit a short time ago and she is hysterical."

The first thought that Donovan had was that it was very fortunate the doctor was there without Spratt having to send for him, and the next that the repeated attempts by the ghost to enter the Porter bungalow were simply to make people believe that the menace came from outside the bungalow. The lake phantom had been, after many years, resurrected to bear any blame necessary for poor Jack's murder.

He had no chance to speak, however, for Leslie opened the front door and stood peering out at the two men.

"That you, Fernly?" he asked. "Oh, come in, Donovan. Helen has been all excited about you. We've had another visit from the phantom. I chased it this time, or attempted to, the moment after Mrs. Porter shrieked that it had torn out her screen, but nary a fluttering crossbone or wagging skull did I see."

Donovan said nothing as they all entered the dimly lighted living room together. Voices issuing from Mrs. Porter's apartment told him that the members of the household were there, and without hesitation he stepped to a room across the hall. In no time at all he came out again. His face grimly determined and lighted with a touch of triumph, he crossed the telephone and ask for long distance.

I T was some time before he got Morris on the wire, and when he did he spoke in a carefully lowered voice which, he knew, would nevertheless carry to anyone who was listening closely.

"That you, Morris? This is Frank. Did you get those bottles I sent you? Good. Have you had time . . . Oh, I thought you would. Give me the dope."

For a moment Donovan listened to his friend's crisp tones, and his face grew brighter while his hands tightened on the instrument, and he forgot that he was staging an act for the criminal.

"Great!" he cried at last. "Nothing wrong with the flask? I thought there wasn't. I'm sending you another sample tomorrow, old man. Coffee this time. All right. Thanks." Hanging up the receiver, Donovan turned with a start to find Helen Ford beside him.

Bending close to his ear she breathed a few words. "The flask has come back. I found it just where it was, in my trunk. Do you suppose——"

Donovan nodded. "Sure. It now has mixed with it the poison that did for poor Jack. But I beat our friend to it. I can prove that the contents of Jack's flask was just straight whisky.

Before morning we'll have this wretched affair cleaned up. I've got your pearls, Helen. Jack hid them where he figured I would find them, in a hollow log just as he used to hide his fishing tackle when we played hookey!"

"Not so loud!" whispered Helen uneasily, glancing about. "You've really got them?"

"You bet!" grinned Donovan slapping his pocket, where the black box reposed. "Listen, Helen. Morris says the water we found on the Trask girl's floor, which was supposed to have dripped off the phantom was plain spring water like they use here in the house! And I know who the ghost is. We'll have the truth of this in no time and then——"

"That thing—it came here again tonight and frightened Aunt Bert so that my uncle sent for Doctor Fernly," shivered Helen. "And you say you know who it is?"

Donovan's face darkened and his hands clenched. "Yes," he said. "I know. Just have a bit of patience, Helen."

As he spoke a heavy step on the porch announced the arrival of the police and Donovan hurried to the door to speak to Spratt. That worthy was looking very grave and he mopped his brow with a large white handkerchief as he greeted Donovan.

"Mr. Donovan, Doc Lee and I both agree without further examination that it is five chances to six that poor Melcher died of an overdose of chloral," he sighed. "The stuff has a melon-like odor and I noted it about Melcher's lips. In other words, he was given knock-out drops."

"You didn't notice anything like that about Jack Ford?" snapped Donovan.

"Never looked for it," admitted the chief ruefully. "You reckon both the lake deaths were brought about by the same means?"

"I certainly do and by the same hand," said Donovan.

Without further delay then, he gave the chief an account of his adventure with the phantom and his talk with his friend in New York, and as he spoke, Porter left his wife's rooms and strode up to the two men, his face dark with anger.

"What are the police doing here?" he demanded, glancing from the chief to the sergeant who lingered behind him in the dusk of the porch. "Is this your work, Donovan?"

"Not entirely," said Donovan dryly.

"Mr. Porter, one of my men who was set to watch out for that lake phantom tonight was murdered down beside the lake, just as poor Mr. Ford was," said Spratt bluntly. "The trail of these crimes leads straight to this bungalow and so I'm here to ask a few questions."

"So you figure Ford was murdered, do you?" snarled Porter glaring at the chief. "Got some fancy notions since Donovan got here, haven't you? I didn't hear any thing about murder when Jack died of heart disease down by the lake."

"I'll just come in and see Mrs. Porter," said the chief, ignoring Porter's manner. "Mr. Donovan tells me she had a visit from the phantom."

"Nonsense!" said Porter impatiently. "Nerves. Donovan got her all worked up at dinner talking about murder. I—"

What he was about to say was cut short by a stifled scream from inside the living room and before Spratt or Porter could move, Donovan, with a muttered curse, was tearing past them to the door of Helen Ford's sitting room. Pushing it open, Donovan was met by a velvet darkness, but he sensed struggling bod-

ies nearby, heard a gasp in Helen's voice, ominous silence from whatever was menacing her.

Donovan had no flashlight and there was no chance to hunt for an electric-light button. Flinging his body forward he fell upon a substantial figure in a cloth coat, and as he grappled with it, Helen spoke chokingly.

"I'm all right. Is it you, Frank?"

"Yes," muttered Donovan as he struggled desperately to hold fast to the figure which was making such mad efforts to tear loose. "Put on the light."

BEFORE Helen Ford, swaying dizzily, one hand on her aching throat where her assailant's hands had closed, reached the electric-light button beside the door, Donovan felt himself hurled aside, and saw a dim form make for the French doors of the sitting room which opened on the lawn. He was out on the grass after the fleeing figure when he brought up smack against Doctor Fernly.

"What under heaven are you after?" asked the physician disgustedly as he seized Donovan by the arms and righted him after the staggering contact.

With a sweep of his arm Donovan flung the doctor aside and dashed forward, to be stopped by a thought as startling as the collision with Fernly had been. What had Fernly been doing right there at that time?

There was no sight or sound of anyone or anything else nearby and the mountain night was silent with a silence that was uncanny. Taking a cursory glance about, Donovan went thoughtfully back to Helen's sitting room from which lights blazed and excited voices issued.

Fernly was waiting for him outside the French doors.

Thrusting his hand through the doctor's arm, Donovan drew him into

Helen Ford's sitting room where, he saw, everyone had collected apparently.

"Just come in and join us, doctor," he said grimly. "We are going to have a showdown, an end to this business right here and now."

Helen Ford ran forward and seized her lover's arm. "Frank, he was after the flask, Jack's flask!" she sobbed, and Donovan nodded. It was apparent that the man he was after now valued his safety above the possession of the pearls for which he had killed.

"Chief," said Donovan as Spratt strode toward him, "just keep all these people here for a moment, will you? Frisk them for weapons of any kind and hold them here under a gun. Believe me, you'll need a gun. No fancy refined methods will go with this bunch now."

As Donovan spoke the sergeant who had entered with Spratt quietly locked the French doors and stationed himself before them, automatic in hand. Outside a rising wind sighed among the trees which crowded the bungalow close.

Mrs. Porter, in a padded dressing gown looking shocked and pale, sank upon Helen's couch, her hand laid over her heart, while her husband, still showing signs of temper, seized the arm of the chief of police.

"Now, what do these high-handed methods mean, sir?" he demanded, his face a deepening purple. "This man who is engaged to my niece has come up here with all sorts of wild yarns about murder. You have no right, Spratt, to take this attitude with my guests. I forbid it. I absolutely forbid any search of our persons!"

"Can't, Mr. Porter," Spratt shook his head, perspiring with misery, but determined this time to make no blunder. "Things have gone so far we got to act. Sorry. If you folks are all innocent in these affairs, it won't hurt any of you."

Donovan left the room as Spratt began his examination of the indignant group, stepped across the living room to the apartment into which he had hurried after his encounter with the phantom, and emerged, holding something wet and clinging and white over his arm. The fingers of his left hand were pressed so tightly over a small hard, round thing in his palm that they ached.

"Well, well, no guns in our midst, chief!" Leslie was saying lightly as he reentered the sitting room of Helen's little suite. "That must be a disappointment to you."

"And meanwhile the criminal or the ghost, if there is such a thing, is having plenty of time to get away," said Fernly with a sneer.

"He won't get away," said Donovan as he held out for all to see the thing he carried over his arm. "And I have the ghost right here. The phantom of the lake. Miss Trask, this weird garment was found in your room tonight just after you and I ran our race in the woods nearby. Perhaps you will explain why you have enacted the part of the ghostly diver and why this ancient story was resurrected by you."

Mrs. Porter gave a slight scream and covered her eyes with her hands while Fernly stepped to her side and took her wrist in his long pliant fingers.

The thing Donovan held out was a white rubber suit, made to fit a woman's body from head to foot. Wisps of something like white chiffon hung all about it and a headgear of white rubber which covered head, face and neck, with holes for the eyes and nose, dangled from two fingers of Donovan's clenched left hand. In his palm he still clutched that round hard something.

MARY TRASK had not risen from her seat, neither had she cried out or made any sound at all. Her brilliant eyes dwelt mockingly on Donovan and the strange garment he held.

"Miss Trask is your lake phantom, chief," went on Donovan. "She knows the truth of Jack Ford's death and also of poor Melcher's. I saw her at the lake tonight before I found Melcher's body and I encountered her later in the woods. A few moments after, I found this suit in her room, dripping wet. I suspected Miss Trask last night after she said the phantom had visited her room and I found her window screen torn from the inside, and not from the outside as it would have been had she told the truth. Are you going to speak now, Miss Trask?"

"I don't know anything about that crazy-looking thing," shrugged Mary Trask. "Someone must have placed it in my room."

"It is my opinion that Jack Ford told you that he was bringing a fortune in unset pearls here to his sister as an engagement gift," went on Donovan quietly. "He would fall for a girl like you. I don't doubt that when we get back to town and I go through poor Jack's rooms I will find ample proof of his friendship with you. In partnership with one of these men present, you devised the idea of bringing to life the lake phantom, in order to swing the guilt of my friend's murder, if it was recognized as murder, to the ghost or the person who played the ghost. Then you sought constant entrance to this house to impress upon the inmates that the phantom was not one of the household and that the menace came from outside. When Doctor Fernly here and the police accepted Jack's death as heart trouble, it was luck you had not expected. But you went on with the phantom stunt in case trouble started.

It did start. It arrived with me. Are you going to talk, Miss Trask?"

"Do we have to sit here and listen to this preposterous charge?" sputtered Porter furiously.

"You bet we do," snapped Spratt as he reached for the white rubber suit. "Jehosophat, I never saw such a contraption as this! It's got grease all over it!"

"It would have been difficult for anyone to have kept the phantom in their grasp, as I discovered tonight," nodded Donovan.

And suddenly, unexpectedly Mary Trask spoke, with a short defiant laugh.

"All right. I admit to the phantom game," she said. "But I don't know anything about the deaths by the lake. I did this for fun. I had the suit. Used it once at college in a diving stunt in a play. The old story of the lake ghost interested me and I thought it would be great to stir it up again and get the house here all upset. So I brought my suit from town one day. The headgear I made from two white rubber bathing caps. That's all. It is so deadly dull up here. I got a big kick out of it."

As she spoke she yawned but not for a moment did she permit her dark eyes to stray toward one of the men.

"You are not going to be frank with us, Miss Trask?" asked Donovan softly. "You are standing by your accomplice? Is that it? It will do no good. I know who the man is. You are a smart woman. You know it will only be a matter of time until we get the entire truth."

"I've told you all I can, Mr. Donovan," said Mary Trask coldly. "I did the thing for fun. I got plenty out of it."

"We'll find that Jack Ford knew this girl well," said Donovan then, turning to the tense group of people. "He told her about the pearls. She told the man she loves, who was in dire need of money, and together they plotted to take the gems. Perhaps, if we find that Ford and Melcher were both given chloral, the man did not mean to kill Jack, only to knock him out. It is easy for someone who does not understand the drug, to give an overdose. Jack's flask will tell us even before the autopsy, what he died of. That flask the guilty man tried to take from this room a short time ago. He tried after he heard me talking with my friend over long distance. You see, he had put the poison in his own flask, had driven part way down the road along which he knew Jack would come, had met him, chatted with him, offered him a drink. After my arrival he lost his nerve. He even ran Jack's car down into the ravine in fear that it might give some hint of the person who had met Jack on his way to this house. Then he took Jack's flask from Helen's trunk and put the poison in it, hoping it would look like suicide if there were an autopsy. And then, in panic, he wanted to remove that poison. He was too late all around. I knew, the moment I got the news of my friend's death, that it had been murder."

"But how—why—" Burns, who had been listening intently, bent toward Donovan. "What made you think it was murder? None of us—"

"Because Jack had written to me that he was taking those pearls to Helen," replied Donovan quietly. "And a large sum of money and his jewelry were found upon his body, but no pearls. Not even Helen knew about the pearls. I wondered who did!"

LOOKING about the room which, with the chief and his sergeant both armed guarding windows and doors, and the white-faced defiant group of people, had taken on the appearance of some sort of trial scene, Donovan proceeded in a level emotionless voice.

"Mr. Burns, why, shortly after I arrived, did you sneak into Mr. Leslie's room?" he asked. "And why did you search the rocks and logs near the spot where Jack's body was found, every time you went to the lake to bathe?"

Halsey Burns replied promptly, showing no evidence of offenses or nervousness.

"I figured, as you did, that Ford had been done in," he shrugged. "I knew him here last summer and I couldn't figure how he could have heart trouble as bad as that. I suspected Leslie. I can't say why. I just did. I had seen him haunting the lake and snooping about the rocks where we found Ford. I figured there was something he wanted. And I happened to know that he had been heavily hit by the recent bad market. That's all."

Leslie's debonair face flushed angrily. "You crook, Burns, that's exactly what I've been thinking of you!" he flared. "I thought there was something fishy about Ford's death myself. I told Donovan so when he arrived."

"Chief," asked Donovan turning to Spratt who was leaning his bulk against the door which led into the living room, "would you agree with me that the man who just made this attack on Miss Ford and who was evidently trying to get hold of her brother's flask, is the guilty person?"

"It sure would look that way," sighed Spratt. "They can't all be in this thing."

"But my flask was taken, also!" exploded Burns angrily. "And it never came back. What would you say to that?"

"I would say that it was a sure proof of your own innocence, Mr. Burns," said Donovan grimly. "Someone tried to throw suspicion on you by making it look as though you destroyed your own flask as you probably destroyed Ford's roadster. It told me that my idea about the criminal meeting Jack and offering him a death drink from his flask, was a straight one. Chief, I have a button here in my hand which I happened to tear off the coat of the man I struggled with in this room a few minutes ago. It wouldn't take a keen detective to see that there is a button missing from Tom Leslie's coat."

Mary Trask gave a sudden harsh laugh, her dark eyes flashing for the first time to Tom Leslie's face.

"You fool!" she cried. "Why couldn't you mind me and leave well enough alone?"

Instead of putting up a fight or an argument, Leslie sank back in his chair with a hopeless gesture.

"You were too many for me, Donovan," he admitted. "I never meant to give Ford such a dose. I only wanted the pearls. He'd told Mary about them. He was kind of sweet on Mary, I'm in debt over my ears and I've got to have money. I've borrowed to the limit and I wanted to marry Mary. We planned this thing together but we only planned robbery. I didn't know chloral was so tricky."

"How about Melcher?" snapped the chief as he snapped the handcuffs on Leslie's unresisting wrists. "You did for him all right. What did you do that for?"

Leslie's face darkened with ugly anger. "I had to," he snarled. "He was too smart. He saw me at the lake looking for the pearls and I couldn't throw him off. He was too ambitious. I couldn't afford just now having a detective suspecting me. So I doctored his coffee in the thermos when I got a chance. Then I heard Donovan talking to that chap in New York and I knew the game was up. I tried to get back Ford's flask which I'd put the chloral into. I guess I was panicky. I was afraid of Donovan. I was afraid from the moment he came."

"So you wrecked Ford's roadster," said Donovan.

"Yes. I was afraid of an expert examination of it."

Leslie's face paled and he lifted his handcuffed wrists and sank his forehead upon them.

"God, when I didn't find those pearls on Ford at all, and I saw that he was dead!" he groaned. "When I knew I'd killed him, and there were no pearls— I didn't dare touch the rest of the stuff. I was scared when I saw what I'd done."

Donovan looked about the room with a quiet smile.

"I guess that's all," he said.

The Chamber of Doom

by

Robert H. Rohde

"If I thought you was ever going to breathe a word, I'd slit your throat right now."

11:00 o'clock—and Johnny Quirk was due to die. The seconds passed as the death-house yammer went up. Suddenly the lights went dim—once— twice—three times—and once again. Then came a murmur from a darkened cell. Had an innocent man died in the chair?

BIG DAN BURR—Dan, Senior, head of the great Burr International Detective Agency—sat comfortably in the executive chamber at Albany with square-toed shoes under the governor's desk and square-crowned derby parked solidly upon it.

Dan was sure of his welcome in that vast, somberly paneled room; far surer than the girl beside him. She sat up straight on the edge of a deep chair that would easily have held two of her, awed by her surroundings, breathless with suspense. Her brown eyes, haunted by tragedy, anxiously searched the governor's face as Burr leaned forward and held a match to the end of his cigar.

"We're here to ask a favor, Joe." Burr spoke easily; he and the governor had been Dan and Joe to each other from remote days when they had fought shoulder to shoulder in a war against crime that the underworld of the big town at the lower end of the Hudson would never forget. "A big favor. It's about this boy in the death house—Jimmy Quirk. You know what happens tonight, Joe?"

The governor's eyes swung to the calendar pad behind the open humidor. He nodded.

"Yes, Dan. Tonight's the night—Quirk's night. What brings you into the case at this late hour?"

"I've been in it. Been in it—under cover—since before the trial. Now my back's to the wall. Quirk is innocent of that killing they're all set to fry him for tonight. I'm pretty sure we can prove it. Right this minute I've got one of my ace operatives—Tom Carson—riding herd on the man we believe is the real murderer. Carson is taking his life in his hands, night and day. If you'll play ball with us, Joe, it's just about a cinch we can clear Johnny."

With thin fingers laced under his chin, the governor turned to stare out the window.

"I'm curious about one thing, Dan," he said. "And frankly, it doesn't predispose me to make any move in Quirk's behalf. The very fact that you're in the case argues that plenty of money must have been raised to save him. It costs a lot to get Burr's International on a job—keep you on it for a solid year."

"Not always." Big Dan smiled. "If that's all that's troubling you, Joe—"

"Who's your client?"

"This young lady here."

"Oh!" The governor studied her. "Beg pardon. I didn't catch the name."

"Quirk!" the girl said faintly.

"Nellie Quirk," said Big Dan. "Johnny Quirk's sister—and one of our own. Nellie runs our switchboard down at the main office. Some day, I guess—if Tom Carson has got anything to say about it, anyway, she and Tom are—"

"Oh!" There was a new quality in the governor's voice and in his eyes as they returned to the girl—quick sympathy. "I'll go as far as I can," he promised her. Then he looked at Dan Burr. "I'm satisfied in regard to the client. But—about the crime. I read the record of the Quirk case just a few days ago, Dan. Couldn't see any reason for interfering with the execution of sentence. Let's see if I've got the facts straight. There was a taxicab involved, wasn't there?"

"Yes. A Red Stripe cab. That's one of the catches, Joe."

"That was it—I remember. The murder was committed in the course of a stick-up. A robber walked into a pawn shop on upper Washington Heights and shot down the pawnbroker's clerk when he tried to get at his own gun, under the counter. Time was about ten at night. Clerk alone in shop. Nobody happened to be passing at that moment, but store-keepers across Amsterdam Avenue heard the shots and saw the robber run north. Right?"

"To the dot," nodded Dan Burr. "The only witnesses were on the other side of that wide street—not straight across, either. The nearest one was pretty close to a hundred feet from the murderer. Their identification of Quirk should have been thrown out."

"It wasn't, though."

"No, it wasn't. Guess it stuck mainly because the robber wore a chauffeur's uniform cap and made his getaway behind the wheel of a Red Stripe cab that was parked around the corner with the engine running. But you don't want to forget, Joe, that more than three hundred Red Stripe cabs were chasing around the streets that night."

"That may be true. But how about the gun—the pistol found under the driver's seat of Quirk's cab when he pulled into the Red Stripe garage in the Bronx a couple of hours later? A shot had been fired from it recently, as I recollect the case. Expert testimony established that at Quirk's trial."

"Sure. A rod that had the number filed off—couldn't be traced from seller to buyer. Got to keep in mind, too, Joe, that nobody caught the number of the cab after the shooting. Also, that Silverstein, the pawnbroker's clerk, was dead before the cops grabbed Quirk and couldn't identify anybody."

THE governor flicked the long ash from his cigar.

"Nevertheless," he said crisply, "when I was district attorney in New York and you were running the detective bureau at headquarters, neither of us would have wanted a better case than the record shows against Quirk."

That brought a sharp cry from the girl; tears started, and she buried her face in her arms.

The governor said quickly: "Excuse me, Miss Quirk. It's a habit of mine, I'm afraid, to weigh evidence as an old-time prosecutor before I reconsider it as governor. The fact that Dan Burr believes your brother innocent counts very heavily. You may be sure of that. I'm just—understand, Dan—summing the state's case against John Quirk out of my recollection. My mind will be open when you present your side of it. But you'll have to admit that the best of all possible witnesses was introduced against Quirk at his trial."

"Rot!" grunted Big Dan Burr. "After Quirk's conviction, my men checked up on every witness the prosecution had." He brought a thick envelope from his inside pocket. "They all admitted it was just the cap and the cab—and general appearances—they went by. Cast your eye over these affidavits, if you don't believe me."

"I'm not talking about human witnesses." The governor dismissed the stack of affidavits with a glance. "I mean the pistol that was found in Quirk's cab. Surely, Dan, you don't dispute the testimony of the pistol experts. Didn't three of them agree that test bullets fired from Quirk's gun bore identically the same markings as the bullets taken from Silverstein's body?"

"That's your trick, too, Joe. It had to be a strong case, or they wouldn't have got the conviction."

"Exactly. And how strong is your case for the defense?"

Dan Burr blew out a ribbon of smoke and meditatively followed its spiral climb toward the high ceiling.

"It's more of a hunch than a case," he admitted soberly. "It wouldn't stand in court for a minute. It isn't worth a sou markee—unless you'll pull an oar in the boat with us, Joe. Remember that Quirk had an alibi witness?"

"Yes. Some young woman. But I've got to tell you that her testimony wasn't very impressive. Not as I read it in the transcript—and evidently not in the eyes of the jury, either. Quirk had told a quite different story in regard to his whereabouts that night before the alibi witness was brought forward. First he insisted—correct me if I'm wrong, Dan—that he hadn't been out of his cab from the time he left the garage until he returned. Hadn't even been at a standstill with it, except when he was taking on or letting off passengers. True?"

"That's right, Joe. Well, Quirk had two reasons for lying that way. First, he was thinking about that little gal of his—was dead set on keeping Helen McCord clear of the whole works. Second, he was thinking about his job, when he told the dicks he had been cruising the whole night long, looking for new fares the minute his flag was up after a haul.

"You see, he didn't know then that the pistol had been found in his cab; didn't know what a tough jam he was in. All he knew was that he hadn't done any worse wrong than sneak an hour out from rolling time for a call on the girl friend.

"The answer to the whole thing, Joe, is right in that hour. Silverstein was shot at ten. Johnny Quirk was with the McCord girl, holding hands, talking about rents and furniture and such like, from half past nine till ten-thirty. They were going to get spliced, see? Everything was set."

The governor's brows drew together.

"It seems you're just repeating what the jury wouldn't believe," he said. "What's the new angle?"

"A triangle." Big Dan Burr reached for the match stand and relighted his cold cigar. "A triangle with a no-good bird named Steve Leadbetter in the odd man's corner."

The governor repeated the name. He shook his head.

"Don't recall Leadbetter being mentioned at the trial," he said.

"Wasn't mentioned. We didn't get a lead on him until after he got into trouble a few months ago. Not until some time after, as a matter of fact. Then Carson had another session with Helen McCord, and she spilled the works. Steve Leadbetter had been hanging around her doorstep a long while. She gave him the gate for Johnny Quirk."

"Ah!" The governor pricked up his ears. "Now you're getting somewhere!"

Big Dan looked at him long and thoughtfully.

"I can't prove a thing, Joe," he said after a time. "Not without you behind me, I can't. A while ago I told you that one of my best men, Tom Carson—"

The girl spoke up, appealing directly across the desk.

"My man, governor! Tom's taken his life in his hands to save my brother. Mr. Burr will explain how."

Big Dan nodded. "Yes, Joe, I'm starting to explain how and why now. And then I'm going to make a request that—well, it'll probably blow your hat off! You always had sporting blood, Joe Robinson, and I hope you'll string in on the gamble."

Out of the corner of his eye he had seen the door to the anteroom ajar. He got up and closed it.

"Always careful, Dan," the governor smiled.

"Always," said Big Dan Burr, "where it's a case of life and death. Now, here, Joe—listen!"

AT 11:00 P.M., Eastern Standard, Johnny Quirk was due to burn. Down in the penitentiary office, crowded with reporters, blue with tobacco smoke, the warden reached to his inside pocket and touched the long official envelope—the envelope that had come from Albany by special messenger a couple of hours ago with the governor's decision on Dan Burr's last plea for Quirk. His eyes clung to the little ormolu desk-clock, chipperly ticking off the minutes.

"Quarter of, gentlemen," he announced, rising. "Time we moved. There is no reprieve!"

Up in the death house, black curtains were being hung over the grilles of all cells but one. The chaplain stood at the unveiled door while Johnny Quirk, gripping the bars hard to keep his loose knees from letting him down, tried to find a voice to tell him for the hundredth time that he was riding on a wrong rap—going to the hot seat for a killing he hadn't done.

"It—it's not a right deal I'm getting, father!" he whispered huskily. "All the experts in the world can say different—but the bullet that killed Silverstein never came out of my gun. I never was in on a stick-up or a hijack in my life. You saw my girl when she was up here, father. You saw Helen McCord with your own eyes. You saw my sister, too. Do you think girls like Nellie and Helen would be with me to the finish if—"

He stopped, choking; tried to moisten his dry lips with a tongue that was itself like leather. They were coming for him. He stared past the chaplain into the sorrowful and faded eyes of Gridley, the white-haired old P.K.

"Padre!" he cried. "Cant' you stop 'em? Don't you believe me?"

The chaplain averted his eyes and said nothing. It was cruel, agonizingly, heart-breakingly cruel, that he could murmur no word of comfort before the slow march toward the door of doom began—but so it had to be.

One of the guards behind the principal keeper spoke up gruffly. "Take it like a man," he advised.

"I would—if I had it coming," said Quirk dully.

Gridley's watch was in his hand.

"Five minutes of," he said, and nodded.

The door of the death cell drew open. Between two keepers, the chaplain ahead, other guards behind, Johnny Quirk went stumbling along the bleak corridor toward the little brown door that marked the end of the world.

The procession had started in a silence broken only by the clump of shoe-leather on concrete and the low monotone of the chaplain, reading. But the silence didn't last. From the next cell below, young Southwaite, the "thrill-slayer," sang out: "So long, Johnny! We'll all be seeing you!"

That was a spark to the powder of ragged nerves. Back of the sable curtains, bedlam turned loose. It was four minutes to eleven—and old-timers within the walls, hearing the death-house "yammer," knowing what it meant, could have called off the time to a second.

IN B block, nearest the death house, house, the racket brought No. 7117 up on his elbow.

"What's the rumpus?" Most first-termers were like that, always sleeping with one eye and both ears open, always on edge. "Hear it, 'Crab'? Is it —a break?"

It was the first time No. 7117 had ventured to address his glowering cellmate by the prison nickname. No. 2122 didn't like that any better than he liked being roused out of a sound sleep. Sleeping was one of the best things he did! Nothing had ever kept him awake while he was lucky enough to have a cell to himself.

"Shut up!" he spat from the lower bunk. "And next time you got anything to say to me, call me 'mister.' You ain't in that bank any more. Up here, you're a punk. Don't forget it."

No. 7117 mumbled a hasty apology. He had been meek under the hard eyes of No. 2122, alias the Crab, ever since he had been checked into that upper-tier B-block cell with him ten days ago, ticketed to a five-to-ten bit for embezzlement.

"Excuse me, mister. Thought you were awake."

"Think all you want. But keep your mouth closed night times—if you want to keep all your teeth in it."

The Crab turned over, but he didn't go back to sleep. Peering over the side of his bunk a few seconds after he had spoken out of turn, No. 7117 saw him sitting up. Echoes from the death house still filled the corridor.

"What is it, mister?" No. 7117 dared to repeat his question. "Gosh, what a racket!"

The Crab, sitting on the edge of his bunk, turned his face upward. The light from the corridor showed No. 7117's thin-lipped grin.

"You'll know what the death-house yammer is, punk, before you get your diploma here. They're burning a guy. That's all."

"God almighty!" The upper voice was awed. "Who?"

"Name's Quirk."

"Quirk? Yes—I read about it, on the outside. Killed somebody during a stick-up, didn't he?"

No. 2122 answered with a grunt. "Yeah. That was the rap. Quirk says he's innocent. What a laugh that is —up here! Who ain't? It wasn't me

said I swiped that nifty new Cadillac up in the Bronx. Naw! It was the cops and the jury said so!"

A pause. No. 7117's voice went shaky. "They—they must be strapping Quirk in the chair now."

"Yep." Gusto in that. "Slitting his pants leg with a pair of scissors. Strapping on the wires. Say, it must be some sight! I'd give sixty days good-behavior time to see it. Won't be long now!"

And it wasn't. The twilight of the cell suddenly deepened as the electric lamp, burning down the corridor went dim.

"Bam!" whispered No. 2122. "That's the one he felt!"

"W-what was it?"

"First jolt of the juice. Last of Quirk."

"It's—over?"

"All but frying him on the other side. In a minute they'll drop another quarter in the meter and give him some more. Watch the light!"

The corridor lamp had come back to full candle-power after the brief dimming. In a moment it dimmed again. Then, with brief intervals, a third and a fourth time.

"Never knew Quirk was that tough," grunted the Crab. "He sure ran up this month's electric bill on the State of New York." His head withdrew. No. 7117 saw his gray-socked feet swing up on the bunk. "Show's over," yawned No. 2122. "No more yap out of you, punk. If you can't sleep yourself, let somebody sleep that can."

Whatever his sins, No. 2122 had an India-rubber conscience. He could sleep.

NO. 7117 couldn't. He lay on his back, arms folded, eyes open, listening to the heavy breathing of the Crab.

An hour dragged away, and No. 2122's rest was broken by another call from above. He raised up snarling.

"Damn you, punk! Didn't I tell you what I'd do to you if—"

"I—I thought you'd thank me this time," stammered No. 7117. "Any time I'm having a bad dream, I'm glad to be snapped out of it."

"What do you mean—bad dream?" The gray socks slid into the light. "I wasn't dreaming at all. Now I'm going to bust your nose!"

A tremor came into No. 7117's voice. "Don't be that way, mister! You must have been having a nightmare. I tell you, you were talking in your sleep."

"Oh, was I?" The Crab was getting up, rubbing a hairy fist. "Well, if I want to talk in my sleep, it's my business. Lay off any back talk."

No. 7117 shrank away from him, crowding the hard wall. He was husky enough himself, but the Crab had set him down early in their acquaintance as a mark for bullying. He insisted: "You were dreaming about—Quirk. Can't you remember? That's funny. You spoke his name. Then you said something about a 'rod' and a 'cab.' That was it. Your very words. 'A rod and a Red Stripe cab'!"

"Hell I did!"

"That wasn't all. You repeated something you said to me when—when they were electrocuting Quirk. Said you wished you could be there to see it. I don't know—you seemed to be dreaming that you had something to do with sending Quirk to the chair."

"Yeah?" said the Crab. His voice was soft, but there was something infinitely more menacing in his speculative look than there would have been in a glare.

"At that, maybe I was dreaming and didn't know it. Tell me some more."

"You—you said that you'd like to have been up there watching Quirk die. 'Finishing'—your own words, mister —'finishing what you started'!"

At that repetition the inertia of bewilderment passed swiftly from the Crab. His eyes blazed. A thick-fingered hand shot out and closed on his cell-mate's throat.

"I did, did I?" The choking grip tightened. "Feel, that, punk?"

No. 7117 was feeling it plenty.

"Uh!" he croaked. "Uh!"

"I could kill you with one hand. And I will—if you ever let a peep of this out. Get me! If I fry for it, I'll squeeze the life right out of you. Up here—in the yard—shoe shop—mess hall—anywhere I can put the clamp on you!"

"Don't! Don't!" No. 7117's eyes were bulging before the pressure was relaxed. "Why should I tell anybody? What would be the harm if I did?"

"Harm? With this foundry full of stools!"

Evidently—that was the plain suggestion of his stare—No. 7117 could make no sense of that.

"How could dreaming make trouble for a man in here, no matter what he dreamed? The whole place is a nightmare, isn't it?"

The Crab's eyes, pale blue, baleful, bored into No. 7117's.

"What the hell are you looking at me that way for? Damn your soul, punk, I bet you're thinking—"

No. 2122 broke off at a sound of approaching steps and slid swiftly back into his bunk. A uniformed figure passed along the corridor—the screw, counting heads. As he passed from view the Crab pushed off his blanket and was up again.

"Don't lie to me!" he grated. "You're trying to dope out something, you little rat, you! I can read it in your face, I can! You're wondering if I didn't maybe spill something real. Ain't it so? Come on! Tell me!"

THE Crab was breathing hard. His face was close to No. 7117's.

"No, no!" protested the man in the upper bunk. "I wasn't thinking anything like that. Remember what you told me the first day they put me in here? You said for me to mind my own business and let you mind yours. That took. Wish now I—I hadn't woke you up!"

"Oh, yeah? And then tomorrow you'd have been blabbing all over this iron-works about me sounding off in my sleep—eyes tight shut and mouth wide open. Maybe you're simple, punk, maybe you're not. But there's a lot of guys going to this school that ain't simple one bit. Guys that would start a whisper going clear up to the P.K. and the warden. Guys that would as soon as not see me burn."

No. 7117's mouth dropped open. "Burn?" he gasped. "For—for dreaming?"

"For talking out of turn. Suppose, punk—just suppose I used to drive one of them Red Stripe cabs? Supposing I hacked out of the same garage that Quirk did? Supposing I and him wasn't such good friends?"

"You knew him!"

"Yeah. I knew him." The Crab stooped and fumbled in the mattress of the lower bunk; when he straightened, the faint light from the corridor glinted on a long sliver of steel, hilted with a wad of sticky tape. "See this, punk? If I thought you was ever going to breathe a word, I'd slit your throat right now!"

No. 7117 cowered back from the honed-down blade. His eyes, though, never left the Crab's. No. 2122 was sure of it then. People had to be smart

—quick-figuring—to cheat banks. In his sleep, he had spilled the works, and No. 7117 was wise to him!

The Crab spent a moment in thought, the slim blade lying across his palm, naked and deadly. The decision at which he arrived at length was the one that nine out of ten criminals would have reached inevitably in the same circumstances.

"All right," he announced suddenly. "I won't leave you guessing. Won't leave you no excuse to run off at the mouth about me and my sleep talk. It was me that sent John Quirk through for the singe. As true as I'm standing here in front of you—as true as I'll ram this sticker right into your heart if you ever breathe a word of it—I put Quirk on the hot spot. Damn him to hell, he had it coming!"

"Y-you—you're talking like a lunatic!" stammered No. 7117.

"Am I? Listen, punk—Quirk's gone, and I might as well get the whole thing off my chest. I guess I'd have to be telling somebody sooner or later, anyhow. Well—the time's now—and you're it! Me and Quirk didn't pull together. He grabbed off a skirt of mine. I hated his guts, see?"

"Y-yes!"

"Then listen some more. I was out with a dirk for Johnny. Didn't know how, didn't know when, but I was bound to get him some day—and get him right. The way it turned out, was like the chance was made to order. Come on, punk. Sit up. Open your ears. You got to hear this."

No. 7117 faltered, and his teeth were chattering. "L-listening."

"I was a hackie," No. 2122 went on, "but I wasn't in the grab just for my health and bean money. A guy driving a cab—cruising all over town—can spot a lot of places where he can pick up a quick roll. Every once in a while, I knock one off to keep in form.

"Well, this night, I walks into a hock shop up in Amsterdam Avenue with my cap under my coat, counting on the gat in my mitt to get me what was in the damper. But the guy behind the counter made a reach and I had to let him have it. I didn't know it then—but I croaked him."

"Killed him!"

"Yep; deader than a run-out pawn ticket. My cab was around the corner, ready for the getaway. Nobody was close enough to lamp the license number. I was sure of that, but a dozen people must've saw it was a Red Stripe. Still, with two or three hundred Red Stripes rolling, that could have been a lot worse. Once I got rid of the gun, the cops'd had about one chance in two hundred of getting anything on me. Do you see it?"

"Yes," said No. 7117 faintly. "I see it."

"Well, while I'm thinking where I'm going to dump the gat, I keep riding. I pick up a fare and haul him down to Sherman Square. That's where the Seventy-second express station is on the West-side Subway, see? When I drop the fare, I'm on Amsterdam Avenue again, going south. Sort of from force of habit, I swung west through Sixty-seventh Street. That's where this jane lives—get me? The jane I was trying to make when Quirk butted in. Quirk's hack was standing out in front of her house, empty—another Red Stripe cab just like mine. It come on me all of a sudden how I was going to get rid of that hot rod."

No. 7117 was sitting bolt upright then. "How?"

"I parked it in Quirk's hack. Under the front seat. Right where the dicks found it when Quirk pulled into the garage. And that's how come Johnny Quirk went on the hot spot tonight.

Now you've got the lowdown on me. Quirk's gone and all you got to think about is your own skin. Think you'll ever squawk, do you?"

No. 7117 spoke without a quaver. He seemed to be bigger, chin squarer.

"Wouldn't make any particular difference," he remarked, "if I did."

No. 2122 gaped. "What?"

A hard hand shot out from the other bunk and fastened onto the wrist of the hand that held the knife; a twist of the wrist loosened the Crab's grip on the taped hilt, and the blade clattered on the floor.

"Not a bit of difference, Leadbetter!" snapped No. 7117 in the new voice. "You didn't talk in your sleep. That was a stall to start you going. But every word that you've said since is down in shorthand—piped out of here through a dictagraph wire, with plenty of witnesses listening at the other end. What you've done, Steve, you've talked yourself into the chair. My name happens to be Carson, and I didn't come in here for embezzlement. I came for the Burr Detective Agency."

Carson was down out of the upper bunk and at the cell door before Steve Leadbetter could move. A kick sent the knife spinning out into the corridor. His call brought the screw running, and he wheeled just in time to meet Leadbetter's spring. His fist lashed out to the big man's jaw, and its crackling impact sent Leadbetter lurching back against the rear wall as the keeper appeared.

"O.K., Mr. Carson?" questioned the screw.

"Perfect!" nodded Carson rubbing his knuckles. "If you'll let me out of here, I'd like to congratulate the warden. Swell piece of theatre, that death-chamber trick. When that light dimmed down by the stairway—say, I couldn't keep from shivering myself."

He saw the car leap into the air. Saw it burst into flames.

Six Diamonds and a Dick

by

Frederick Nebel

Author of "Hell's Pay Check," etc.

It wasn't where the jewels were that worried Cardigan—he knew that all the time. He couldn't prove it, though—not until the crowd at the casino got their spots crossed and midnight murder showed up in the cards.

CHAPTER ONE

The Blonde in Blue

THE girl in the slate-colored silk tights gave a fair imitation of the East Indian Nautch. The man at the bass viol plunked the strings and the trap drummer worked hard and grinned like a fool. A moving spotlight changed colors and followed the girl around the oval-shaped floor. Beyond the radius of light, sixty tables were white cases where men and women, the majority in evening clothes, took nourishment from tall glasses in which ice tinkled.

Cardigan, nursing a Corona-corona. raised his left wrist close to his face and looked at the illuminated dial of his watch. The expanse of his boiled shirt was as wide as the average man's breadth is from shoulder to shoulder. He weighed close to two hundred and his stomach was as flat as a griddle cake.

He rose and picked his way among tables to the lounge. The Dago waiter looked after him with a dark malignant stare. In the lounge high-backed gilt chairs stood against mauve-colored walls, a crystal chandelier tapered from the ceiling, carpets an inch thick muffled footfalls.

A tall man who looked like a diplomat but wasn't, took a drag on a cork-tipped cigarette and put himself in front of Cardigan. Cardigan stopped, lounged on his heels with hard easy grace.

"What's eating you, Gould?"

"I'm getting tired of this, Cardigan."

"Well, do something about it."

Gould had a thin dry-gray face, prematurely gray hair that was slicked back so tightly that his head looked like a skull. Only his eyes were dark and shiny with a surface glare that lacked depth, like lacquer. He laid long attenuated fingers lightly on Cardigan's arm.

"I mean what I say, Cardigan. You've been doing a Dracula around here for the past three hours. You haven't taken a whirl at the wheel or the tables and every now and then you take a walk around the place like you owned it."

"So now what?"

"I don't intend standing here in the lounge room arguing with you. The door is—you know where the door is." His voice was thin and quick and oddly brittle. The framework of him looked brittle.

A grin threw Cardigan's leather-brown face into many wrinkles. "I'm not ready to leave yet, Gould. I understand your overhead is ten thousand a day. Don't try to chuck me out and raise your overhead."

Gould's left eyebrow quivered. "I've got to know where we stand. I've got to know what the hell you're doing here. This is a high-class joint. I've got to be careful."

"I'm telling you, honeybunch, that what I'm doing here has nothing to do with you."

"You're tailing somebody."

"Wouldn't that be a surprise!"

Gould's thin voice shook. "Who the hell are you tailing?"

At the other end of the lounge was a broad door of mirror glass overlaid with whorls and modernistic angles of bronze. Beside the door stood an attendant. In a chair a few feet from the door sat a chunky tuxedoed man with a face hard as nails. In the archway to the foyer stood another man. The three men were watching Cardigan and Gould.

Gould was saying, "I warn you—"

"You don't have to warn me. If you don't want me hanging around here then put me out. And I'd like to see you put me out. You scare me, you do, Gould. You scare hell out of me."

He went past Gould. The man at the mirrored door squinted pale eyes, opened the door. Cardigan went through.

Hum of voices, click of dice and chips, click of a small white ball in a whirring roulette wheel. Women in glittering gowns, men in evening dress. Dispassionate-eyed croupiers. A cashier with a big wallet under his arm; he appeared through a small door from time to time and went to a table where a player was checking out.

Cardigan's roving gaze fell on a burly man who was playing roulette. A Spanish-looking woman was with him. Her blue-black hair fitted her like a casque and the green gown she wore followed every undulating curve of her body. The burly man had close-clipped sandy hair. There was a scar on his forehead that glinted like a sliver of silver. The man was quite drunk.

A short, thin girl brushed against Cardigan. "A blonde—in blue. She went upstairs."

Cardigan said nothing. He moved on through the gambling rooms and came at length back to the mirrored door. He pushed out into the lounge, took the circular staircase aloft and went out on a wide veranda. Below, at the foot of the bluff, the Mississippi rolled through the night.

A girl was standing by the veranda rail, looking out into the darkness. A dimmed porch light made a faint glow on her fuzzy blond hair. The damp river breeze ruffled her blue gown. She stood motionless, tense. Muffled was the constant throb of the jazz band below. A train went by at the river's edge, far down the bluff.

CARDIGAN took a step out onto the veranda floor. The girl whirled, her dress corkscrewing about her legs, her red mouth open. Cardigan stopped. In her hand was a glint of metal. Cardigan could see the convulsive rise and fall of her bosoms. Her face was white as a ghost's, her eyes wide and staring.

Cardigan went close to her, put his hand on the gun, twisted slowly this way and that until her fingers let go. She did not move. The fingers that had held the gun remained splayed. Her breath started to come in intermittent shudders.

Suddenly she gasped and collapsed. Cardigan caught her and let her down gently to the floor. Her mesh bag fell to his knee, slid off and fell to the floor. He let her lie. He opened the bag, ransacked it. He left bills and change, cosmetic compact. He took out a neat sheaf of white cards, thrust them in his pocket. He thrust her gun in his pocket.

Footsteps made him look around. Gould was there. And another man.

"What's this?" Gould clipped.

"Lady fainted," Cardigan said, and stood up.

The man with Gould had his gun out. He jammed it against Cardigan's back.

Gould bent down. He lifted the woman in his arm. "Come on," he said.

The man with the gun prodded Cardigan and Cardigan followed Gould into a room where Gould laid the woman down on a divan. The sound of the jazz band throbbed in the room. The woman on the divan stirred, groaned. Gould went into a bathroom and came out with a wet towel. He patted the woman's head. He looked up at Cardigan.

"You're funny, Cardigan."

"Like a crutch, huh?"

"I'm going to see what this song and dance of yours is all about— Hello, miss. Better?"

Her eyes, open now, rolled around in their sockets; rolled slower and then stopped rolling, to steady on Gould's narrow gray face.

"I—I must have fainted," she breathed.

"What did that guy do to you?"

"Where?"

"The big boy there?"

She looked at Cardigan for a long minute.

Cardigan growled, "Don't be an airdale, Gould. I found her lying out there."

"You shut up," Gould said.

The woman passed a hand over her eyes. "I—just fainted. It was hot downstairs and I came up for some air."

"What did he say to you?"

"I don't know. I never saw him before. Just let me alone. Let me rest—please. I'll be all right."

Gould's forehead puckered. "This is funny." He got up and looked at Cardigan. "I said this is funny."

"I heard you the first time," Cardigan said. "What kind of a come-back am I supposed to make?"

Gould's left eyebrow twitched. He made a nervous, impatient gesture with both hands. "Go on. Go on get out now . . . . Leave her alone in here a while, Sam. Go on, Cardigan. But by God, this is funny!" He pivoted toward the woman, biting his thin nether lip. "Are you sure this guy—"

"Please—please let me rest. I tell you I just fainted. It was hot . . . and I fainted."

Gould sniffed irritably and went to the door with a nervous doggedness. He opened it. Cardigan and Sam followed him into the corridor and Gould, closing the door, shook his bony forefinger threateningly under Cardigan's nose.

"I'm getting damned tired——"

"Don't wave your mitt under my nose, Gould!" He threw Gould's hand down violently and his mouth became sullen.

Sam started to crowd him. Cardigan swung on Sam abruptly and bit him with a hot gray stare.

"And you, baby, think again before you yank that roscoe on me!"

"Says which?"

"Sh—now—sh!" muttered Gould petulantly. "Out in the hall, you saps you!" He waved to indicate the lack of privacy.

Cardigan rumbled, "Well, tie this lapdog outside then."

Gould screwed up his face into an expression that was intended to be ferocious. Cardigan chuckled. Gould blew out an exasperated breath and Cardigan passed him and rocked down the corridor. He entered the gambling rooms again, mingled with the crowd around the roulette wheel, touched the elbow of the short, thin girl. She moved her left hand and he looked down at it. In her palm was a slip of paper on which was scrawled, "$4,000." He turned and passing behind her said, "Beat it." In a minute the small, thin girl left. He was in the foyer when he saw her leave and enter a taxi. Five minutes later he got his hat and coat from the check room and was shrugging into the coat when Gould appeared. Gould stopped and regarded him narrowly.

"Goom-by," Cardigan said.

Gould didn't say anything. He kept biting his thin nether lip in nervous irritation. Perplexed indecision strained in his eyes.

AT a quarter to twelve Cardigan braked his shabby roadster in front of the Hotel Andromeda. He went through revolving doors into the lobby. There were many men and women strolling around in evening clothes. There was supper dancing in the Peacock Room off the north wing.

He sat down in a leather divan and watched the main entrance for five minutes. Then he got up and crossed the lobby to where the small, thin girl sat. He dropped down beside her.

"Any luck?" she said.

"Maybe." He took out a sheaf of small white cards and held them so she could see.

"That's the blonde, huh?"

"And not peroxide, sister. She pulled a swoon on the veranda. She had a gat—in her hand. Whether she was going to do the dutch or was getting set to go after White I don't know. I took it away from her. Who was the Spanish number?"

"Somebody called her Miss Monteclara—Nita Monteclara. But that's a lot of *braunschweiger*. Her name's Becky Steinwein. She models for underthings. The maid in the dressing room gave me the lowdown unasked. She's taking this chap White for a farethee-well. The blonde looked daggers at her all night—and there was murder in them blue eyes, suh."

Cardigan squinted. "And White went in the red for four thousand?"

"By his inamorata's hand. She played everything but the corners and he kept cheering her. Pardon me if I seem to yawn."

"Hit the hay, Pat. See you at the office."

Small and trim, pretty in a quiet, certain way, she went to the elevators.

Bush, the Metropolitan dick, bumped into Cardigan deliberately and said, "So that's your new operative, Cardigan?"

Bush got rid of a hollow, uncertain

laugh and Cardigan left him standing in the center of the lobby.

CHAPTER TWO

The Diamond Trail

WHEN Cardigan came heavily into his office next morning Miss Gilligan, his stenographer, said in her always startled voice, "Oh, Mr. Cardigan—oh, Mr. Prier of the Jewelers Cooperative Indemnity telephoned and asked—"

Cardigan, heading for his private office, said, "Call him back," and closed the connecting door behind him.

Miss Gilligan put through the call.

"Hello, Mr. Prier," Cardigan said. "We got some breaks last night . . . . Well, don't get excited. We just found the jane White jilted and the headache he's running around with now . . . . I'd rather not mention names . . . . Yes, White's still spending like hell. Four thousand last night up until the time I left . . . . Well, that's a problem. Either he fenced the stuff as soon as he came out of stir or he's living and playing on the stuff. . . . Yes, it's getting my strictly personal attention . . . . 'Bye."

He hung up, lit his first cigar of the day, gathered together a number of sheets and went into a long room where four desks stood in a row. Three men were working over reports.

"Morning chief," they chorused.

"Hello, gang. Blaine, that client's yelling that we're holding him up. Spend another day on that stolen radios case and if nothing breaks we'll sign off. You've covered about everything and we're not going in for cut-rates . . . . Hennessy, you've got to wangle a photostatic copy of the Dixon Hotel register for June 10, 1929. Don't go over fifty bucks . . . . Katz, I want a record of Ludlow's bank deposits during August. Drop the Flemming case. He's reconciled to his wife."

When Cardigan returned to his private office Miss Gilligan was standing in the doorway. She said, "A Mr. Ullrich to see you."

"What's he want?"

Miss Gilligan shrugged.

Cardigan dropped to his swivel chair heavily. "Well, shoot."

Mr. Ullrich almost bounded in. He was a roly-poly man with cheeks like red apples, a big-toothed grin in a small mouth, dancing blue eyes.

"Good-morning, Mr. Cardigan! Good-morning to you, sir!"

He extended a stubby arm, gripped Cardigan's hand hard. He yanked a fat cigar from his breast pocket.

"I'm smoking," Cardigan said. "Sit down."

"Yes, yes! Well, well, Mr. Cardigan, this is a grand day! A grand day to be alive!"

Cardigan eyed him curiously. "Senator Ackerman's right hand man?" he tried.

Ullrich slapped fat palms on the desk joyously. "The old eagle eye, Mr. Cardigan! Yes, sir!" He sat back in the chair facing Cardigan and rocked with laughter.

Cardigan's eyes narrowed. He said nothing. He crossed his big brown hands on his flat stomach, creaked his swivel chair gently to and fro and took slow puffs on his cigar.

"Well!" said Ullrich, getting his breath. He rubbed his fingers back and forth on the edge of the desk with a gentle, caressing motion. Back of the laughing bubbles in his eyes was a wily, speculative look. "Well, Mr. Cardigan." He looked up with his bright, dancing eyes and tongued his cigar back and forth between grinning teeth "Senator Ackerman, you know, has his country home in Lancaster County. Lovely place, Mr. Cardigan. Ah—you were out in the county last night, were you not? Yes, yes, of course. I came here to—— How is business, Mr. Cardigan?"

"Swell.'"

"So. So indeed! Well, well!" Ullrich took three quick puffs on his cigar, grinned into space. "Ah—Phil Gould was a bit upset. You know Phil: kind of jumpy and nervous. Since—since the Civic Service League started to percolate in the county."

Cardigan was impersonally blunt. "We're not working for the Civic Service League, Mr. Ullrich."

Ullrich's chuckle bubbled and he made vague gestures. "Of course, of course. Well, you see, out in the county, we like to keep things running nice and smooth. Phil's a good sort. Only he gets worried—and when he gets worried—"

"He runs to Senator Ackerman," nodded Cardigan. "And why? Because the senator is one of the big backers of Gould's gambling casino. So now what?"

This bluntness teetered Ullrich for a minute. Then he said, "It's just— well, Phil was worried the way you were—"

"I'm not interested in the casino," Cardigan said. "I'm not working for any civic uplift organization. Why I was there last night is my own business."

"You know, Senator Ackerman is a good man to stand in with."

"My boss is in New York and they never heard of him there."

Ullrich stood up, his face wreathed in smiles, his eyes shining. "Then that is all, Mr. Cardigan." He pulled at his breast pocket. "Do have a cigar."

"Thanks, but they look too heavy."

Ullrich shook hands violently, went out buoyantly.

Pat sauntered in saying, "Who was sunshine and happiness?"

"Don't think because you wear skirts, sister, you can bust in here an hour and a half late."

"Boo!"

"That's a nice hat you have on, Pat."

THE Shelby Arms was a nondescript apartment house on Washington Boulevard. The chemical cleaners hadn't touched the bricks in years. Cardigan entered the small, stuffy lounge, climbed three steps to a mezzanine and stopped at a chest-high desk. A fat woman sat behind it, knitting.

"Miss Carmory's apartment," Cardigan said.

"There's no switchboard. She's in 411."

The elevator was self-operated. Cardigan got in. The doors wheezed shut. He pressed a button numbered 4. The elevator wheezed upward. He opened the doors when it stopped and entered a narrow, dim corridor. He poked around in the shadows until he found a brown door with 411 on it.

The blonde opened it. There were circles under her eyes; the lids were puffy. She was pretty in a faded-flower way. She had a nice chin and wore a pepper-gray ensemble and a silk blouse of lighter gray. She regarded Cardigan with round blue eyes wide open and expressionless. But in a split minute her mouth loosened and a hurt look came into the eyes. There was something oddly harried about her but at the same time her air of passivity was definite.

"Come in." Her voice, like her shoulders, was listless.

Cardigan pushed through the doorway, took a single-room suite in with one casual glance. His hair stood out from his ears like a shaggy mop. His jaw was big, brown, heavy. A floor board creaked beneath his weight.

The girl stood looking with tired eyes at a window and said, dully, "I knew you'd come."

Cardigan looked in the bathroom, started toward the kitchenette. The girl shrugged.

"I'm alone," she said.

His "O.K." was low, resonant. He sat down on a straight-backed chair, crossed one leg over the other, closed his left hand around the ankle and sat regarding the girl with a deep, thoughtful frown. Presently she turned and looked at him.

"So you knew I'd come," his low, deep voice said.

She nodded and let herself down slowly into a divan. She rubbed her hands slowly together and said nothing.

He said, "If you were going to turn that rod on yourself last night I'm glad I stopped you. If you were getting steamed up to turn it on Burt White— well, that's six of one and half a dozen of the other."

"Burt White?"

"Or maybe the Spanish flame that's turning him all hot-and-bothered these days."

Her lips made a round O and remained that way for a minute. Then she whispered, "Who—who are you?"

"Those playboys out at the casino last night were itching to hand me a rough deal. Gould had a brain-wave and decided that I was there on a big tail. He hopped around like a hen on a hot griddle all night."

She nodded. "I know. After you left he quizzed me again. I said— well, what I said when you were there."

"Good girl."

"Well, you could have told about the gun. Thanks for helping yourself to my cards."

"Manicurist, eh?"

"Who are you?"

Cardigan put both feet on the floor, leaned forward, resting elbows on knees. "Three years ago six unset diamonds were lifted from a diamond merchant in the Hotel Midlands. Value of seventy-thousand dollars. The diamonds were insured by the Jewelers Cooperative Indemnity. Catch on?"

She said nothing in a blank-faced way.

Cardigan stood up, took three steps, jammed hands into pockets and planted himself in front of her. "Burt White was in the hotel at the time. He had a room in the rear, eighth floor, looking down on Bennington Court. All right. The diamond merchant's room was busted into, he was slugged—in the dark—and a guy got away with the diamonds. At 12:40 A. M. At 12:35 White tried to get a telephone number. Party didn't answer. He tried again at 12:43. No answer. The defense claimed that a man couldn't have got from Room 709 to 818 in three minutes. White got off on the robbery charge but just for spite they sent him up for three years for concealed weapons. A man said that at 12:45 he saw a woman hurrying out of Bennington Court. The defense proved that at midnight this man left a speakeasy plastered to the eyebrows and the clerk in the hotel where he lived said he fell in the lobby at 1:00, still plastered. So that killed that. Still the diamonds had disappeared. The indemnity company took it on the nose. Two weeks ago they engaged me to jump on the merry-go-round. You get me?"

SHE kept staring down at Cardigan's feet. "I thought you were a detective of some kind."

"How's to play ball?"

She got up slowly and walked the length of the room. She turned and looked at Cardigan and smiled wearily, shaking her head. "I'm afraid you're up the wrong tree," she said.

"No one knew who White's girl friend was. They tried to catch on through letters to him when he was in stir. There were no letters. He figured that out too. We got him lamped the minute he came out. We found out last night who his heart was. I said— *was.*"

She colored. "Burt White? Who is Burt White? I don't know him. Who is he?"

"Ask me who is Nita Monteclara."

Her color deepened. Cardigan liked the way her chin tilted. She said, "I don't know what you're talking about, please." Her voice throbbed.

Cardigan strode to her. Shaggy-headed, massive-shouldered, he towered threateningly above her, an ill wind in his eyes. "I know you're lying, Miss Carmory. You tell a lie bum as hell. I've got White figured out and I've got you figured out. I know he's chucking money away and I happen to know that when he came out of stir he was stony. We've been smack on his tail all the time and we've found that in two weeks he's spent fifteen-thousand bucks. That ice was fenced while he was in stir by his pal or he's fenced it since he got out or he's borrowing till he can fence it. You've been singing, 'Lover, Come Back to Me,' and the punk lams on you for—"

Calmly she said, "Please, you are wrong. This is all like a story to me."

"There's some dough in this for you if—"

"I work for a living." She looked at her wrist-watch. "I have an appointment at 11:00."

He searched her pallid face with glittering eyes. His wide lips tightened against his teeth. "You're White's ex. At the casino last night you watched every move he and the Monteclara flame made. You were going to do something with that gun. For God's sake don't hand me a run-around like this. White's ditched you and why you're worrying about him I can't see. You look pretty O. K. to me. That guy's a louse four ways from the jack and I've got the finger on him but I need more evidence."

She smiled gently. "I'm sorry I can't help you."

She was tranquil now—too tranquil. Back of her almost beatific calm a load of emotion was suspended by a single thread. Her face was too white, her eyes too rheumy. She moved past Cardigan and went into the little dressing room. He stared at the open door through which she had gone. No sound issued. After a minute he took a few steps and reached the doorway.

She was standing in the little cubicle. Standing with her hands clenched at her sides. Her lips puckered. Tears rolled down her face. Silent sobs ripped at her bosom and pain traced its way across her face. Her body began to shake. It trembled all over. Her legs trembled. Her mouth opened and the sobs raked out—hoarse and unimpeded now. Restraint tried to fight them back but emotion was greater. The sobs came faster and her lips quivered but she remained standing there, her heels together, her arms at her sides her fists knotted.

"O God . . . O God . . ."

"Listen—"

"O God . . ."

"Please . . . I was kind of rough. . ." He made a half-hearted gesture with his hand; he ran the hand through his hair. He started toward her. He gave it up.

He stood frowning not unkindly. He felt oafish and uncomfortable.

"I'm a bum," he growled.

He turned and went back into the bed-sitting room, got his hat. He went to the door, opened it and passed into the corridor. He took the stairway down. As he reached the lobby floor he saw Mr. Ullrich enter the elevator. The indicator stopped at the fourth floor.

CHAPTER THREE

Cardigan Walks Out

AT noon Cardigan shouldered into the lobby of the Andromeda. Pat joined him and they went into the Coffee Shop for luncheon.

"Tell me a story," Cardigan said.

"I popped over to Adrienne's, the lingerie shop where the Monteclara woman models. I looked at some lingerie. I looked at it on Nita. She's neat to look at and don't think she isn't. She uses an accent that she thinks is Spanish but she goes wrong on the Spanish J. I acted dissatisfied. I mentioned a kind of lingerie they didn't have but they said they expected it any day. I asked them to send Nita to my hotel with some samples."

"So I suppose you'll buy yourself a lot of undies now and charge it up to investigation expenses. You're not a moron."

Pat winked. "You keep scowling that way and some day you're going to scare me. I reasoned that if I could get her in my room I could lay some conversational traps. If necessary"— she raised a neatly plucked eyebrow— "I could get rough—in a feminine way. Please pass the tabasco."

Cardigan nodded, frowned hard at the table top. "The Carmory woman got under my ribs. There's no buying her. She denied knowing White or anything about him—and then she busted out crying. I never saw a jane cry so hard. So I cleared out."

"Weakling."

"As I was leaving I saw Ullrich go up in the elevator. The elevator stopped at her floor. I parked across the street and Ullrich came out ten minutes later. The jane came out five minutes later and took a cab to the Congress Place Hotel. I pumped the house Shamus there—Willard—and Carmory had an appointment with a dowager of the buter-and-egg trade. Manicure. She's known at the hotel—and liked. She had appointments there that carry her over till 4:00 this afternoon."

"Just a poor woiking goil."

"Don't be a damned cat. Helen Carmory's a sweet jane that's getting a raw deal but she's dope enough to keep her trap shut. The only thing I'm afraid of is that she'll bump off either White or the Monteclara—or maybe herself.

"Senator Ackerman's guts must hurt or he wouldn't be sending his mouthpiece around trying to find out what I was doing at the casino last night. This laughing jackass Ullrich would be just the guy to throw a wrench in the whole shebang."

Pat said, "By the way, when I left the office I saw Ullrich talking at the corner of Sixth and Olive with a great old friend of yours."

"Who's that?"

"Detective Sergeant Bush."

Cardigan laid down his fork and glared at Pat.

She said, "Well, why look stilettos at me?"

Cardigan cursed, took a savage poke with his fork at a chunk of meat. "He once acted as Senator Ackerman's bodyguard. They're like this." He crossed his fingers.

Pat leaned forward. "Don't look. Bush is in the lobby now looking this way."

A man's voice said, "Why, hello, Mr. Cardigan."

Cardigan stood up. "Hello, Mr. Reams. . . Miss Seaward, Mr. Reams."

He stood chatting for a few minutes with Reams, sat down when Reams departed and said, "Head of the Civic Service League. I once investigated a poverty case for him."

P AT left before Cardigan, and when Cardigan went into the lobby five minutes later Bush buttonholed him. Bush had two stock expressions; he could either look very hard and mean or he could assume a fixed smile brimming with suspicion. This time he wore the latter and poked Cardigan in the ribs.

"Big business, eh, Cardigan?"

"I thought there was a bad smell around here."

Bush poked Cardigan in the ribs again, stuck his blunt hard jaw close to Cardigan's chest. Cardigan jabbed him in the stomach and Bush said, "Oomp!" and made a face.

"You're soft, Bush, like dough. Why don't you drag your pants out of easy chairs once in a while?"

Bush always resented any slur against his physical condition. His face got hard as granite. "You might be on a case, big boy, that's going to get you a pain in the neck."

"You're giving me a pain right now —and not in the neck."

"Yah!"

"All right, make funny noises."

Bush took hold of Cardigan's lapel. "I could give you some good advice, Cardigan. You think you're pretty hot. You think that agency you work for is just about the most powerful in the United States. Don't—" he prodded Cardigan's chest—"think so."

Cardigan stared hard at him while taking two slow puffs on his cigar. "You get this, Bush. You tell a certain party that if anybody slams into my parade I'll start the biggest political upheaval that you or anybody else ever saw. It's damned funny that I can't go about my business around here without having you master-minding all over the place."

"I'm just telling you—"

"You could tell me that you're the swellest cop on the force and I'd believe that too. In a horses's neck I would! Go chase yourself around in circles till you get dizzy, fat-head."

Cardigan left the lobby and went through the doors like a blast of wind. For a minute he walked with a rolling, hard-heeled gait and anger crackled in every line on his weathered face. For a minute he was oblivious to the noontime crowd. His attitude toward Bush contained far more of disgust than genuine hatred. He carried a healthy contempt for Bush that a long series of petty interferences had evoked.

When he walked into his office he found Miss Gilligan blindfolded and lashed to her chair. Miss Gilligan was a spinster. Cardigan said nothing. He crossed the small office, took off the blindfold, removed the bonds.

"Oh," exhaled Miss Gilligan. For a moment she looked dazed and slightly awry. Then she said, "Whew!"

"Who did it?"

"I was inside in your office going over some files. I didn't hear anybody come in. Of course—between 12:00 and 1:00—I was the only one here. Then when I came in here that rag was pulled around my eyes. He must have been behind that bookcase. There was another one. They put me here and then I heard them going through the file cases. Then one of them came back and gripped me by the neck. He said, 'Are there any more files?' I said, 'You better go. I just pressed this button under the desk with my knee. It notifies police headquarters.' He got scared and called the other one and they went out.''

The button she alluded to was once used to call her when the desk had been in Cardigan's office. Now it was out of use.

"Good girl," Cardigan said. "You didn't get a look at them?"

"No. But one of them lisped."

Cardigan made a fist, rapped the knuckles slowly on the desk. "Somebody still has a guilty conscience. Busting into my office, eh? Take a look, Miss Gilligan, and see if anything's been lifted."

Nothing had been taken.

"Do you know who they are?" Miss Gilligan asked.

"I think so."

"They ought certainly to be arrested."

Cardigan muttered, "I've got a better way."

AT 11:00 that night Cardigan was climbing into plain cotton pajamas when the telephone beside his bed rang. He crossed the room pulling up his pajama pants, knotted them at the waist as he sat down on the bed, and then picked up the telephone.

"Yeah . . . . When?" His face became leaden; his voice dropped to a low note when he said, "I'll be right over."

He got out of his pajamas, into undershirt and shorts. In three minutes he went down in the elevator to the basement garage, climbed in his old roadster and tooled it out. Where Lindell crosses Grand he swung right and went south on Grand, crossed the bridge and burned the wind. Five minutes later he pulled up at a dark intersection as two men were lifting a stretcher into an ambulance. A small crowd had gathered.

Cardigan climbed out of the roadster and got a look at the white face on the stretcher. He turned around and Bush and Haas were looking at him. A couple of cops kept yelling at the crowd. Bush made a spitting sound and smoke popped from his lips.

"What do you think of this, Cardigan?"

Cardigan looked back at the ambulance. His brown face was expressionless. "What happened?" he said.

A cop said, "I was up the block when I heard the shots. Three shots. I came runnin' down here and there she was layin' in the gutter. See the blood there? She was layin' there. A guy says he saw a black sedan go past the next block, only another guy says it was a blue coupe and another guy says it was a dark red convertible. So you can tie that and whaddaya got? A knot. What I mean!"

Cardigan looked at Bush. "How is she?"

"How would you be with two shots in your belly and one through your leg?"

The ambulance bell clanged. The ambulance roared away and the crowd lingered.

Bush, wearing his sly leer, said, "Want a lift, Cardigan?"

"I've got my own?"

"Then we don't need a taxi. Haas and me are going your way."

They crowded into the roadster beside Cardigan. Cardigan swung the car around and headed north. Bush was in the middle. He seemed pleased with himself. Cardigan didn't say anything. He stared grimly through the windshield and exceeded the speed limit.

Bush said, "Goddard's went with her. She may come to and say something but the doctor says not a chance. Me, I'm kind of interested in you."

Cardigan remained silent.

"Very," Bush added.

Cardigan looked like a man who was thinking hard. He said nothing. He seemed unaware that Bush was speaking. He reached Lindell and stopped at the corner.

"You go east," he said. "I go west."

Bush made his voice very soft, "Aren't you going to drive us to headquarters?"

"Not that I know of."

"Oh, yes you are."

Cardigan said nothing. He clicked into gear, swung right and drove east, slowly. Ten minutes later he pulled up in front of police headquarters.

"Do come in," Bush said.

Cardigan remained silent for a while, then shut off the ignition and growled, "You ought to have your head examined and find out what you use in place of a brain."

There was a neat, quiet office on the third floor. Bush closed the door after Haas and Cardigan had entered and then brushed his hands lightly together. He went to a desk and called the hospital.

"I see . . . . Yes, stay there anyhow, Goddard, until it's all over.

H E hung up, relit his dead cigar and sat on the edge of the desk, swinging one hard, stubby leg. Haas hadn't spoken yet. He watched Bush in a manner that implied he would act according to Bush's wish.

"Now what's behind it?" Bush said. He was at ease. He overdid the fact that he was at ease.

"You're the whole police department, it seems. And you ask me?"

"You knew her, Cardigan. I tailed you this morning when you went to that apartment house. I asked the woman at the desk who you went to see. She told me. I didn't think it was anything, so I left. We found her handbag tonight. The names were the same."

"You didn't see anybody else go in after me, did you?"

"I didn't hang around." Bush narrowed one eye. "Who else?"

"I don't know. I just thought somebody else might have been hanging around."

"Who bumped her off, Cardigan?"

Cardigan looked surprised. "Who bumped her off! How the hell do I know?"

Bush stuck his jaw out and came up close to Cardigan. "I want to know who put the finger on Helen Carmory."

"I don't know."

"You called on her this morning, damn you!"

"I was in her apartment about fifteen minutes. When the murder was pulled off I was home. You know that because you phoned me and I was there. Have I denied that I was at the Carmory place?"

"What were you doing there?"

"I knew Helen Carmory. I was out to Phil Gould's casino last night and Helen Carmory fainted on the veranda upstairs. I happened to be there. I picked up some things and stuck 'em in my pocket. I forgot to give them back. I gave them back this morning. Start working on that."

Bush forgot his smile. He grated, "I don't believe you."

"That doesn't knock me over."

Bush took a handful of Cardigan's vest. His face worked. "I've got enough of you, Cardigan! I've got just about enough! Since you came to this city three years ago you've been handing me a kick in the slats every chance you got! By God Almighty, this is one time when you ain't—"

Cardigan barely moved, yet he straight-armed Bush in the chest and Bush went reeling backward, knocked over a chair and landed on his back, his short legs flying. Haas looked sour and leaped in front of Cardigan with a blackjack. Red color was flooding Cardigan's face, his mouth was crooked and a little open, showing set teeth.

Bush scrambled up, his trouser legs wrinkled, the cuffs halfway up his lower legs showing his socks. His eyes popped. He had his blackjack out and his lips were sputtering wetly.

"You—you—you damned son-of-a——" he choked.

Cardigan's body engulfed Haas like a tidal wave and Haas went down. Cardigan's fist whipped in a short chopping blow. It caught Bush on the jaw and Bush slammed against the wall. Haas was up, off balance, but he took a wild swing with his blackjack and glanced a blow off Cardigan's head. Cardigan went down.

Bush rubbed his jaw and hefted his blackjack and Cardigan got up and said, "There's one word I don't like to be called."

The three of them stood breathing heavily.

The telephone rang. Bush answered it. When he hung up he said, "She just died. Never came to. Now, Cardigan—"

"Shut up!" Cardigan's voice carried a whip. "I told you I was at her apartment this morning. I told you why I went there. That's all I'm going to tell you and if you think you

can hold me on that then you'll have to rewrite the criminal code."

Bush snarled, "I'll hold you over night and take a chance on that. I'll hold you over night. I'll hold you for striking an officer! Ha! How's that?"

"Fast but not fast enough," Cardigan shot back at him. "I can pull out of this. Right now! And I can make you take it through the nose!"

"Yeah?" snarled Bush.

Cardigan pointed to the phone. "Get Ullrich down here."

"Get—" Bush stopped short, gasped. The room suddenly became silent. Then Bush spluttered, "Why, dammit—"

"Get Ullrich," Cardigan hammered out. "He's not my friend. He's yours. But get him."

"To hell with you. You can't bluff me."

"I'm not bluffing. Get him. Get him or get Inspector Lewiston in here and I'll break up this little clique of yours. If you're going to pinch me because I called on Helen Carmory this morning then, by cripes, you're going to pinch Ullrich!"

"That's a stinking lie!"

"Get Inspector Lewiston and inside of half an hour he'll have Ullrich down here. I asked the woman at the apartment house what apartment Ullrich asked for. She said Helen Carmory's. In just three seconds you telephone Lewiston or I walk out that door."

When Cardigan walked out Bush looked dumfounded.

CHAPTER FOUR

"How Much Do You Want?"

IT took five minutes for Cardigan to reach his office on foot. The building was dark. He turned on a light and began pacing up and down heavily. He kept combing his shaggy hair with his big brown fingers. There was a sharp, concentrated look in his eyes.

Presently he sat down and called a telephone number. After a while the operator said, "Party does not answer." He hung up and sat drumming his fingers, nibbling at his lip, staring hard into space. He made another call.

"Sorry, Pat. . . . Yeah. I'm down at the office. How's to run down? As soon as you can powder your nose."

Pat was one woman in a thousand. Fifteen minutes after the phone call she walked in. She looked wide awake, neat, comely. She wore a droll smile that always hinted that the world was a funny old place but all right so long as you took it as a joke.

"At this hour you get me down to your private office. Helen Carmory was bumped off."

She said nothing, but her smile vanished.

Cardigan slapped the desk. "Bumped off! Out on the South Side. About 11:00. She lived about half an hour. Never came to. Bush flagged me over there and then hauled me to H.Q. and began acting up."

"White, huh?"

"Says the hunch. Bush hasn't got an idea in the world that White's mixed up in it. But he may find out. There's no telling what Helen Carmory left behind. We've got to work fast. Seventy thousand in diamonds is in or has passed through White's hands. It's one of the biggest jobs I've ever had. There's ten thousand in it for the agency. It's my job to get that ice and I'll beg, bribe and coerce to get it! If Bush gets a lead, finds out White is mixed up in the murder—and gets him —we're going to be left holding the bag. With a murder rap hanging on

White he'll never spring about the loot."

Under the skin Pat was all woman. "You're playing a dangerous game, chief. You've got a big political clique wondering about you. Is it worth it?"

"Sister, I like my job. The head office sent me out here because 'Boss' Hammerhorn thinks I'm a swellelegant guy. He wired me to hang onto this job till my guts hurt. I liked the way he put it. And I'm in it—this job. Up to my neck. I'm holding good cards and—" he took a slow swing and buried fist into palm—"I don't like Bush." His teeth set and he flexed his lips over them. "That's that, sister."

Pat sighed, shrugged. "O. K."

"Now look. I rang Nita Monteclara's apartment. No answer. You run over there—take those master keys out of that drawer—you run over there, crash the place and turn it inside out. Letters. Photographs. Addresses. If you don't find anything hot wait there—hide somewhere—and if the worse goes to the worst get rough with the jane. Get Tom McWaye on the wire. His house — Jefferson 0024."

Pat telephoned and handed the instrument to Cardigan. "Hello," Cardigan said. "You, Tom? . . . . Hello, you legal lion. I might bust into trouble in the next twenty-four hours. Me or my assistant Pat Seaward. I want you to be ready to pull your legal tricks if the works get gummed . . . . Thanks, kid . . . . Goom-by."

He hung up and said, "All right, Pat, on your way."

She went to the door, turned, said, "Don't run too high a temperature, chief."

He grinned, said nothing. Pat went out.

Cardigan rolled the roadster through the night on Broadway, hummed through the South Side, crossed the River Des Peres and hit the open highway. The night wind was damp, sometimes the windshield became clouded. The road rolled up and down gently. The stars were small and far away and the countryside was empty, black, with the moon gone. Occasionally headlights burst over a rise in the road, a car went past with a vicious swish. The roadster's top clapped, hooted; the grass by the roadside looked pale in the glare of the headlights.

At a lonely crossroads Cardigan turned left and struck a dirt highway. A little farther on he veered left at a fork and followed a narrower, rougher road that went up over short, choppy hills, fell away in short, steep grades and tortuous curves, leveled off and meandered through sparse timber and broken fields.

Two stone gate-posts supported small globes of light. Beyond, in a grove of trees, loomed a large, rambling stone building with many windows lighted. Cardigan pulled up in a parking space and a uniformed attendant opened the roadster's door. About fifty cars were parked there and the muffled beat of a jazz band came from the building.

CARDIGAN walked to a white porte-cochére where half a dozen uniformed men stood around. He climbed broad stone steps, entered a large vestibule and showed a card of introduction. He was passed into the sumptuous foyer, and the louder beat of the jazz band throbbed in his ears; lovely women drifted past in alluring decollete and the perfume of them hung pendant in the air.

He stood there and lit a cigarette. He was keyed up. He was anything but an iceberg and he could feel the blood warm and quick in his veins. One thing he had—presence, and it did not pass unnoticed by the women. He dwarfed the average man.

In a minute he moved, passed through the archway into the Louis lounge. A man sitting and a man standing by the mirrored door looked at him. The man in the chair stirred, crossed one leg over the other. The man at the door shifted his feet. Behind Cardigan was the restaurant, the throbbing jazz band, the laughter of women commingled with the tinkle of glass, the *shush-shush* of dancing feet.

Cardigan entered the gambling rooms. They were more crowded than on the night before. Smoke hung like a fog about the crystal chandeliers. The little white ball bobbed in the spinning roulette wheel. Cardigan's eyes roved. He passed on into another room.

White teeth were laughing behind carmine lips. Nita Monteclara threw dice with wild abandon. Burt White stood at her shoulder. A cigarette drooped from his thin-smiling mouth. From time to time he looked up, jerked his almost colorless eyes over the crowd.

Cardigan moved away, looked at his watch. It was halfpast one. Phil Gould came toward him. Gould's thin white hands were at his sides. His face was white and narrow with nervous muscles twitching near his lips. His voice was a low whisper.

"You!"

"Now, now."

"I want a word with you."

"Sure."

They went out into the lounge and Gould jerked his head, muttered, "My office."

It was the famous "armored" room: walls, floor and ceiling of reinforced concrete; the main entrance door of heavy steel, with double locks; slanted steel blinds over the windows; a small steel door that led to a passageway into the gambling rooms. Through this door money was brought, deposited in the vault against the back wall of the office. It was no great secret. Once a scribe had written it up in the Sunday magazine supplement of a newspaper.

A pale-faced youth worked over a ledger; another worked at an adding machine. There was a loud-speaker through which warning could be yelled from any part of the building.

"You've got to clear out of here tonight, Cardigan," Gould said in his quick, brittle voice. "You've got to. This is one night when you've got to get out."

The clerks were trained. They did not look up. They kept on working with smart precision.

"I'm sorry," Cardigan said. His voice was slower than usual.

Gould scratched his jaw irritably. "You've got to! Listen, this is straight: you're going out of here or you're going to get put out."

Cardigan darkened. "I'm here on a job, Gould."

"As if that's news! Maybe you thought I thought you came here to play marbles or something."

"I'm on a job. A big one."

"So then you think you're going to play cops and robbers in my place, huh? Nuts you are, Cardigan, and that's flat."

"I'm not going to do a thing here. That's God's honest. What I'm going to do I'm going to do somewhere else. But the tail starts here. It's my job, Gould. It's a red-hot and you're not in any way connected with it. I know I've got a reputation as a wise-guy, but this time I'm on the level. I'm telling you the truth. I'm swearing to you that I'll pull no monkeyshines here."

"What I said stands," Gould bit off.

"I'll meet you halfway. I'm heeled. I'll leave my gun with you till I'm ready to leave. That's fair, Gould."

"There's no chance at all of meeting me halfway, Cardigan. Are you going to walk out of here like a nice guy or are you going to be taken out?"

"So you're sold on your own ideas, eh?" Cardigan's mouth tightened. "I'll tip you, Gould, that you're stepping on your own toes. I can hurt you if I want to. I've got enough stored away in my noodle to hurt you and some guys bigger than you are. You can throw me out. Of course you can, with the army of heels you've got around here, but you do it and you'll sing your swan-song."

Gould shook his head bitterly. "Tonight—you've got to clear out—that's all." Gould turned on his heel, walked to a desk, picked up some papers and studied them carefully.

CARDIGAN moved to the door. Gould dropped the papers and joined him, opening the door and eyeing Cardigan coolly. Cardigan went into the corridor and Gould followed closely and Cardigan walked slowly with his brows bent and a hint of malevolence in his eyes. He reached the foyer and the chatter of women standing in little groups. He looked distinctly unpleasant and there was a glimpse of wind rising and falling in his eyes.

"Thay, Phil—"

Cardigan stopped, turned around and saw a wavy-haired blond youth accosting Gould. Gould muttered something and the youth shrugged and stepped back, looking at Cardigan. Cardigan suddenly went toward him.

"Did you say something?" he growled.

"I didn't thay a thing."

"Oh, you didn't *thay* a thing. You——"

Gould touched Cardigan. "He spoke to me, dope."

"Yeah. And he busted into my office at noon and took a look over my files!"

"Sh!" Gould muttered. "Keep your voice down."

"Who thaid I buthted——"

Gould hissed, "Ned, scram!" Suppressed anger bit into his words. No one ever fought in the open at the casino. No one ever argued out loud. It was that kind of place.

Cardigan rasped under his breath, "And I'm damned if I'm going to leave here till I'm good and ready!"

He pivoted and strode away from Gould. Gould did not rush him. Three hard-eyed men looked to Gould for a signal but he did not give it. Each of the three men had a hand in his pocket. But Gould was afraid—afraid of something. He was reluctant, apparently, to stage a fight in the sumptuous foyer of his elaborate casino. His face reddened and his thin fingers moved nervously in his palms. A dozen women, half a dozen men, were unaware of this taut, bitter drama.

Cardigan walked right into the lounge, turned and looked back through the archway. He could see Gould rooted to the floor. It was no effort to pick out Gould's men. He knew that at another time, in a place less public —Gould's office, for instance—he would have been jumped, manhandled, chucked out a side entrance.

The front door swung open and Detective Sergeant Bush came in. Bush did not see Cardigan. Bush's face was worried and he went directly to Gould.

Cardigan stepped away from the arch. Explosive thoughts began crackling in his brain: Bush must have gone to Helen Carmory's apartment, found something there—perhaps a picture of White, or a letter, or some clue that was hot when he found it and that led him here to the casino.

Cardigan had not expected this. He hoped for at least a six-hour jump on Bush. It was open and shut that if Bush collared White for the murder the whereabouts of the diamonds would not be divulged—with any benefit to Cardigan, anyhow. White was a murderer, if Cardigan's hunch held water, and Cardigan had no intention of letting White get away with it. But on the other hand he had a job to complete, a robbery to solve, loot to regain.

A couple came out of the gambling rooms. The mirrored door swung shut. Cardigan strode toward it. The stony-faced attendant opened it and Cardigan entered the feverish gaiety. He was jostled right and left. The hour was late and many of the guests were drunk, but there was rarely any disorder at the casino.

Cardigan did not see White. He covered the three gaming rooms slowly but purposefully. Nor did he see Nita Monteclara. He returned to the lounge, walked the length of it and lingered in the entrance to the dining room. The pair weren't there. He turned and went up the staircase and stood at the top looking the length of the corridor toward the open porch doors.

He walked to the doors and looked out. The veranda appeared to be deserted. He went out and strolled along the broad rail. It was dark here. Farther on the veranda turned around the side of the building. Cardigan followed the rail around, then stopped.

Ten feet away a man and a woman were embracing. They broke, and Cardigan knew they were White and Nita Monteclara. He said nothing. He pretended he had not seen them. Turning away, he scowled into the darkness. Far down the bluff the river rolled by. His right hand rose and crossed his chest and he felt the bulge of the gun in his spring holster.

Voices and footsteps came out on to the veranda and Bush and Gould walked toward Cardigan. He took a few lazy steps toward them. They recognized him.

"What are you doing out here?" Bush growled.

"What are you?"

"I can go where I damned well please."

"So can I."

"Oh, can you?"

"As a matter of fact," Cardigan said, "I've got more of a right to be out here than you have. You're a metropolitan cop and your business ends there. You haven't an excuse in the world to be out here in the county."

HE walked away from them, drawing them after him, and entered the corridor. A door opened almost abreast of Cardigan and a head thrust out. The head bobbed back, its owner bumped against someone behind, there was swift confusion and the door swung open.

Cardigan got an eyeful. He saw Ullrich, the man who had bumped the other. He saw tall, lantern-jawed Senator Ackerman, a few other men. He saw half a dozen girls—young, heavily rouged. And there was a long banquet table, many bottles, many buckets of ice.

Behind Cardigan Phil Gould sucked in a breath.

No one made an attempt to close the door. Ullrich's face was a round blank moon. Ackerman was frowning. The other men quieted down. One of the girls was doing a clog to radio music.

Gould gripped Cardigan's arm. "Come on, Cardigan."

"Shut up," Cardigan grumbled.

Then Ullrich's face brightened, became wreathed in smiles. "Well, well, well, sir!"

Cardigan shrugged free of Gould, stalked into the room.

A girl cried, "O-o-o, what a big meany you look like."

Another said, "Any minute now, Gertrude, I expect to hear him growl and then see him start biting."

Ackerman half turned, muttered, "Be quiet. Go into the other room."

The girls entered an adjoining room, some of them giggling.

Cardigan leaned back against the open door. His stare was baleful. Gould came in rubbing his hands together nervously. Bush remained standing in the corridor, a fretful, bewildered look on his face.

Ackerman said, "Come in, sergeant."

Bush came in and assumed an angelic expression.

"Close that door," Ackerman said.

"I'm not staying that long," Cardigan said.

"Close it."

Cardigan moved and Ullrich closed the door.

Ackerman, a tall, bony man, crossed the room, closed the connecting door and came back to face Cardigan.

"How much do you want?" he said.

"What makes you think I want anything?"

Ackerman was blunt. "Don't beat about the bush. How much do you want for your silence?"

"If my silence were at stake, you nor anybody else could buy it. What the hell gave you the idea I was after a shakedown?"

"I'm not mincing words, Cardigan."

"So you think I am? Dammit, I told Ullrich today that your business didn't interest me. He didn't believe it. Two guys crashed my office and bound my stenog and looked through my files. One of them's downstairs now. Man alive, if I wanted to spring it I have enough on you to get you slammed out of the State Senate overnight. And I'm not keeping it under my hat because I like you, which I don't, but it wouldn't get me anywhere. But I'll tell you this: if there's anymore hocus-pocus pulled off around me I'll get mean and low-down and land on you and your whole scatter like a ton of brick."

He whirled and reached for the doorknob. Gould blocked him and looked at Ackerman for some signal.

Ackerman droned, "Don't get hotheaded, Cardigan. Let's talk this over sensibly."

Cardigan was biting Gould with somber eyes. "Get away from that door, Gould."

"Now please, Cardigan," Ackerman said.

Cardigan grabbed Gould by the throat, flung him sidewise with terrific violence. Two men grabbed Cardigan from behind, held on grimly. Gould lay on the floor panting.

Ackerman bit off the end of a cigar. "Let him go," he said.

CHAPTER FIVE

The Crossed Spot

WHEN Cardigan reached the lounge below he looked through the archway and saw White and Nita Monteclara leaving. He got his hat and when he passed out through the door he saw a black sedan swing around the pebbled drive. He took his time on the way to the parking space. He drove slowly through the gates and laid his gun on the seat beside him.

He doused his lights after a minute and picked his way carefully along the dirt road. From time to time he spotted the tail-light of White's sedan. When the sedan turned right on the paved road Cardigan slowed down, rolled along leisurely and then put his lights on just before he made the turn. He picked up speed gradually, saw the tail-light on a rise beyond.

In a few minutes he was aware of lights shining in his rear-view mirror. He paid no attention until he noticed that the car maintained an even pace behind. Cardigan speeded up, and as he did so the car behind followed. When Cardigan eased up on the throttle the car behind dropped back. Several times Cardigan did this and on each occasion the result was the same. It occurred to him that Bush was still watching his every move.

White's car maintained a steady speed of about forty-five. Cardigan crept up on it and the car behind crept up on Cardigan. The road made a wide turn. Cardigan looked back, cursed, and came to a decision. He stepped on the throttle and shot away. When he passed White's sedan the roadster was doing sixty. He looked back and saw the third car cutting out to pass White. He pressed harder on the throttle and the clock-like speedometer went to sixty-five, on to seventy. The wind hammered the top.

The other car was after him. When Cardigan turned the dashlight off the needle was quivering at seventy-five. He dared not look back. He had to keep his eyes on the road. He took chances and cut corners, turned on the spotlight to see better. The roar of wind and motor was deafening; the frenzied clapping of the canvas top was enough to rattle a man's nerves. Ultimately the car's speed was eighty, but settlements a mile beyond would cut that.

Suddenly he heard a crash. Saw his spotlight go out, saw the rear of it torn open. His mouth flew open. There was a sharp *ping* of a sound. He saw a hole in his non-shatterable windshield. An oath ripped from his lips and he jammed himself far down into the seat. Lead snarled against metal somewhere behind. Cardigan flattened the accelerator against the floorboards and hung onto the wheel.

He drew away from the pursuing car. He knew now that it was not Bush. Bush was a cad and a petty nuisance but he wouldn't go in for murder. Cardigan did not look back. He blasted through a small settlement, screeched around a curve. He roared past a truck. The heat of the motor came up into his face. Filling stations flashed by. Houses grew. The open country was behind.

At three o'clock Cardigan braked his steaming car in a wide avenue, turned off the ignition. He strode quickly from the car a matter of twenty yards, then turned into a flag walk and entered a small apartment house. In the deserted lobby he paused to look in a notebook, then took a stairway up. On the fifth floor he began looking for door numbers. He stopped in front of 509, put his head close to the door.

"Pat!" he whispered. He listened a moment. "Pat, this is Cardigan!" he whispered again.

The door whipped open and a gun steadied on him.

"I just wanted to make sure," Pat said.

"Good girl," he said, and pushed in. "Lock it."

They were in the dark.

"Find anything?" he said.

"No. Isn't that jane ever coming home?"

"It's my hunch she'll be here soon—with White. Turn the lights on so I can get the lay here."

Pat switched them on and remained standing by the switch. Cardigan went to the bedroom, came out, looked in the bathroom, the closets.

"All right, kid, turn 'em off." Darkness engulfed the room. "Don't hide behind any chairs," Cardigan said. "Stand right here in the center of the room."

"I'll lock the door first."

"You take care of the jane."

"Oh, I'll take care of the jane."

TEN minutes later a key grated in the lock. The door swung open. The man and the woman were in dim silhouette against the glow in the corridor. The woman sauntered in. The man, directly behind her, turned the light switch and kicked the door shut with his heel.

"Reach," said Cardigan.

"Oh!" cried Nita Monteclara; and to Pat, "Why, you're—you are the—Oh!" Definite recognition added to her shock.

White kept his elbows at his sides, raising his forearms. His black felt hat was rakish over one eyebrow. He was quite a big man, with a hard pallor, colorless eyes. The scar glinted like a strip of metal on his forehead, just above his left eyebrow.

"Pinch, huh?"

"Raise 'em higher."

"This is an outrage!" cried Nita. "I weel not permeet—"

"You pipe down," Pat said quietly. "Cut out stamping the hoof and in general shut up. Sit down there."

White said, "Well, well?" to Cardigan.

Cardigan went close to him, pressed his gun firmly against White's stomach, removed White's gun and took a few steps backward. White never budged. His eyes shone like glass that has been slightly smoked.

"Well, well," said Cardigan. "I want those diamonds."

"What diamonds?"

"The Hotel Midlands job the cops failed to hang on you three years ago. Six diamonds."

"Aren't you funny?"

"Am I?" Cardigan took one step and laid the flat of his left hand across White's face.

"Oh, dear!" wailed Nita.

White stopped against the wall, lowering one hand to feel his face. "Who the hell are you?" he muttered.

"Cardigan, private snoop for the insurance company that was fall-guy over that theft. I want that ice, White. I want it and I'm going to get it. I haven't any time to spare. I'm going to get it if I have to break every bone in your body."

Nita snapped, "This is my home! You have no right—"

"You," said Pat, "had better act indifferent."

"But this is the outrage! I weel—"

"You hear me, White!" Cardigan was growling.

Cardigan's slap had left red marks on White's face. White remained standing with his back against the wall. "I don't know what the cripes you're talking about. Can't a guy come out of stir and go straight?"

"I've been keeping tabs on you for two weeks, White. I know that you've been spending jack like some big bomb and machine-gun man. You came out of the hoosegow stony. How come?"

White snapped, "You got nothing on me! I did my stretch for packing 'at pop-gun. I did it and now what's the big idea of you making cracks?"

"Where'd you get the dough to throw a party at Filone's? The dough to bust out like a rash in a new Chrysler? Where'd you get the dough to stake the dame here for whirls at the games at Phil Gould's casino? Go on —go on and tell me that your maiden aunt died."

"I got friends. I c'n borrow."

Cardigan wore a frigid smile empty of humor. "Only on good security, White. Got a job? No. Any money in the bank? No."

White's temper was rising slowly. "To hell with you! You've got no right to quizz me. You've got no right a-tall to bust in here and hold my girl and me like this—"

"You tell them, honey," Nita said, forgetting her accent.

"I'll tell 'em!" White blurted, his neck muscles bulging, his eyes striving to stare down Cardigan. He pushed his hat back. Sweat was on his forehead. Sweat made his white scar gleam. His initial coolness was ebbing fast.

"You'll tell me where that ice is, White; that's what you'll tell me," Cardigan said dully. "You dirty half-wit, I've pieced the whole puzzle together. Helen Carmory got the ice when you dropped it from you hotel window to Bennington Court. Five hours ago you bumped her off because this new heart of yours—"

"You liar!"

"Am I? Maybe you've got an alibi where you were."

"At Phil Gould's. He'll tell you."

"Will he? He'll tell me the truth because I've got enough of Gould and his bunch to send them up. He'll have to squawk to save himself. I've got him and Ackerman and the whole shebang tied in a knot. Gould can't afford to fake your alibi. I'll leave the murder pinch to the cops. I'm not after you for the murder of your former flame. I'm after the ice you chucked to her from that hotel window. You'll tip me off or you and this jane go in for the rap together."

Nita cried, "Not me!"

"Yes, you will," said Cardigan. "You'll take it right on the nose with your boy friend. Sergeant Bush has a hunch. He followed the hunch out to the casino. Gould can't stand by you because Ackerman won't let him, can't afford to. They'll chuck you to the wolves to save your hides."

White gritted, "They can't. I know too much about them."

"That's too bad. Then they'll put the cross on both of you. I'll take you out there—both of you. Come on."

"No," cried Nita in a frightened voice. "No—no!"

"I want those diamonds," Cardigan said doggedly.

WHITE moistened his lips. His breath came unsteadily. "I can't! I'm in the hole for twenty-two thousand. If I don't meet the debt—"

"I want those diamonds."

Perspiration dripped from White's chin. "How do I know you won't squawk?"

"I'm making no bargain with a killer, White. My job is to get the diamonds first. When they're in my hands I'll give you a ten-hour start, then I'll have to drop a hint to the cops."

White mopped his face. "It's no go. I'll take a chance. Gould will have to stick by us."

Nita cried, "But you heard this man say Gould—"

"Shut up, Nita," White snapped.

"I won't! You've got to keep me out of this, Burt! I had nothing to do with it."

"You tramp, you knew what was coming off. You stayed in that room at the casino so you could swear I was with you. I gave you five-thousand

bucks to do it. We got to take the chance. I don't believe this guy."

"I do!" cried Nita. "Anyhow, I will not take the chance. You've got to protect me, Burt. You've got to!"

"Shut up, damn you!"

Nita stamped her foot. "I won't! You have the diamonds. You were waiting for Max Bloomberg to come back from New York so he could buy them—"

"Why, you dirty—"

Cardigan gripped him by the throat, kept his gun pressed against White's stomach. "You're getting just what you deserve, White. Helen Carmory's death was a mistake. She looked swell to me. Are you going to fork over or are you going into a sure pinch with this jane turning color on you?"

"To hell with you!"

Nita cried, "He wears a money belt. They're in—"

"You two-timing—"

But Cardigan dropped him with a blow to the chin. White slumped to the floor and Cardigan bent down, ripped open vest and shirt, found the money belt, extracted a chamois pouch containing six diamonds.

White got to his feet, his face flushed and sullen. He rubbed his chin. His eyes were glassy. He thrust his hands into hip pockets. His face looked murderous.

"Beat it," said Cardigan, opening the door.

White moved to the threshold. He straightened up, turned and regarded Nita. His face softened. A strange smile came to his lips.

"Good luck, Nita," he said. "You were right. I was a louse. Forgive me, baby."

"Oh, Burt, I'm glad you understand."

She stumbled to the door, gripped his shoulders. "I'm only a woman, Burt,

I'm not as strong as you. I couldn't stand it. Kiss me, Burt."

His hands came out of his hip pockets. There was a quick movement. Then White spun and darted away. Nita mumbled something while she swayed in the doorway. Her swaying body blocked Cardigan. He grabbed her and turned her around. Her eyes were wide. There was a jack-knife sticking in her breast. White's hands had been in his hip pockets—

"Oh—" Nita's whimper was very weak.

Cardigan felt her body relax, saw a queer fixed look in her eyes that only the near-dead wear. He let her down to the carpet, threw a look at Pat, said nothing. He lunged through the door, down the steps. He heard the front door bang.

White's car was parked in the driveway alongside the house. White must have known it would be futile to try using it. He ran up the street. He saw Cardigan's roadster and leaped for it. The key was in it, the motor was warm and started easily. He did not know it was Cardigan's car, did not know who owned it. But he meshed gears savagely and got away.

Cardigan went no farther than the lobby. From the closed vestibule he could see White getting away. And then he heard the roar of another motor. A black touring car swept by.

A minute later the sound of guns hammered in the street. Cardigan sprang to the terrace. He saw his roadster leap across the curb, across the sidewalk; heard the crash of metal as the car slammed into a stone wall; saw the car leap into the air flinging aside torn metal; saw it burst into flames—while the touring car sped on.

When Cardigan returned to the apartment five minutes later Pat said, "I phoned a doctor, but it's no use. What was all that racket?"

Cardigan stared at the dead woman. "One of fate's little jokes. A mob that thinks I know too much tried to get me on the road in from the casino. They didn't have luck. So they just tried again. Only White was in the car. They got him."

Pat spread her hands. "What a mess, chief!"

"The double cross all around. White was in deep. He could never have got out. And Gould's heels got him instead of me."

"But what a mess, chief—for us!"

Cardigan pressed her arm, then patted it. "Don't you believe it, Pat. This is easy. We didn't fire a shot. Just keep your mouth shut and let me do the talking. We had a job to do. We did it."

He crossed the room heavily, picked up the phone, said, "Police headquarters."

Waiting, he smiled at Pat. He didn't look worried.

"What a man!" she said. "What a man!"

The Crime Machine

A Vee Brown Story

by Carroll John Daly

To that upstairs room came the notes of the Gangster's March—weird, staccato, crackling. As the music reached its highest pitch an arm swept downward and two guns spoke. Vee Brown, killer of killers, had changed the chorus to a melody of death.

I knew that I was looking at a dead man but I stood there frozen to the spot.

83

OF COURSE I paced my apartment nervously. In five minutes I was to meet and associate myself with the most dangerous, the most feared—and if Jack Ferris, editor of The Morning Globe, was correct—the most relentless hunter, and even killer of criminals. And it was this aptitude for killing; for meeting gunfire with gunfire, which had interested The Globe in the activities of this detective who carried the mildest of names—Vee Brown.

Vee Brown, after some pressure—in which Jack Ferris threatened to expose him as a ruthless killer—had agreed to permit a reporter to accompany him on his man-hunts and let the public see, through The Globe, that the new era in crime demanded that the hunter meet the hunted with his own weapons.

But there was more behind The Globe's interest in Vee Brown than the recording of his cases. Jack Ferris had told me that Vee Brown enjoyed an outside income that permitted him an apartment on Park Avenue, together with a high-priced car and chauffeur. The source of this income was not known to Ferris. It was part of my job to discover it. What with the poilce investigation; the enormous bank balances of discredited officers, Ferris was anxious to be assured that in killing the enemies of the State this detective did not also kill the enemies of himself. Those criminals, perhaps, by whose crimes he had profited. But that, of course, was mere speculation.

Vee Brown had made one stipulation. That he could choose his own assistant from The Globe. And he had chosen me.

Why had he picked me? Certainly the name Vee Brown was unfamiliar to me. But why confuse further an already overstimulated imagination, when this Vee Brown himself would call on me any minute and take me out into the night—in a hunt for a killer?

And Vee Brown came. There were short quick steps, and a small, slim, dark-haired man stepped through the doorway.

I was half across the room when I stopped and stared. Then grasped the hand that was extended toward me.

"Vivian—Vivian Brown!" I gasped. "Such an idea never entered my head. And you! Surely—"

"Quite correct—Vee Brown." He grinned. "The 'Vivian' was dropped years ago. Honestly, now—Dean, didn't you even suspect me?"

I shook my head. How could I? Oh, I recalled Vivian Brown now—when I was face to face with him. But to connect the acquaintance of my college days with the gun-toting, gun-using detective was hard to do even now. Vivian Brown, who had failed at things physical! Yet I recollected his gameness. It had been admired—and joked about too. Vivian Brown's insistent and useless attempts to force his frail body into college sports.

It was half an hour before we were through reminiscing and Vee Brown came down to business.

"I didn't like it at first," he told me frankly. "This being dragged through the press. And then your name bobbed up in that 'big game' feature. We weren't very close at college, Dean, but I admired your athletic accomplishments—and perhaps, now, there was the boyish itch to reverse the tables. Johnson had his Boswell, Sherlock Holmes his Watson, and—" he looked at me shrewdly with those penetrating black eyes, "Napoleon had his Waterloo," he finished.

Did he suspect, after all, the very thing that Ferris sought? The unfounded wealth back of Vee Brown's salary as a first-grade detective. But he was talking again. "You wonder how I got into the thing—eh, Dean?"

And I did wonder.

"Purely through my failure to make the mental desire conquer the physical weakness of my body. It is drilled into us that all men are created equal. I didn't believe it. Then it finally came home. We were created spiritually equal. That was the Divine power." He leaned forward. "But it took man, who made the pistol, to put the physical powers of each of us on an equal basis. Get the point?" He wagged the index finger of his right hand before me. "It's all there. I worked on it day and night for years. The difference between life and death lies only in the pressure of that single finger and the brain that controls it."

I jerked back in my chair. His hand had flashed down and up again with such rapidity that it seemed simply to waver slightly in the air. But now the hand held a heavy revolver, and the finger that had wagged in the air no longer caressed an imaginary trigger— but a real one.

I LOOKED again at Vee Brown; his clear black eyes; his fine intelligent features; and the quizzical, somewhat humorous twist to his thin lips. He would not be my idea of a criminal, but neither would he be my idea of a fearless hunter of men—although there was something animal-like and graceful about his movements.

"Do you work entirely alone?" I asked.

"Entirely alone, and independent of instructions since I have been assigned to the district attorney's office." He came to his feet and walked across the room to the piano in the alcove. "I might talk to you for hours, but you see it all yourself. You play?" he asked suddenly.

"No. I lease this apartment furnished. The piano came with it."

Without a word Vee Brown sat down and strummed a few notes. "That's something I never mastered." He laughed harshly, rose from the piano, and lighting a cigarette stood before me.

"You are going to see and feel sudden and violent death tonight," he said.

"Do you always go out with the purpose of killing a man?" I asked.

"I never go with that purpose." He shook his head. "Nor have I ever regretted a death. Tonight it's 'Killer' Regan. He shot the watchman and the cashier at the Hudson Terminal Theatre. She identified his picture before she died. He shot her three times in the stomach, though she never made a cry or move."

"You know where he is?" I asked.

"No, I don't. But I'll know tonight." His speech became more rapid and his tone more vehement as he talked. "Regan killed without reason. And he knows I know, and knows that I'll seek him out. And he knows that I'll shoot, and I know that he'll shoot. If there are any odds they're all in his favor. I'm getting information that may be true and may be false, or may be simply a means of cornering me— to be shot down as that defenceless girl was shot down." He paused a moment, jerked out his watch, snapped it open. "Come! It's close to midnight, and there's much to do."

"We're temperamental—all of us," Vee Brown said as we left the subway and walked toward Sixth Avenue. "I'm thinking, and my thoughts are all of the girl who died with a stomachful of lead." He paused a moment, then jerked out the words. "It's never pleasant to think, before the deed, that you might take a human life—unless you've built up a wall of hate."

"Don't you ever feel that there's another way?"

"I have no plans," he cut in quickly. "No specific instructions. Just an order. This time, to bring in Killer Regan—wanted for murder. And my order calls for me to produce a man or a body."

"Is—Regan in here?" I think that my voice shook slightly as we turned into a hallway beside a pawnbroker's shop.

"No." Vee Brown shook his head. "This is my bureau of information—and misinformation. The clever police clues and reasonings and deductions that decorate the newspapers are, with few exceptions, the squeals of stool pigeons. An unsavory system, that? Granted—but a necessary evil."

We passed down a narrow, ill-lit hallway, paused before a door on which Vee Brown tapped. A moment of silence; the shuffling of heavy feet, and a tiny hole in the door as a panel fell back.

"This will be Irving Small," Vee Brown whispered, as the door opened and we slid through the narrow passage.

For a moment we stood in blackness. The door closed, a lock clicked, and a dim electric lamp flashed from under a worn shade upon an old table. I saw the bent figure peering at us in the darkness. He opened his mouth as if to speak, closed it again; and I caught the flash of watery blue eyes.

"My assistant." Vee Brown spoke sharply as the little man still watched me.

"I understood there was to be only one." Irving Small raised the lamp and held it out toward me as far as the silk cord would permit.

"You understand 'two' now," Vee Brown said simply.

"He goes too?" The yellow lips of the pawnbroker smacked.

"Yes—he goes too."

"It ain't safe. Leastwise, it's doubly dangerous—for you."

"I know that. But he goes nevertheless."

The clawlike fingers opened and closed long after Irving Small placed the lamp back on the table. He stretched out his right hand and took something from the hand of Vee Brown. For a few minutes his back was to us. He was counting softly to himself. Then he spoke over his shoulder. "It ain't any more than last time. Regan's worth more than that. It ain't very much."

"It's better than a cold, damp cell."

"Ehe—but not worth the price of a long box."

Another moment of silence, and Irving Small spoke again. "He's a desperate man. I hope you've left nothing behind to—that tells ill of me."

"Nothing. You've had my word on that."

"Ehe—I've had that." The lips smacked again—and then, "He's at Magna's. Second floor—last room—over the pianie. This is the night for it. He'll leave tomorrow. Magna's is watched. If you hold a police parade there'll be no show."

"There'll be no parade," said Vee Brown."

And that was all.

I BREATHED easier again when we reached the street. I was learning much about police work. Vee Brown had wanted information, and he knew where to get it. And he had bought it as he might buy any commodity.

"Stuffy place." Vee Brown stretched. "That's part of the system, except that I have my own private information bureau. It wasn't through luck hat I first found Irving Small. It took time, and much work. But now—I hold twenty years over his head any time I wish to speak. I know you won't mention this until the usefulness of Irving Small is over and he has betrayed me."

"And that he might betray you I should think would be a real fear."

"It is." Vee Brown nodded vigorously. "I haven't the least doubt that he doubled on me tonight. I know that he was Killer Regan's fence."

"Then we won't go to—to Magna's." I guess I felt relieved.

"On the contrary, we will go straight to Magna's."

I pushed the question of his suspicion of Irving Small and why he walked into a trap, if he suspected treachery.

"Why—" he looked suddenly up at me as we passed a street lamp, "traps are a most interesting study. The game is—to get the bait out of the trap before the trap is sprung. Tonight the bait is Killer Regan."

"You'd walk into this trap—and drag me with you!"

Vee Brown stopped and swung on me suddenly. "You don't have to come." His eyes flashed and his lips set tightly. "Your editor has hinted that I shoot men down in cold blood, without giving them a chance. If you want to learn the truth you've got to face what I face—or you've got to believe what I tell you. It's not too late to turn back."

I guess several things shot through my mind as we faced each other there on the deserted street. But what decided my quick reply was the curl of his lips and the sneer in his voice.

"I'll go with you," I said. "But I hope you're playing a man's part tonight."

He hesitated—and when he spoke again the curl had left his lips and the sneer gone out of his voice.

"I am not acting as a man tonight," he said, "but as a machine—maintained by the State. A crime machine." Then suddenly, "Are you armed?"

I nodded my reply, for a high-caliber automatic was one of the first things I obtained when I left the office of Jack Ferris, city editor of The Morning Globe.

"That's Magna's," Vee Brown told me as we passed a dilapidated, neglected three-story building. "There's a fence and a gate in the rear, which is used for a hurried exit when the police make a raid. That'll be our entrance."

Well back down the side street was a dirty driveway which gave entrance to a storage warehouse. The wide wooden gates opened enough for our bodies to squeeze through. For some time Vee Brown remained at the crack in the big gate, peering out on the side street.

"Not a watcher—not a light—not a sound," he muttered as he shook his head. "Very clever or very stupid." He took my arm as we passed along the six-foot wooden fence. Somewhere, close to the middle of the block, he paused. "Since two of us are going in, you'll have to play your part," he said. "The little gate is about ten yards down. If you find it open, walk in. If you don't—climb over."

"And you?" For a moment the thought came that I was to be the bait that would spring the trap. But I didn't say more. It was the contemptuous tone of his voice as he dismissed my question that made me act. I simply turned and hurried down the alley toward the gate.

The gate was not locked. It gave easily beneath my pressure, but there was a dull squeak to it that sounded doubly loud in the clear stillness of the night. I thought that I heard the soft tread of feet beyond the fence. It was then that I first sought my gun and jerked it into my hand. The gate opened inward; I thrust it open and stepped back, raising my gun. But no figure darted out at me; no voice called for me to stand back; no——. And I heard it. The scraping of feet—and once a dull thud against the fence, further down the alley. I looked back in the direction I had come. The night was clear—it was only ten yards to where Vee Brown had been standing. He was gone.

FOR perhaps two minutes I hesitated between entering the gate and retracing my footsteps to the street in a search for Vee Brown. Again I heard the footsteps, a steady tread this time, that came toward me and the gate. Should I stay and face the one who came, or—— It was too late to decide. The owner of those feet had already reached the gate and stood in the opening. I half dropped my gun.

"Come!" The figure spoke. It was Vee Brown. He was straightening his tie and rearranging his coat. A tiny trickle of red showed on his forehead.

"I missed him by a foot when I swung over the fence," Brown explained. "Timed it wrong, I guess. His feet against your squeak at the gate. I thought he'd search you out, and by dropping over the fence we'd have him between us. But he didn't. He sought the house." Brown's thin shoulders shrugged as he wiped the blood from his forehead. "After all, it was a close call—and I got the breaks."

The explanation in Vee Brown's cryptic words came to me as I followed him. The alley inside the fence was narrow. Fifteen or twenty yards down it we stepped over the body of a man. I shuddered slightly and looked down at the silent figure.

"He's not dead—just knocked cold." Brown answered my unspoken question as he jerked me by the arm. "We must hurry now. Our presence is expected. When this outside man doesn't report, suspicion may be felt within."

He was a different man now. His words came in quick, sharp, spasmodic jerks, and he seemed to raise his head and listen between each sentence.

As we hurried down the alley I could hear a hum that grew louder and louder. Then I knew that it was voices—many voices. Almost at once it died away and the tin-pan notes of a piano drifted to us, above the steady beat of a trap drum. I didn't have to be told that we were approaching one of those many dives that dot the city under the name of 'night club'.

The music and the sound of dancing feet became almost deafening as I followed Vee Brown down a short flight of stairs and into a cellar.

"Stick close—and behind me." Vee Brown stretched out a hand to guide me as we crossed the damp, ill-smelling basement. "It's here that we strike the first blow, I think." I hardly caught his whisper. "And we must make it before the music stops. Now!"

I heard a door open before us, saw the dim light and the white face; the thick lips of the man who blinked at us, trying to pierce the darkness.

"Is he——" The man started, and stopped. His lips parted; his narrow eyes tightened to two slits, and a hand jerked to his side. But he never called out—he didn't have a chance. Vee Brown sprang forward; his hand flashed up. Metal shone for a moment in the light, then steel collided with bone—and steel won. Without a groan the man toppled forward into Vee Brown's arms. I saw Brown's feet slide back as he braced himself and eased the inert body to the floor.

The cellar door swung closed behind us with a dull slam—and the music stopped. Again the hum of voices and laughter, and the clink of glasses. But this time it was very close; almost as if we were in the room with it.

"You'll make note of that," Vee Brown whispered, close to my ear. "Remember that I struck with the barrel —not the butt. I don't want to appear a fool, in the paper. It's only detectives of fiction who are free from the danger of a bullet running up their sleeves." And there was a high-pitched note to his voice—and a slight ring of pride too, I thought.

"What was that?" He sung suddenly, raising his gun. But I had heard nothing. At least, nothing but the buzz of voices. For a full minute Brown tried to listen as we crouched back in the darkness.

"I could almost swear a figure moved —back there." He shook his head, and I thought that much of the elation had gone out of his voice. "Let's go on," he said finally. "I can't stand this waiting—this inactivity. It hounds and depresses me. I wouldn't mind so much being knocked over by Regan—but to be trapped here by this sort of flesh!" And he actually pushed the unconscious body slightly with his foot before he stepped over it.

"Inactivity" and "waiting." I could have laughed at the absurdity of the complaint, but I didn't. I said nothing; scarcely breathed as we slipped along the dimly lit hall, turned a corner sharply and stopped before a flight of stairs.

"I've been this way before," Brown told me as we waited, our backs against the wall. "Every step is charged with its own natural burglar alarm. We'll have to wait until the music starts again. Every step groans loud enough to wake the dead. The dead!" he repeated, as he nudged me in the side.

"How do you like it?" he whispered—and I thought there was a challenge in his voice. "One flight up— last room—right. And Regan; Killer Regan, who put the lead into a young girl's stomach. Always think of that, Dean. Put your mind constantly on something like that, in the man-hunt. It steadies the nerves. And even now, when we flatter ourselves on doing well so far, we cannot tell. For often the obstacles that we overcome are planned just so—for us to overcome. No. The question for us to figure out is—are we coming to 'get' Regan, or is Regan waiting above to 'get' us? And in your honest answer to that question lies The Morning Globe's opinion of the paid man-hunter of the law—Vee Brown."

FOR seconds that seemed like hours we remained in silence at the foot of the stairs. In the room beyond the voices churned incessantly; in the hall behind us a man lay unconscious; and above—

My heart gave an involuntary leap. Did the man who put the lead in the dead girl's stomach lurk at the top of that black stairway?

I jerked erect. Vee Brown gripped me by the arm. The music had started—and so had we. Quickly we were mounting the stairs.

The old boards gave up their dead. Would others hear them? Would they announce our arrival to listening ears at the top of those stairs? Vee Brown didn't hesitate. In fact, we increased our speed. I reached for a step that wasn't there, half stumbled, felt the hand upon my arm jerk me erect—and we were at the top. At the top and still going; moving along the dark hall to the rear room, right—and Killer Regan.

Would the gunman be in bed?

Would he be waiting for us at the door? Had he been listening at the top of the stairs and was now crouched back in the darkness? Would—

I sucked in a deep breath. I heard the knob of a door turn—and the slight squeak of hinges. Then saw, almost at once, a thin strip of light. Certainly Vee Brown did not waste time.

I could see into the room now; dimly illuminated by the soft glow of a heavily shaded lamp. The room was divided as the suites in cheaper hotels. There was a large arch effect, with a curtain pole across the top—but no curtains. Through this I could see the end of a bed and, I thought, the shape of a foot beneath the covers.

As I slipped through the doorway behind Vee Brown I heard him close the door gently. Then the click, as the key turned in the lock. If Killer Regan was in that room his escape was cut off—and I also thought, with a gulp, so was ours.

Vee Brown slipped the key into his pocket, and stepping across the room thrust a hand against the curtains before the window. He turned suddenly at my exclamation.

"There's a man in the bed." My voice seemed to come from a long way off as I clutched Vee Brown by the arm.

"Really. How observant!" Vee Brown glanced casually at the bed, knelt and looked beneath it, and stepping to a closet door swung it open.

I walked cautiously to the bed, my gun raised.

Vee Brown joined me. His gun hung by his side. He didn't move cautiously. He strode rapidly by me, reached the bed and threw back the covers. A couple of pillows and a pair of shoes were beneath them.

There was a thud behind us, as if feet had jumped upon the floor.

"Quick—right—behind the arch!" Brown jerked out the words. And I? I jumped to the left, collided with Brown, and saw the sad sort of smile on his lips as he muttered: "It didn't really matter, Dean. I'd advise you to drop your gun at once." And I heard the revolver that he carried in his hand drop to the rug. It was then that I saw the shadow that crossed the light and heard, too, the voice—gruff, vicious, with a ring of triumph in it.

"That's good advice, bozo. Drop the gun and stick up your hands. I was sitting pretty, on the fire-escape. If you'd opened them curtains the show'd be over now."

Mechanically my fingers opened and the gun fell to the floor. Funny. I didn't have the same sensation of fear now that the thing had happened. My first thought was—what a story for the paper! And my second thought, and hardly as pleasant—who would write the story, and would I read it?

"I didn't expect such a pleasure," the voice went on behind me as I stood with my hands in the air—Brown beside me. "Who may you be?" A gun in my back punctuated the final sentence.

"A cub reporter from a paper. Leave him alone, Regan. He—" Brown began.

I heard the curse, saw the shadow, and caught the thud as the man's arm swung through the air. Vee Brown swayed slightly, his arms half lowered —but they went up again at a sharper command.

"We'll have no advice. One more peep and I'll slap you away for good. It's a great moment, Mr. Vee Brown— and a personal one." He raised his voice above the din of the orchestra that shrieked out its music from below. "Swing around—both of you, and I'll boast a little myself—that Killer Regan's bullets weren't found in your backs."

WE turned and faced him. Certainly if I didn't know fear before, I knew it now. Rat-like eyes; dominant chin and coarse, evil lips. There wasn't one redeeming feature in that hard, mean face. For the moment I thought of the girl with the stomachful of lead. Regan had finished searching me and was now searching Vee Brown for weapons. And I acted. My body slipped forward and my hands lowered. Threatening perhaps, but it was involuntary. Maybe I was going to spring on Regan—maybe I wasn't. I don't know.

Regan's left hand shot up and his gun cracked beneath my chin, straightening me. In a dazed way I knew that I still stood on my feet. And I knew too that Regan had backed us into the other room. But I also knew, with a little feeling of satisfaction, that Regan watched me carefully—and that, though he finished patting Vee Brown for weapons, his search was but a perfunctory one—his eyes ever switching to me.

"You let him go, Regan," Vee Brown nodded his head toward me. "He's from a newspaper. Nothing to do with you or with me."

"You're from a paper?" Killer Regan raised his voice again, for we must have been directly above the orchestra now, as the music was almost deafening. "Well—you'll have something to write for them. Something about Killer Regan. You can face a bit sideways and watch the show." Regan stepped around in front of us again, a gun in either hand now. "I'm going to shoot this boy detective to ribbons. There's one thing about frying a lad that has its good points. You can't burn him more than once."

Killer Regan raised his right hand. His chin shot forward; his thick lips curled. Vee Brown stood straight and tense, his eyes full on Regan's—and his hands stretched high.

"You guessed at me and brought the picture of my mug to the girl I croaked." I could see the gathering of hate in Regan's eyes as he talked. "She'd never have lived long enough to mark me if it wasn't for you. You've been a terror to them what lacked guts, but now—" His gun shot forward, his finger tightened upon the trigger, and deadly silence fell upon the room. The music, below, had stopped. Regan dropped the muzzle of his gun slightly.

"What—" Vee Brown smiled as he faced death. "Must have music with your murders, eh? But you won't be the first man who talked himself out of killing me. Now—if you had an ear for music you'd have shot sooner and talked less." Involuntarily, it seemed, he stepped to the right.

"You stand your ground!" Regan's sharp little eyes ran from Vee Brown to me, and both his guns raised and waved menacingly. "If you want it now, why—"

"But you don't care to disturb the peace, and—"

Vee Brown stopped. Regan grinned. The orchestra, below, had crashed into life again. I knew the piece. It was The Gangster's March, that had lately taken the city by storm. And I read death in Regan's face. I had never seen it in a man's face before. In animals, perhaps. But I recognized it just the same. Not just a deadly purpose; not the will that forces a man to do something particularly loathing to him. No. It was a lust—a desire to kill. I saw his tongue slip out and lick at thick, dry lips. There wasn't a bit of doubt that only a second stood between Vee Brown and sudden and violent death.

I half closed my eyes, then opened them again. Vee Brown spoke.

"Don't be foolish, Dean," he said. "There is no danger to you. Keep your hands up."

Killer Regan's rat-like eyes flashed toward me for a split second; mine shot toward Vee Brown. And it happened. Just as the music reached the weird, high, cracking notes—like the staccato of machine-gun fire— Vee Brown plunged his right hand suddenly downward. Down and out. And that hand, which had started down empty, now contained flashing steel.

They fired together, I think. The roar of the bullets was lost in the clash of the instruments below, but plainly I saw the two spurts of orange blue flame.

I didn't jump forward. I didn't even lower my hands. I just stood there, frozen to the spot. For a moment I saw nothing but the dull white smoke, the blurred faces of two men, and the little pool of blood on Vee Brown's forehead, that broke suddenly and forming a tiny red stream rolled down his face. But Vee Brown still stood upon his feet.

Mechanically my eyes turned and rested full upon the face of Killer Regan. There was a gray, powdered, spattered hole right in the center of his forehead. And those eyes, that were malignant and glaring bright, now were dull, glassy, distant, filmy things.

I knew that I was looking at a dead man, yet he stood upon his feet. He didn't sway back and forth. His hands opened and his guns dropped to the floor. Then his knees bent—slowly, almost carefully—till they reached the floor. For a moment he knelt so, as if in prayer—then pitched forward on his face.

VEE BROWN shrugged his shoulders and knelt beside the dead gunman. With an effort he turned him over on his back.

"Lucky I planted that gun in my sleeve," he said. "But I felt, dear Mr. Regan, that you were on the fire-escape. And that's the disadvantage of having a newspaper pass judgment on your ethics. How much easier to have shot through the curtains before the window!" He wiped the blood from his forehead. "Well—you missed and I didn't. But I don't like this playing to the gallery. Yet, the public must have its thrill."

He smiled at me as he stood up.

"There's your story—and hard to get a better one, even if we had rehearsed it." And then, the smile broadening into a grin, "You can put your hands down, Dean," he said quietly. "You were always my idea of a hero—and you look rather silly now. I should—" He stopped as he stepped over the dead murderer, one foot on either side of what had been Killer Regan. The music below had suddenly changed. The notes were soft and alluring now.

Vee Brown stood so, his right hand raised in the air, his index finger keeping time with the music, his shoulders swaying slightly. The sad smile had changed to a pleased, wistful sort of a smile, and his eyes were bright and—yes—laughing.

"Hear that, Dean," he said softly. "Even that gang of melody murderers can't take the beauty away from it. Can't you feel it grip you, like a southern night?"

"I—It's pretty." My voice came from between cracked, dry lips.

"Pretty!" He swayed back and forth above the dead man. "Why—all New York will sing it by tomorrow night. It's a masterpiece." He began to hum softly.

And I? It was loathsome—revolting. Here he had killed a man, and now stood above the body and discussed a new melody. I shuddered, half turned my head, took a step forward—and stopped, swaying dizzily. Things began to dance about the room; the hot blood rushed to my forehead; the floor began to rise—and I stretched out a hand.

Vee Brown was across to me—a hand beneath my elbow.

"I forgot, Dean. I didn't do it for bravado. There! Brace up, old man. As he led me from the room and down the stairs and out into the alley, he said, "Think of the dead girl and the stomachful of lead."

But I was thinking of something else. Of the dead man on the floor; of Ferris and his suspicion of Vee Brown's supposed wealth; of the song that was still on Vee Brown's lips. As if he read my thoughts he cut in on them.

"It's the music that gets me, Dean. There are two men in me, I think. An outer and an inner man, and the one is the relief for the other." He looked at me with that wistful, twisted smile as we reached the street and he hailed a taxi. "You didn't think of me when Ferris spoke the name Vee Brown. You knew me as Vivian. Now—what you wish most to know, and Ferris wishes most to know, stares you in the eyes every day; assails your ears on the radio and from every night club. Even the restaurants that have music. Don't you see—don't you understand yet?" He looked at my blank face. "Vivian. I'm Vivian. Why—the name is blazoned out on the most popular of our sentimental song sheets."

"You—you!" I gasped. "Vivian, the song writer. Who people wonder about, and whom the publishers won't —So that's where you get your money."

"Yes. That's the other side of me, Dean. The outlet for this passion of hunting criminals. Or perhaps the sentiment in my songs is—But I don't know. I don't know which man I really am—or if I am a mixture of both. It's a rather lonely life. You'll keep my secret and—and my shame." He was grinning now. When he left me to enter an all-night drug store to telephone police headquarters the grin was still there—and he was humming.

Vivian Brown. Vee Brown the anonymous writer of sentimental song hits! Hard to believe that? But why? After all, it was easier to believe that this slim, almost delicate little man was Vivian the song writer, than it was to believe that he was Vee Brown, hunter and killer of men. "Master of Melody" they called Vivian.

Killer of Men—Master of Melody. What a — But above all, I was thinking that I was through, Morning Globe or no Morning Globe—public or no public. Yet, thoughts are flitting things. I looked up as Vee Brown came from that drug store, still grinning and still humming, and despite my thoughts I knew that I was not through—but just beginning.

ONCE A CROOK

by

Oscar Schisgall

"You've got to steal!" That was the order
waiting for Dave Loree when he left the pen.
He could not refuse—for his brother's life
depended on his answer—and crookdom
was bound to claim its own.

**With a mighty leap
Loree reached him,
seized the weapon,
jammed it down.**

CHAPTER ONE

"I Mean Business"

THE state prison occupied a commanding site on the crest of a hill; and when Dave Loree stepped out of its gates, he surveyed, like a monarch, a vast and glamorous panorama of farmlands.

The sight lit leaping fires in his eyes, and he drew a mighty breath of joy.

"God!" he whispered. "It's good to be out!"

The guard behind him said curtly: "Yep. Reckon it must be, after two years. Why don't you wait for the prison bus and get a lift? You're two miles from the railroad station."

Loree shook his head. His glowing gaze swept avidly over far horizons.

"I'd rather walk. I've got to stretch my legs. They——they're cramped!"

Because he understood this fervor of youth, the guard smiled wryly. He proffered his hand.

"All right," he said. "Good luck, kid. Hope you never come back."

"I won't!"

Dave Loree swung down the road with a lusty, vigorous stride. Spring wind, laden with the pungency of newly tilled soil, rushed out of the valley to welcome him, and he drank of it profoundly, happily. It set his blood to tingling. He let his coat hang open, the better to receive the breeze. He even drew off his hat, so that the coolness would flow through his masses of curly brown hair.

The road wound downhill until, halfway to the village, it disappeared between walls of fragrant pines. When he reached the trees Loree saw, at some distance ahead, a small, black coupe. It was parked innocently enough. Through its back window he could discern the shoulders of two men.

But he granted the car little attention. It was the future that beguiled his mind. He yearned eagerly to grapple once more with life, to wrest from it something finer than it had so far yielded.

Why shouldn't he? He was twenty-three——big, sturdy, capable. Though prison had calloused him, it had not succeeded in poisoning his soul with bitterness. Even the warden had noticed that. He had said: "I hope you're going to make a clean start!" The words, strangely, were an echo of Loree's own resolve——to start fresh, clean!

He approached the coupe with the soaring spirit of a young crusader.

But when he was within ten feet of the car, its door swung open, suddenly, and two men stepped into the road. Queer men, they faced Dave Loree and grinned. They kept their hands in the pockets of their overcoats.

"Hi, Dave."

And he, recognizing these companions of a darker era——"Squinty" Pike and Joe Scarlatti——halted in amazement. A tremor of excitement rippled through him, left him rigid.

For an instant not one of them spoke.

Squinty Pike's grin was like a satyr's, thin and cunning and incisive, revealing irregular yellow teeth. He had a lean bony face perched on a lean, bony body and looked dangerously consumptive.

"Me and Joe," he said, "is the reception committee."

Loree glanced quickly at the other man. Joe had the squat, huge-chested figure of a wrestler. His Corsican countenance, shadowed by the brim of a black velour hat, was thick and muscular, daubed by a pair of startlingly red, fat lips.

"Hop in, Dave," he said, with a sideward shake of his head. "We're driving you to Springfield."

Dave Loree did not move. "Nick

Brody's orders?" he asked, his voice low.

"Right!" Scarlatti assented.

"Well, I'm not going, Joe."

"Huh?"

"I'm through with Brody's racket."

Joe Scarlatti and Squinty exchanged a surprised yet humorous glance. Then Squinty scoffed: "That's what you told the lawyer Brody sent to see you in the big house."

"Yes, and I meant it."

Squinty laughed derisively. "Don't be a sap! A guy with your talent would be a fool to waste himself!"

"Exactly how I feel," grimly agreed Loree. "That's why I'm going straight."

"Yeah? When Nick Brody has a dozen juicy jobs all cut out for you, just ripe to be plucked?"

"I did one job for Brody, and it landed me in that house up the hill. Now I'm through."

LOREE actually resumed walking, but Joe Scarlatti abruptly stepped in front of him. And Joe's smile, in half a second, became a scowl.

"You're crazy!" he rapped out. "Don't you realize Brody is giving you a chance to make yourself some real dough?"

"I don't want it."

"But you got to come and see him, anyhow!" determinately.

"Why?"

"Because he wants you, that's why! He sent us special to get you!"

Dave Loree shook his head. "Nothing doing," he said flatly. "You tell Brody to count me out of his mob. I'm going, Joe. I've got to make a train."

And he would have turned to march on without further parley had not the thick-set Joe Scarlatti moved once more to block him. This time Joe's eyes narrowed uncannily. They gleamed.

He pulled his right hand out of his pocket. It gripped an ugly little automatic the muzzle of which he pointed straight toward Loree's stomach.

"Get into the car!" he ordered softly. "I don't want to hurt you, Dave, but—get into the car!"

Loree stared.

Precisely what prompted him to act he could never clearly explain. What he did was instinctive; or probably the venting of sudden rage. It came even before Scarlatti finished talking, as quickly as a blink.

Loree's fist flew up!

It was a mad, reckless thing to do. Yet this very recklessness—so utterly unexpected, so impulsive—saved him. Joe, unprepared for that violent response, had no chance to dodge the blow; no time even to realize it was coming. Before his wits could impel his fingers to shoot, Loree's fist crashed on his chin!

"Damn!" Joe gasped.

His head jerked upward. He winced in pain, staggered back. Momentarily his arm lost its strength. It sagged, the automatic pointing ineffectually at the ground.

After that, having leaped into this madness, Dave Loree could not stop!

There was Squinty Pike to remember. In his amazement, Squinty had not yet drawn a weapon, but Loree could not risk waiting. He whirled toward the lean man. And as he turned, his arm swung through a semicircle and smashed a furious blow full into Squinty's abdomen.

"Oof!"

Squinty shut his eyes. Physically he was weak. The punch not only exploded the breach from his lungs but put him for a time quite definitely out of the fight. He reeled back to bump against the coupe. Both hands clutched wildly at his stomach; his face was horribly contorted by a grimace of agony.

"He's out!" thought Loree.

By this time, flushed and fiery-eyed, he was again following the burly Joe. He had to follow! His very life now depended on speed and decisiveness!

Scarlatti was just recovering his balance. He was not facing Loree, for he had been spun half around by that first punch. As he blinked the daze out of his eyes, he started raising the revolver.

With a mighty leap Loree reached him. His left hand seized the weapon, jammed it down. In the same violent lunge he brought his right fist from behind and drove it straight at Scarlatti's jaw.

It landed—crack—just below the ear. Joe's knees crumpled, almost collapsed. He floundered sideways, one arm groping out like a blind man's. For an instant the jolting blow obliterated his senses. He did not even feel the automatic being wrenched out of his grip.

And that changed everything.

HALF a minute later Dave Loree, breathing hard, his eyes aflame, stood with one foot on the running-board of the black coupe. He held two automatics—the second having just been snatched from the pocket of Squinty Pike who still sat in the road, gasping to retrieve his breath.

"Stay where you are, Joe!" Loree rapped out harshly. "I mean business!"

"You damn fool!" Scarlatti rasped. "Maybe you don't know it, but you're putting yourself in one swell spot!"

He had regained his wits and his balance. His rugged figure seemed little the worse for the blows it had sustained. But there were red splotches on his face, and his vivid fat lips quivered in fury.

"Wait," he flung out savagely, "till Brody hears about this! It'll be too bad!"

"I told you I'm through with Brody."

"But he ain't through with you, see?"

For a tense moment Dave Loree peered at the thick-set man searchingly. Ten feet separated them, and this margin of peace the automatics promised to maintain. Then, abruptly, Loree demanded: "What's making Brody so doggone anxious to have me back in the mob?"

"Who the hell said he's anxious?"

"He was anxious enough to send you and Squinty for me!"

Scarlatti sneered. His fingers twitched at his side. He wanted very much to hurl out some harsh and contemptuous retort. But it occurred to him, of a sudden, that a smooth tongue and subtle flattery might achieve what he and Squinty had failed to do. So, after some hesitation, he shrugged with an air of yielding a point.

"Well, all right. I'll admit he wants you," he granted. "He needs somebody who knows how to open a safe scientific, see? I told you he's got a dozen juicy jobs lined up for you, and they're not in Springfield, either! Geeze, Dave, he thinks you're a wizard in your line! Why don't you go back and give him a chance? Brody can do a lot for you!"

"He's done enough," snapped Loree. He was scowling; but despite himself he emitted a dry, hard laugh. Characteristic of Brody, he thought, to want to profit by the ability of those he could domineer. By his system he had successfully built up not only a powerful gang of supporters but also an impressive personal fortune.

"You tell Brody I'm through with safe-cracking!" he said. "He knows I've a kid brother to look after, and I can't do that in jail! From now on I'm playing safe—and straight! Get me!"

He scarcely listened to Joe's hoarse reply. Instead he stepped into the coupe and slammed its door shut.

"You'll find your car parked at the station," he promised over his shoulder. "You and Squinty can walk down as soon as he feels better. As for the gats, I'll throw them into the creek down below. Good-by!"

Joe roared, sprang forward. Even Squinty turned to splutter in panicky protest. But the black coupe leaped away and went whizzing down the hill.

It was two years since Loree had touched the wheel of a car, yet he drove confidently. There was a queer smile on his lips. Occasionally he glanced back at the two enraged, gesticulating figures he had abandoned, but soon a bend in the road obscured them.

Well, that was that!

He inhaled a vast breath of relief. It was a strange way to begin his venture in freedom, yet it was certainly better than returning to Nick Brody—and crime.

From somewhere far out in the valley floated the whistle of a train. Loree pressed the accelerator. He had, he realized, lost time; but with the coupe he could still catch that train for Riverton—his home town—and peace!

CHAPTER TWO

The Black Sedan

WHEN Loree hopped off the train in Riverton he did not anticipate immediate trouble.

He wanted, before all else, to enjoy this thrilling sense of release. He was home! And free! He wanted to forget Nick Brody and Joe Scarlatti and the desperate life they signified. There were, he knew, better things ahead of him.

But as he gazed about the familiar platform, with half a smile, the impulse to exult was checked, and he was at once snatched back to uneasy tension.

For he saw Silas Taggart, the local chief of police, coming ominously to meet him.

Loree stiffened.

It was twilight—a purple dusk in which the station lights seemed oddly feeble. And though he could not yet distinctly see Chief Taggart's features, he sensed in them a hostility that did not brighten the gloom.

"Well, Dave! So you're back."

That was Taggart's greeting, curt and hard. He devoted several seconds to an appraisal of the young man who had spent the first twenty-one years of his life in Riverton. Then, as the train started to roll away, he asked a very significant question: "How long you expecting to stay in town?"

"Why—" Loree hesitated in surprise. "I don't know. I hadn't planned on leaving, exactly."

"No? Well—I'm hoping you won't try to stay more than twenty-four hours."

Loree's astonishment became a stare of utter incredulity; then of dismay.

"What—what do you mean, chief?"

"We may as well understand each other," snapped Taggart. He was a sharp-featured man of sixty and not given to futile hedging. "Crooks 've never been welcome in Riverton!"

"But I—"

"You're no exception."

An instant Loree could not speak. Something leaped into his throat, choked him. This, then, was his longed-for homecoming. He had to look away from Taggart's small, uncompromising eyes. On the murky platform a few figures whom he vaguely recognized were watching him, but not one of them moved to approach. They remained aloof and forbidding, as tight-lipped as the police chief. Clearly, they had not forgotten the young man who had illegally opened a local safe; nor did they appear disposed to forget.

Loree's mouth was suddenly dry; he swallowed.

"I—I understand how you feel," he said, not very steadily. "But listen, chief. I've got to think of my brother. It—it's because of Stevie I came back. I can't make arrangements for him in only twenty-four hours."

"You don't have to," declared Taggart. "John Cornell and his daughter are taking mighty good care of the boy. You know that."

"Yes, but now that I'm free—"

"You're damned lucky having him with a decent family like the Cornells instead of in some institution! I was talking to John Cornell about it today. He's perfectly willing to keep your brother till you get settled somewhere else."

"But I can't ask them," Loree protested, a little desperately, "to go on taking care of Stevie when—"

"Well, suit yourself," flatly interrupted Silas Taggert. "It's my business to see that you're out of town by this time tomorrow. Just remember that. Good-by."

The chief turned obdurately and walked away.

FOR a while, as he stared after the man, Dave Loree remained motionless, a wraith in the deepening dusk. He wanted, somehow, to emit a harsh laugh. But no sound escaped him. A growing fury, blended with despair, held him silent. Was this, then, the sort of reception he must expect?

After a time he jammed his hands into his pockets and strode away, quickly. He dared not give expression to the sudden bitterness that churned in him. Bitterness, he knew, was poison.

"Dave! Oh, Davy!"

At the sound of that unforgettable voice—reaching him as he stepped off the platform—Loree halted. A curious prickling sensation quivered through him. He looked around at the blue roadster that had just stopped, at the girl jumping out of it, waving her gloved hand.

The sight of Julia Cornell left him rigid. His temples began to throb, and he felt ridiculously hot.

Julie, almost running toward him, was as slender and gracile as a sylph. Her tan polo coat and her saucy beret emphasized the exquisite suppleness of her young figure. With her hand finally in his, and an eager welcome bubbling on her lips, she gave Loree a radiant smile. It all but made him forget, for a second, he was now an ex-convict and no longer the boy she used so gaily to mock in Riverton High School days.

"Gosh it is good to see you again!" she exclaimed.

"It—it's great to see you, Julie," he muttered huskily. The warmth of her greeting, after the frigidity of Taggart's, dazed him. He felt as if he were playing two opposite roles in a fantastic drama.

"Stevie is just dying to see you," said Julie Cornell. "I promised I'd rush you right home. And dinner's waiting, too. So let's go!"

As he followed her, almost mechanically, he asked: "How—how is Stevie now?"

"Splendid! You won't believe your eyes when you see the progress he's made with his new crutches!"

She led him excitedly to the roadster, which she insisted on driving herself. And as they started for the Cornell home, through gray twilight, Loree regarded her anxiously from the corner of his eyes. Riverton, he suspected, would never condone her graciousness to a criminal.

During the past two years he had seen her quite frequently. Every month, unfailingly, she had brought his young brother Stevie to visit the big red house on the hill. And though the sight of her loveliness had always filled Loree with a strange, yearning ache, she had never seemed as beautiful—and as hopelessly unattainable—as she was now.

He stared hollowly into the golden path of the headlights as they stabbed the gathering darkness.

While she drove, Julie talked cheerfully—not of prison, not of crime, but of Stevie. A week ago, she said, they had given him a rollicking party on his fourteenth birthday. He had actually been able to play with the other boys; and she was certain that within a few years he would conquer the paralysis that had stricken him in childhood.

Loree turned to her. "You and your dad," he said earnestly, "have been mighty good to him while I was in— away. I don't know how—how I'll ever be able to repay—"

"Nonsense! We love having him!"

"I don't know what would have become of Stevie if it wasn't for you. Nobody else—" he thought bitterly of Brody's gang, who had called themselves his friends—"bothered about him."

"Oh, forget it now! You ought to see how excited he is about your coming. He's been telling everybody— neighbors, friends, even the postman— you were arriving today!"

At that Loree's mouth hardened. He understood now how Chief Taggart had been apprised of his coming. The news must have circulated through the town like scandalous gossip. Everyone knew—

Abruptly Dave Loree stopped thinking.

IN the gray darkness ahead he saw the Cornell house—a stately, white Colonial mansion set behind venerable elms and birches. As they drove on, his heart began to thud. In a few moments he would be hugging Stevie— crippled, soft-eyed young Stevie—for whose sake he had opened a safe and gone to prison. Loree moistened his lips. His fingers began to patter nervously on his knees. He felt queer. He felt shaky. He—

And then, suddenly, the tension was snapped. In its place rushed a dreadful torrent of surprise and apprehension.

The roadster had swerved into the horseshoe driveway. Loree saw old John Cornell on the veranda steps, brandishing Stevie's crutches, talking wildly to Martha, the ancient housekeeper.

Of Stevie himself there was no sign.

Cornell's agitated manner—a veritable panic—froze Dave Loree with indefinable fear. He jumped up. Julie stopped the roadster with a jerk and stared. And her father—tall, white of hair, wild-eyed—came running down the steps, desperately, still gripping the crutches.

There was no greeting. John Cornell shouted: "Stevie—Stevie's gone!"

Loree, his face white, demanded hoarsely: "What do you mean, gone? Wh-what's happened?"

"He was waiting for you at the gate!" roared Cornell. "Martha says she heard him scream! She—she looked out the window and saw three—"

"Three men grabbed him!" cried Martha herself, hysterically. "Pulled him out and—and threw him in a car and—it raced away!"

Mechanically, in a pallid stupor, Dave Loree stepped out of the roadster.

Julie followed. His very speech was paralyzed. Unutterable terror was battering savage assaults on his heart. His eyes were haggard, stupefied.

"Sam's phoning the police!" blurted Cornell.

Sam was the handy man. But Loree scarcely heard. He stared tragically from John Cornell to the waddling housekeeper on the veranda—herself colorless, almost sobbing.

"Did—did you see those men?" he managed to force out in a husky voice not his own. "Know them?"

"In this darkness? No! They—"

"Did you see their car?"

"It was a sedan—black—big—"

"How—how long ago?"

"Why, hardly five minutes! Just before you came!"

On desperate impulse Loree whirled around and actually bounded back into the roadster. His face was gray as rock. Julie had left her motor humming. As he seized the wheel he called vibrantly to Martha: "Which way did they go?"

"Left! Toward Springfield!"

He slammed the gears into first speed and let the car leap off with a roar. John Cornell, bewildered, moved to accompany him, and Julie cried a frightened, uncertain: "Dave! Wait!"

But he shook his head and whizzed dangerously around the semicircle of the horseshoe drive. Over his shoulder he yelled something, but they did not catch it.

He swung left into the highway, bent a white countenance over the steering wheel, and jammed down the accelerator to its limit. If the black sedan had a start of only five minutes, there was a wild chance—

Dave Loree sat desperately rigid.

On that drive he violated all speed laws. His narrow, blazing eyes were fastened on the road ahead, thrown into brilliance by the glaring headlights.

An increasing wind tore past him with a shrill **whoo-ee-ee-ee!** The speedometer's trembling arrow pointed to 50 . . . 55 . . . 60. There it quivered a while, then slowly, as if fearfully groping into the unknown, pushed farther and farther, nearing the 70 mark, hesitating before it, touching it gingerly first—then clinging to it.

Loree did not even glance at that speedometer. He pressed for more speed, and more; and groaned because it seemed to him the car was crawling.

THE road to Springfield, fortunately, was a smooth concrete highway. He could fly along with little danger, save at crossroads. And whenever he approached these, his horn screeched mad warnings.

A black sedan.

His eyes pierced the road ahead in their despairing quest. Each time he saw a new tail-light, he charged toward it with revived hope. But every car offered a fresh disappointment, and he raced past it—leaving outraged drivers to gape after him in amazement.

Then a new fear agonized him.

What if the black sedan had turned off the main road?

That, he realized, was most likely. Stevie's abductors would not remain on the highway, with its manifold risks of being stopped.

But which side road?

He had already passed a dozen. And on the twenty-mile stretch to Springfield, he would pass a dozen more! The futility of this mad chase began to appall him. He wanted to groan. He was racing insanely, he saw, without knowing where he was going. Perhaps every mile now was carrying him farther away from the hope of finding Stevie.

Stevie—

He had a torturing vision of the boy,

crippled and helpless, struggling against three men. The picture overwhelmed him with terror, and he blotted it from his mind.

Why had they taken Stevie? Who had taken him? Certainly anyone who knew the boy's circumstances could not have kidnaped him for the usual motive of obtaining ransom. Good Lord, if that were the only reason, Riverton offered the children of a score of wealthy families!

Loree drove on desperately and tried to force clarity into his chaotic brain. He passed car after car, peered into each of them, raced by to seek the next.

And then, of a sudden, he was struck with a possibility of the truth. The idea crashed upon him like a bolt of lightning. It dazzled and dazed him. It left him quivering between horror and rage.

Nick Brody!

Brody—in Springfield! Certainly abduction was not beyond him and his crowd! Suppose Joe Scarlatti and Squinty Pike had telephoned a report of the affair near the state prison. Suppose Brody, in grim fury because Loree had ignored his orders, had sought this means of retaliation—or better, this method of forcing Loree to come to him! Suppose he had taken Stevie as a hostage, a decoy!

It was a crazy idea—grotesque. Yet it offered the only hint of an explanation Dave Loree's turbulent mind could conceive. It filled him with wild fear.

But he knew now where he was going. He was driving to Springfield to see Nick Brody!

CHAPTER THREE

"You've Got To Steal!"

NICHOLAS BRODY lit a green-dappled cigar. He extinguished the match with a show of deliberation and tossed it into an amber tray on the end-table beside his chair. Then he smiled, with a mixture of contempt and amusement, at the two angry men who had just entered his library.

"Well," he said, crossing his legs, "you sure made a mess of it."

"I tell you," heatedly protested Joe Scarlatti, "we couldn't help it! That bird was nuts! I had my gat practically in his ribs when he hauls off and plants one on my jaw. Think I was expecting anything as dumb as that?"

"Dumb or not, he made a monkey of you. And what about you, Squinty?" Brody inquired with amiable sarcasm. "Were you asleep on your feet?"

"Geeze," the lean man exclaimed, "it all happened so fast I didn't get a chance to do anything! He bumped the wind clean out of me!"

Brody chuckled, but there was more harshness than mirth in the sound. "A fine couple of muscle men!" he jeered softly.

"Aw, listen," objected Scarlatti, his thick-set face flushing. "How the hell could we guess that guy was going to be so crazy with a gat sticking in his—"

"All right, all right," Brody interrupted impatiently. "I heard enough. The only sensible thing you two did was give me that long distance call about what happened. It gave me a chance to—to fix things a little."

Joe was startled. He exchanged a puzzled glance with Squinty Pike, then peered narrowly at the complacent Brody.

"How?" he muttered. "What d'you mean, Nick?"

"You'll see by and by. Tomorrow, after he's had time to worry a while, I'll get in touch with Loree and make him a new proposition." Brody smiled shrewdly at his cigar. Then, abruptly, he rose, put the cigar between his lips, and walked to a window. He parted the curtains and gazed into the darkness thoughtfully, yet with that peculiar smile persisting—while behind him Joe and Squinty stared in wonder.

He was a heavy man, Nick Brody—a strong man. He had reddish jowls that hung rather loosely over his collar, but that was the only sign of flabbiness about his ponderous figure. His eyes were small and keen and crafty. His hair, though thin, was still dark. A lock of it had been trained to dangle over his forehead, where it partially concealed a jagged scar.

In his way, Brody was the product of a new era in crime. He dressed well, lived quietly here in a suburb of Springfield, and outwardly appeared to be a successful merchant. Indeed, he owned two popular restaurants and belonged to a respectable enough country club. But these activities he maintained merely to screen more lucrative and more fascinating affairs—affairs he really enjoyed.

For at heart he was a gangster, with a gangster's love of illicit power.

He had organized a crowd of men who dabbled in any racket that promised quick profits. If Brody personally took the lion's share of those profits, no one could reasonably object; for in times of stress he could always be relied on to provide good lawyers and bail. It was a tribute to his cunning, as well as to his local influence, that he himself had never yet been indicted on any serious charge.

Now he smiled reflectively through the window, hardly hearing the conversation of Joe and Squinty behind him. But Brody had been there scarcely a minute when something happened.

He snatched the cigar from his lips. He grew rigid. He stared in amazement, and an ejaculation tumbled from him.

Joe Scarlatti asked quickly: "What's up?"

Brody blinked through the pane. Suddenly he jumped back, allowing the curtains to fall. He turned, and his small eyes actually glittered.

"Loree's out there!" he said tensely.

"What!"

"Just hopping out of a car! You two get out!"

"Get out?" resentfully cried Squinty. "Say, listen, I want to see that guy! If he comes here, I'm gonna square myself for that—"

"Shut up!" whispered Brody. "You heard me—get out! Into the next room! Don't come out unless I call you. And if I do call, come damned quick—with your rods handy!"

"Rods?" scoffed Joe Scarlatti. "We ain't got any—"

But Brody was already at the hall door, calling to an unseen servant: "Pete! When Dave Loree rings, send him right in here!"

Then he spun around. His big face was agitated, the muscles writhing, the eyes flashing. His fingers nervously twisted the cigar. Jerkily he nodded toward a second door.

"In there, Squinty! You too, Joe! I want to see this baby alone!"

Bewildered by this sudden confusion and half inclined to protest, Joe and Squinty nevertheless obeyed. They were addled. Also, the sudden brutality in Brody's countenance awed them. They hastened, almost stumbling over each other, into the adjoining room.

A second Nick Brody hesitated, peering sharply about the library. Then he strode to an ornate table. He perked open its drawer, extracted from it a small revolver, and slipped the weapon into his pocket.

After that, with an excited little smile and a flare in his shrewd eyes, he waited.

DAVE LOREE all but plunged into the room; at the sight of Brody he halted.

One might have imagined he had run the twenty miles from Riverton. He was breathing heavily. His eyes blazed, and because he had dropped his hat in the roadster, the curly brown hair above his pallid face was wildly disheveled.

Brody spoke in mock surprise: "Well, well! This is unexpected! How's the boy, Dave?"

"Where's Stevie?"

"Eh?"

"Stevie! My brother!" Hoarsely, without hedging, Loree shot out the question that seethed in him. "Somebody kidnaped him! I got an idea you know—"

"Me? Better sit down, Dave."

"Sit down, nothing!" Loree cried huskily. "I want to know about Stevie!"

Suddenly, then, Nick Brody's jaws became hard and ominous. His brows contracted over glittering little eyes. He snapped sharply: "So you want it straight, do you? All right. You don't have to worry about the kid. He's O.K."

"He—" Loree checked a gasp. He was staggered by this cool admission of guilt. "Why, you dirty, yellow—"

A wave of insane rage crashed over him. For an instant he went completely berserk. He started a belligerent lunge across the library.

But before he had taken two paces he confronted a small, deadly automatic. It was leveled steadily at his heart. And because he knew the character of the massive man who held the weapon, he halted.

"Better go easy," quietly warned Nick Brody. "I'm not Joe Scarlatti."

A moment Loree stared at the revolver. Then, with a rigid grip on himself, he raised burning eyes to Brody's.

"Where've you got Stevie?" he demanded in a choking whisper.

"For the present, that's my business."

"Brody, if—anything happens to that boy—"

"That depends on you."

"On me?"

"You heard me. Nothing's going to happen to him as long as you're reasonable."

"You—"

"Let me do the talking," grimly advised Brody. He stood beside the library table—an uncompromising bulk with the automatic in one hand, the cigar in the other.

Loree swallowed with difficulty. He realized, of a sudden, that he needed composure and craftiness to cope with this man, and he struggled to crush the chaos in his mind.

"Well?" he whispered.

Brody smiled in that cold, mirthless way of his.

"We're alone," he said, "so I don't mind being frank. I'll talk turkey. But you understand that if you ever try to repeat any of this, I'll call you a damned liar."

"Go on!" came tensely from Dave.

"All right. Dave, I figured that when you got out of jail we could get together on a friendly basis. That's why I sent Joe and Squinty to meet you—"

"With gats."

"Well, the important thing was to get you here for a talk. But you put a fast one over on them. They phoned me about it. So I thought things over and finally sent a few of the boys to pick up your brother. I sort of figured that was the best way to make you reasonable. Of course, I didn't expect to get in touch with you till tomorrow. But as long as you're here now, we may as well get this thing understood and settled."

LOREE clamped his lips shut. Purple veins were swelling about his temples. He seemed much older now than his twenty-three years.

"Go on, Brody. What do you want?"

"I've got quite a few jobs lined up for you, but there's one in particular I want you to pull now."

"I've told you a dozen times—"

"Sure. But this time is different, isn't it? I mean, with Stevie likely to get hurt—"

Loree's face paled; he did not reply.

"So let's be sensible," urged Brody, talking firmly. "I need you, Dave. I don't mind admitting that. When you worked in the Cornell safe factory, you learned something mighty few men know nowadays. You're the only one I know, frankly, who can open a safe by ear. And that's why I've got to have you!"

Still Loree remained silent, waiting.

"This job I want you to pull," the big man resumed, "is on a wall safe. What's more, it's on a Cornell safe! That ought to be gravy for you."

Having said that, Brody appeared to relax slightly. His revolver, however, kept at his hip, continued to menace his visitor's chest.

"How about it, Dave? Is it a bargain?"

"You mean if—if I rob this safe, Stevie comes back?"

"Exactly."

"And if I don't?"

Brody shrugged. "Why go into that? You won't give your brother such a break."

The implied threat sent a chill through Loree. He wished he could fly at this man. But he saw, with horrible clarity, that Stevie's life now depended on his own acquiescence. He said bitterly: "Brody, you're the dirtiest rat I ever knew! To kidnap a paralyzed boy—"

"That sort of talk," sharply interrupted Nick Brody, "won't get you anywhere!"

"How do I know you will send Stevie back, even if I do agree?"

"I promise to play square."

The irony of this assurance stabbed Loree with a sense of despair. He saw little guarantee in it. Mentally he groaned. Would this man ever send Stevie back, alive? Wouldn't he dread the possibility of Stevie's identifying the thugs who had abducted him?

It seemed that Brody divined and derided the unuttered fear. He shook his massive head contemptuously.

"Don't think I'm afraid to send the kid back to you," he said. "He'll never be able to describe the men who've got him. They were masked when they nabbed him at Cornell's place. And in the house where he's being kept now, everyone who goes into his room will be masked. No, I'm not scared about having him go back, Dave. In fact, I'm hoping you'll be reasonable just so's I can send him back. You know damned well I won't want to be mixed up in—murder."

Murder! It was the first mention of the word. Brody now was frankly threatening to kill Stevie unless his terms were granted. The horror of the ultimatum devastated Dave Loree's resistance. He felt dizzy and stretched out his hand to seize the back of a chair. He fought to bring lucidity into his rioting brain.

"So," he said hoarsely, "I—I've got to steal, have I?"

"Put it that way if you like," assented Brody, with a nod. "You've got to steal! How about it, Dave?"

Checkmate. Loree saw no escape.

He knew that all his resolutions to go straight were futile mockeries in the face of this situation. To Brody, however, he did not yet reply; could not sufficiently control his voice. And the big man, perhaps misconstruing his silence, added generously: "And another thing, Dave. You know I always give my boys a fair split. You pull this job for me, and I'll hand you five grand in cash—just to encourage you on some other ideas I've got planned. You could do a lot with five grand—for Stevie and yourself—couldn't you? Come on. What d'you say?"

Loree relinquished his grip on the chair. He hardly heard the offer of money. What mattered solely was Stevie—Stevie's life. If only he knew where to find the boy; if there were some way of forcing Brody to divulge the place! But these were futile thoughts. He whispered huskily: "If I pull this job, Stevie comes back immediately?"

"Positively!"

Loree inhaled a deep breath. "All right, Brody," he said. "You win. What's the job?"

Instead of replying Nick Brody turned his head slightly, and there was a note of gratified triumph in his voice as he called: "Joe! Squinty! Come in here!"

CHAPTER FOUR

Once a Thief—

IN Riverton, meanwhile, Julia Cornell and her tall, white-haired father were in their living room, tensely discussing the disappearance of Stevie with Chief of Police Silas Taggart. Lean, hard-featured, and scowling, the police official was a difficult man to convince. He sat shaking his silver-grey head obdurately.

"Somebody's trying to get at Loree through the kid," he insisted. "You can't just accept as coincidence the fact that Stevie was kidnaped on the very day Dave got out of prison. I'm willing to bet Dave himself knows a lot more about it than he admitted."

"Impossible!" Julia exclaimed in exasperation. "He can't know anything!" She could not endure the chief's inexorable hostility toward Loree; his innuendos and accusations.

"Well, then," Taggart retorted, "where is he? Where did he go? How did he know where to go?"

Julia shook her head hopelessly. It was more than an hour since Dave Loree had whizzed out of the driveway in her roadster, and no word had come from him yet. Chief Taggart had, of course, broadcast to all neighboring towns the report of Stevie's disappearance; and presumably the police everywhere were watching for a black sedan with three men and a crippled boy.

Of Loree, however, there was no news. And it was preposterous to suppose he was merely driving about aimlessly all this time, on the chance of finding his brother.

"I'll tell you where he is!" snapped Taggart. "He knows very well who took the kid, and he's gone to see for himself!"

John Cornell, striding anxiously about the room, paused to deride this idea.

"Why should he do anything like that?" he challenged. "If he knew who had taken Stevie, he would have seen to it that the police went after the boy."

"Don't judge a crook's sentiments," curtly advised Taggart, "by your own."

Julia half rose, her young face flushed in anger. "Dave," she whispered fiercely, "is no crook!"

"No?" It came sardonically. "I

suppose he spent two years in jail just to study conditions?"

"Two years ago he was——"

"Himself," grimly finished Silas Taggart. "Once a crook, always a crook."

At that John Cornell—an erect, really distinguished figure, though profoundly uneasy now—stopped in front of the police chief and eyed him gravely. It was odd, in its way, that two people like Julia and her father should be defending the reputation of an ex-convict.

Firmly Cornell said: "Chief, I'm afraid you don't understand Dave Loree. I don't profess to deny he did commit a crime. But—I've known him since he was a boy, since he was left with the responsibility of looking after Stevie. I know that he is not inherently a criminal."

"Then why," Taggart demanded "did he crack the Jorsen safe two years ago? As a prank?"

"I can explain that."

"That's what his lawyer said, but he went to jail just the same!"

"Dave," Cornell continued in a low, hard tone that commanded attention, "had a good job in my factory. He learned a great deal about safes——"

"Too much, I'd say!"

"And he was slated to rise. At that time my daughter and I were in Europe, you recall. Hornung, the man who remained in charge of the factory, had some sort of dispute with Dave—a personal matter, I gathered—and fired him. I didn't know about it until my return, which was too late. When Dave lost his job, he had no money. He had spent practically everything on Stevie's doctors."

Taggart smiled cynically. "There's a sob story connected with every crook, if you look for it."

"Yes, and we'd probably make much better men of them if we did look for it!"

To this Taggart made no reply. John Cornell resumed in that inflexible tone: "Here in Riverton Dave couldn't find work. He went to Springfield. But with the unemployment situation as it is, he ran against one blank wall after another. He had to think of Stevie, and that made him desperate. I mean desperate in the full sense of the word, chief! Finally, when he was at the very end of his rope, he ran into some Riverton boys who steered him into an opportunity.

"They introduced him to members of a local gang. I'll say for Dave that he never would give the names of those men; a few of them were pretty decent and offered to lend him money. Then they tried to persuade him to put his knowledge of safe locks to some use. He refused until his last cent was gone, until the support of Stevie became an impossibility. Then—well, yes, then he finally committed a crime. And he was caught before he could get out of the house—sent to prison for two years. But it was a crime to which he had yielded as a last desperate resource. I know he has regretted it. I know he wants to go straight, and I stand ready to help him."

Julia's eyes, as she watched her father, were lustrous with unutterable pride and gratitude. Chief Silas Taggart, however, remained cryptic. It was not the first time he had heard the story. He rose, picked up his hat.

"You certainly have confidence in him, Mr. Cornell."

"I have."

Taggart grunted as he started for the door. At the threshold he paused and looked back narrowly.

"Well," he rapped out, "I hope that confidence won't be misplaced! If Dave Loree tries a second crime—and gets caught—it's going to mean a mighty long, long stretch in the state prison!"

IN Springfield at this precise moment, curiously enough, Dave Loree was actually listening to the plans for his second crime.

He was seated now. He felt steeled against the inevitable. If cracking a safe was the only way of saving Stevie, then a safe must be cracked! He shot a swift, hard glance from Squinty Pike to Joe Scarlatti; after which he peered back at Brody who, perched on the edge of the library table, was talking succintly.

"It's the Ferrold house," he was saying. "I guess you know the place—just this side of Riverton?"

Loree nodded.

"The Ferrolds have a guest—a Mrs. Martindale," Brody went on, "who's got some of the sweetest doodads I've seen in years. There's a string of pearls and a diamond brooch I'm particularly interested in, understand. She's worn them to a couple of affairs at the country club."

Again Loree nodded, his gaze now fixed on the floor.

Brody snapped: "It cost us a cold five hundred smackers to get under the skin of the Ferrold butler. But for five C's the fellow loosened up and told Joe here the jewels are being kept in a wall safe in the library. That safe is hidden by a portrait of Mr. Ferrold. You can't miss it."

"Is the butler going to fix it so I can get in?"

"Oh, no. He wouldn't go that far. The guy's yellow. You'll have to manage a window, I guess. Joe will see to it that you have any tools you may need."

"I see—" thickly. This was precisely the sort of job that had sent him to prison two years ago. His fingers rigidly gripped the arms of his chair.

"Well, then," said Brody, "suppose we set it for—"

"Tonight!"

"Eh?"

"Tonight!" Loree insisted. "I—I want Stevie home before morning!"

Brody appeared startled. As a matter of truth, he had not planned to have the robbery occur until later in the week, on a night when the bribed Ferrold butler could assure him of safety. Yet Loree's haste, when he considered it, did not entirely displease him. The sooner this affair was completed, the more comfortable he would feel—and the richer.

He rubbed the side of his nose, frowned. At last he nodded acquiescence.

"Well, O.K. If you think you can pull it tonight, go ahead. It's all right with me."

Loree rose, his eyes flaming slits. "But get this, Brody," he whispered. "If Stevie isn't home safe and unhurt, by morning, I'll—"

"Cut it out!" the big man snapped. "You don't have to threaten me, Dave! The minute you turn Mrs. Martindale's stuff over to me, I'll phone to have Stevie sent home. And that's straight! Now beat it. Joe and Squinty are ready to go with you."

This last rather disconcerted Loree. He had not counted on being accompanied. He frowned at the two men distastefully, then demanded of Brody: "Can't I swing this alone?"

"That's up to you. I figured you might want help."

"No! All I want is a car," Loree snapped. "I won't use the one I've got downstairs—it's Miss Cornell's. As for the rest, I'm doing this thing on my own!"

Nick Brody readily consented to let

the black coupe be used; it was the car Joe and Squinty had driven earlier in the day. But as he spoke, his eyes narrowed craftily. For a moment he studied Loree in silence. Then he slid off the edge of the table and came forward two steps, his chin drawn in, his manner wary and suspicious.

"Listen, Dave," he whispered tersely. "I'm letting you go alone. But if you try any tricks—if you try in any way to double-cross me—you'll never see that kid brother of yours alive again! Is that clear?"

It was very clear. Loree's face, as he acknowledged the terms, was pale and grim and hard. He rent a final glance at the three men. And then, stiffly, he turned toward the door—and crime.

ONE o'clock in the morning. A pallid moon, groping timidly among clouds, dropped an eerie radiance on the Ferrold home. An alleged copy of a minor French chateau, it was hidden among trees on a dark side-road. Since halfpast eleven it had shown no lights, but Loree had prudently waited.

Finally, having twice circled the place in reconnaissance, he now approached it closely to examine its windows for a means of entrance.

And a bit of devil's luck accompanied him.

He discovered he would have neither to jimmie a sash nor to cut glass. One of the narrow cellar windows in the rear had a shattered pane! He had only to thrust in his gloved hand to unlock it and let himself into the house.

As he knelt there, his eyes afire, his heart thumping, Loree presented a rather terrifying figure. On Brody's advice, he had bound a handkerchief about his face as a mask. His hat brim was pulled low over his forehead. Indeed, he looked to be the typical desperado.

He opened the window softly.

Though he knew no one was about, instinctively he darted a swift, searching glance over his shoulder. Then, soundlessly, he thrust his legs into the aperture, turned, and lowered himself into the Ferrold cellar.

His whole being thundered. From his pocket he drew the flashlight Joe Scarlatti had slipped into his hand. He shot its narrow golden beam into the blackness, sent it sweeping around until it fell on a wooden staircase. With that goal in sight, he started forward on his toes.

Inwardly, behind all his caution, Dave Loree abhorred the whole exploit. He had to lash himself into it, ignoring the rebellious clamor of his nerves and conscience. Even now, as he moved up those steps, a thousand uncertainties, contradictions, and plans roared in his head.

Was there any conceivable way of saving Stevie without doing this thing? How?

Suppose he went to the police and brazenly divulged everything he knew. Suppose he brought the authorities to Nick Brody and openly accused the man of kidnaping. What then?

Brody, he knew, would simply stare in amazement and declare his accuser a madman. Certainly he would never confess his guilt; would never admit he knew where Stevie might be found. And Loree had no witnesses to the things Brody had said to him. If he did turn against the gang leader now, there could be only one result for Stevie—a tragic result.

That course was unthinkable.

True, another possibility offered itself, but it was so wild and implausible that he was tempted to discard it even as it occurred to him.

What if he took both the police and the Ferrolds into his confidence? Asked that he be permitted to deliver the jewels to Brody, so that the man might release the kidnaped Stevie? Later, with the boy safe, Brody could be seized and the jewels recovered.

To this fantastic scheme there were, however, too many objections. Paramount among them was this: the Ferrolds, being utter strangers, after all, would be perfectly justified in refusing to risk their valuables by entrusting them to an ex-convict for the enactment of some dubious and hare-brained idea. And thereafter, with the family warned, all chances of obtaining the jewels would be gone. And Stevie would be—

No. Loree realized he had but one feasible plan, desperate but unavoidable. It was based on meeting Nick Brody's terms. He had to go on with it!

He climbed the staircase, softly opened the door, and emerged in a butler's pantry.

Here he paused a few seconds, while the flashlight revealed his surroundings. At his left was a dining room. He crossed it cautiously, lighting every step of the way with that thin yellow beam, and moved into a corridor. Ten feet farther he found himself between the wide doors of a drawing room and a library.

It was in the library, Brody had said, he would come upon the safe.

LOREE entered quickly, excitedly. The golden ray of his flashlight darted through the darkness. It crept over bookcases, explored the walls, until it stopped abruptly on the portrait of an exceedingly corpulent man.

Mr. Ferrold's? With every muscle tense, every nerve strained, Loree tiptoed over soft carpet. When he reached the picture, he slid it aside a few inches and— Yes! Stared at the familiar dial of a Cornell safe!

Something in him jumped.

He drew a hard breath. Exasperatedly he wished the violent throbbing of his temples would cease. For a while he listened rigidly for any possible sound in the house. But he heard nothing to alarm him.

Loree swallowed hard. He slipped the flashlight into his pocket. Slowly, with infinite caution, he removed the portrait from the wall and placed it on the floor.

A moment later he pressed his ear close to the dial and began carefully to turn the disc. He wondered if in two years he had lost much of his former skill. Above the handkerchief-mask his eyes narrowed attentively. He turned . . . listened . . . turned . . . listened . . . caught the almost imperceptible sound of a tumbler dropping into place.

Minutes passed. Not many of them, really, yet to Dave Loree they seemed aeons.

This, he had discovered, was a simple enough safe, one of the older Cornell models. He had opened hundreds like it—legally. Certainly he ought to be able to open this one!

And he did.

The task required fully twenty minutes, but he succeeded!

At precisely halfpast one he thrust an agitated hand into that small hole in the wall. His flashlight flooded its interior with golden brilliance. He saw papers, a packet of money—and did not touch them. The only thing he took was a silken sack. He trembled a little as he opened it. The beam of his tiny torch played dazzlingly on lustrous gems.

Loree did not commit the folly of yielding to either haste or exultation. He closed the safe, replaced the portrait as it had been, and assured himself that he had otherwise disturbed nothing. Then finally, with the sack of jewels in his pocket, he turned and tiptoed away.

Two minutes later he slipped once more through the small cellar window. He had to pull himself up; and outside, when he straightened to peer about with flaming eyes, he was panting. Under the handkerchief his face was colorless. His chest was filled with heavy thuds.

It seemed incredible that only a dozen hours ago he had left prison with a staunch resolve never to commit another crime! When he realized how much had happened in those twelve mad hours, he shuddered. The fates, he felt, were laughing at him derisively, jeeringly.

Of a sudden he lunged into a run. He ran swiftly, his shoulders hunched, across the Ferrold grounds to the road; and up the road to the distant clump of bushes behind which he had concealed the black coupe.

So far success!

But—what would happen when Chief Silas Taggart learned a Cornell safe had been opened near Riverton on the very night Dave Loree, expert cracksman, returned to the town?

CHAPTER FIVE

"Just To Go Straight"

NICK BRODY stared at the jewels with eyes that glittered eagerly.

"Attaboy! I knew you could do it!" he said.

He had impatiently awaited Loree's return; and now, in his own library, he momentarily ignored the young man while he spread the precious trophies of the night on a table. The white light of a reading lamp fell on them, evoking all their brilliance.

He smile—a peculiarly hard, triumphant smile. Because Joe and Squinty had long ago departed, he was left to enjoy this achievement alone. He fingered the loot in silence, as if weighing it, until Loree snapped: "Well, Brody?"

The big man glanced up and grinned. "This is the stuff, all right. It—"

"The devil with that! How about Stevie?"

"Stevie?" Brody appeared startled and a little aghast, as though he had quite forgotten his captive. But his grin quickly returned; reassuringly, he nodded. "Oh, sure. You can have him back, Dave. I'll play square."

Nick Brody gathered the collection of jewels and dropped it into his pocket. Then he picked up the telephone on the table and called a number. As he awaited a connection, he smiled at Loree affably.

"Remembering this number," he said, "won't do you much good, Dave. It's not the place where the kid's being kept. It's just a speakeasy on the other side of town. One of the boys is waiting there for my orders."

Loree did not reply. He did not even stir. He stood watching intently.

"By the way," Brody continued after a moment, "I promised you some cash for this—"

"I don't want it!" Dave said tersely.

"No? Well, that's O.K. with me. Only I figured we might get together on a friendly basis for future . . . Hello!" He broke off to give his attention to the telephone. "Phil? Let me talk to Jeff, will you? Yes."

There was an interval of strained silence, while Brody's spatulate fingers pattered on the table. Speculatively he fixed his eyes on Loree. And suddenly, when a voice crackled in the receiver, he straightened.

"Hello, Jeff! Nick calling. Listen! Everything's all right here . . . Yes, he did. Just a minute ago . . . Now get me. You go over to the house and tell the boys to take the Loree kid back . . . Right now, yes. They can drop him where the Pikeville Road crosses Springfield Highway. Yes, at the corner. I'll tell Loree he can pick the kid up there in half an hour. O.K. . . . Right! Make it snappy, Jeff!"

Nick Brody replaced the telephone. Once more he smiled at Loree, with the air of a man who had been generous.

"Well, that's that," he said. "My boys 'll drop the kid at Pikeville Road and Springfield Highway, and you can pick him up on your way back to Riverton. He's all right, except for a bad scare. Now are we square?"

"No!"

"Eh?"

Slowly Dave Loree's face paled, became grim. Its muscles began to bulge ominously, and his lips formed a tight gash. A thousand thoughts were surging through his mind. Now that Brody had ordered Stevie's release, the boy's safety was probably assured. Loree's body stiffened. As long as he prevented the big man from rescinding his instructions, he was free to talk—and act!

His eyes narrowed, blazed. He spoke very softly, through his teeth: "Brody, now that it's settled, I—I'm going to give you the beating of your life! And after that—"

Nick Brody started in amazement, caught his breath. His eyes widened, and his large face lost a little of its color. He snapped harshly: "You—you crazy, Dave?"

"I must be for giving you a chance to put up your arms!"

"Why, you damned fool—"

As he spoke Brody moved his hand. He did not raise it to fight. He sent it to his jacket pocket, where he had his small automatic.

But Loree saw that movement. Even as it started, he charged. Savagely, with all the pent-up fury of the night in his lunge, he threw himself at Nick Brody! He drove out his fist.

The big man tried to dodge. But he was too late. A terrific blow crashed against his jaw. He went staggering sideways, half drawing the revolver.

Dave Loree saw the butt of that gun as it appeared. He seized it with his left hand, jerked violently on Brody's fingers, and—

There was a shot!

The bullet cracked into the floor.

And Loree struck again. His second blow landed full on Brody's ear. The man groaned, reeled dizzily. For an instant he had no strength—and in that instant Loree wrenched the revolver from him, cast it away. He wanted no weapon. He wanted only to pound this man into submission! He wanted to vent his accumulated rage in a torrent of wild, punitive blows!

Nicholas Brody, however, was no weakling.

His bulk bumped heavily against the wall. On the rebound he seemed to find his balance. His eyes blazed crazily, and his face was puffed. He whirled around, crouched.

"Damn you!" he shouted. "If you think you can—"

The rest Dave Loree did not hear. For Nick Brody charged.

HE came with the ferocity of a mad bull, his head lowered, his arms ramming. Loree tried to stop him, but the fury of that attack sent the younger man staggering back. As he retreated, he lashed out fiercely. Yet he did not seem to hurt Brody. Instead, he was himself shaken by a deluge of violent blows to the head and face and chest. Brody hurled those huge fists without aiming, letting them crash where they could.

Somehow Loree rallied. He jumped

to one side. The half-second respite, in which the big man turned to follow, offered a chance to find footing and steadiness.

And then——the fight really started!

They stood almost toe to toe, driving at each other savagely, brutally. Blood suddenly gushed from Brody's nose.

They moved about the room, over-turning chairs, shattering a lamp, but constantly hitting. And they were near the table again when, of a sudden, Loree heard a hoarse yell.

It came from the upper floor of the house!

And he remembered, with a chill of horror, that Brody's servant, Pete, must be hearing this, must be coming! If Pete rushed in and saw the revolver——

That desperate thought settled matters.

Abruptly Dave Loree did a most un-expected thing. He ceased driving his fists. He ran backward, four quick steps that carried him almost ten feet from Brody!

For an instant the big man paused, nonplussed, sucking in horrible breaths. His bleeding face was agape. But rage quickly suffused it again. He cursed, lowered his massive head, and charged.

That was precisely what Loree had prayed would happen.

He poised himself. Gathered all his strength for one last, furious blow.

A terrific, whizzing uppercut! It started behind him and swung through an arc to come up and meet the big man as he plunged. It did meet him!

Squarely on the jaw it landed——with a sickening thud——the hardest punch Dave Loree had ever delivered!

Even as rugged a figure as Nick Brody could not withstand that terrific smash. It straightened him. Sent him reeling back with a cry of agony. His eyes were tightly shut. He hit the wall and dropped like a rock——and lay still!

Loree, however, could not afford to pause then. Already he heard Pete on the stairs. He spun around and dashed wildly at the door.

Pete really never knew what happened.

He realized only that a tornado struck him as he turned into the library. spluttering, and suddenly plunged him into blackness.

A moment later Dave Loree, his cheek bleeding, his whole countenance torn and blotched by Brody's punches, was at the telephone.

"Operator! I——I want to talk to Police Chief Taggart in——in Riverton! No, I don't know——the number!"

As he waited he stared dazedly about the library. It was in ruins. Nick Brody lay in a corner, unconscious, his arms hiding his bloody face.

Inhaling a tremendous breath, Loree tried to steady himself, but it was a hard thing to accomplish. He wiped the blood from his cheek, pushed back his wild hair. And suddenly he heard a crackling voice in the telephone: "Hello?"

"I——I want Chief Taggart!"

"Taggart talking!"

"Chief! This——this is Dave Loree! Listen! Nick Brody's mob kidnaped my brother! They——they're bringing him to the corner of Pikeville Road and Springfield Highway now! If you can get there in a——a few minutes with some men, you may nab the whole gang! But for God's sake, take——take care of Stevie!"

"What on earth——"

"C-cant stop to explain now! I'll be in Riverton within an hour! And I ——I'm bringing Nick Brody!"

IT was exactly 3:30 in the morning when Dave Loree brought Julia Cornell's blue roadster to a screaming stop in front of the Riverton police station.

Disheveled and fiery-eyed, he jumped out, scarcely aware of the other four cars parked at the curb. As he ran up the wide steps his face was flushed with a mixture of anxiety and eagerness and hope—for Stevie.

Six men in uniform were there, under the command of Chief Taggart himself; and four dilapidated, handcuffed creatures whom Loree instantly recognized as old members of Brody's gang!

Loree halted. A wave of relief surged over him. The police, then, had been in time!

He did not notice that at his appearance the clamor in the place had abruptly subsided. Everyone stared at him.

"Where—where's Stevie?" he asked.

With a nod of his graying head Chief Silas Taggart indicated a rear room.

"He's in there with the Cornells," he said. "He's all right. But look here—"

Loree, however, was in no mood to look anywhere before seeing Stevie. Impetuously he started for the back door.

"You said," called the chief, "you were bringing Brody!"

"Oh!" Loree halted, spun around. A hard little smile gripped his features. To the astonished police chief he tossed a bunch of keys. "The keys to Miss Cornell's roadster," he said. "It's outside. You'll find Nick Brody locked in the bottom of the rumble seat!"

And then Loree plunged into the anteroom.

Stevie!

Yes, Stevie was there! Seated in front of Julia Cornell and her father! Holding the crutches old John Cornell had brought to the station.

At the sight of Dave Loree he cried out, raised his arms, let the crutches fall unheeded.

For a second the older brother stood rigid, utterly unable to move. A huge lump clogged his throat. His eyes began to smart queerly. Then, with a low, throttled cry of his own, he sprang forward. He caught Stevie in his arms and hugged him tight. Hugged him with the fierceness and passion of knowing he had been saved from tragedy.

Just what Loree said during the next few minutes, he never recalled. Nor did he realize what Stevie answered. Theirs was a confusion of joy, obliterating even the memory of that crime at the Ferrold house. But at last Loree was able to step back and demand: "Did—did they hurt you, Stevie?"

"Not much, Dave, honest they didn't!" the boy exclaimed. "But gee, you should've seen the excitement when they brought me to the crossroads! They carried me out of their car and sat me on a rock and said I was to wait there for you. And then, just as they were getting back into their automobile, the —the cops jumped out from everywhere! There were shots and yells and fights and—gosh, it was bettern' a movie!"

Loree grimly smiled.

"But no more experiences like this for us, Stevie," he muttered. "We've had enough. We're going away somewhere to start a nice, quiet life—"

"Away?" Stevie gaped in amazement. "But why, Dave? Why do you want to go away? Mr. Cornell here says you can have your job back—"

Dave Loree shot a quick, startled look at the white-haired man. He looked at Julia too, more intently, more searchingly. Something in her eyes pleaded as eloquently as Stevie's voice that he remain here.

But after a moment Loree shook his head with a trace of bitterness. "It— it would be nice," he whispered. "Only —well, I'm afraid Chief Taggart won't like the idea very much. He's given me twenty-four hours to get out of town."

"You leave that to me!" snapped Cornell. "If I give you a job——"

Then he stopped, staring blankly at the door.

CHIEF SILAS TAGGART himself was there, as stern as an Indian. A singularly ominous frown tautened his countenance. He peered straight at Dave Loree with eyes as hard and brilliant and cold as diamonds.

"Loree," he rapped out, "come here!"

Dave Loree felt a stabbing premonition of what was to happen. The Ferrold burglary—— He turned slowly.

"Yes, chief?"

"Come out here! Not the rest of you, please! Just Dave!"

Loree went, rather stiffly. He moved past the grim chief, entered the crowded room beyond—and halted as he faced Nick Brody!

Brody stood between two policemen, a tattered and disreputable figure. His swollen, blood-smeared countenance held the most malevolent glare Loree had ever beheld on a man.

He did not speak. It was Chief Taggart who talked, in a curt, sardonic voice.

"Loree, we've had quite a scene. It seems this man Brody doesn't want to go to jail without you. He says you opened and robbed the Ferrold safe tonight!"

There it was!

Yet, oddly enough, the direct accusation did not cause a change in Loree's expression. He merely turned his head to fasten a narrow look on Taggart.

"The Ferrold house?" he repeated. "Yes!"

"Have they reported a robbery?"

"Not yet. Officer Cary——" Taggart nodded to a man telephoning in a far corner——"is talking to Mr. Ferrold now! I want to know what you've got to say, Loree!"

"Nothing."

Chief Taggart's mouth became an uncompromising slash.

"You realize, Loree," he said, "that if you did rob that safe, it means a second offense for you, and a mighty long stretch in——"

But at this moment Officer Cary called across the room in a deep, resounding voice— "Oh, chief! Ferrold just looked into his safe! He says there hasn't been any robbery! Everything's still there!"

Nick Brody gaped. His mouth opened, and he tried to speak. But not a sound escaped him. His face became purplish, mottled, dumbfounded. He stared from Officer Cary to Taggart; from Taggart, in a kind of outrage, to Loree.

And Loree, meeting the big man's stupefied stare, smiled in a grim, merciless way. He wished very much he could tell Brody: "You were locked in the rumble seat—unconscious. You don't know that on the way here I stopped again near the Ferrold house and put the jewels back in the safe! It was the only way to beat you, Brody!"

He wanted to say that, but he didn't. Instead, he stood quite still for a moment, then looked at the somewhat dazed, though frowning, police chief. He knew that without a robbery there was no case against him. And so he spoke quite calmly: "Any objection to my going back to Stevie now, chief?"

"Why—er—no, I guess not. But——"

Dave Loree did not wait to hear the rest. He turned his back on Brody and his men. For the last time, he hoped!

As he moved toward the little rear door, his thoughts flew ahead. Flew to Stevie, to Julia Cornell, to the chance for a new, clean start in life!

"Lord!" he muttered. "What a struggle just to go straight!"

HOT ICE

by Norman H. White, Jr.

A shot rang out. Then to the clamor of alarm bells, armed guards came pouring in. For there on the floor lay the diamond merchant—a neat, round hole bluing the center of his forehead.

AS the messenger boy tucked the receipt into his uniform pocket and hurried down the shabby stairs of the lodging house, Jack Williams looked curiously at the letter in his hands. With a puzzled expression he hurriedly tore it open.

The pallor of dark places and thick walls was still on Williams' thin face. The hands that were holding the letter were slender and white—not the hands that a man of twenty-two should have. But these things might be expected for the gates of Sing Sing had closed behind his back only the day before. Until the arrival of the messenger a few moments ago he had thought that no one in the world knew or cared where he was.

Jack's dark eys, set deep under level black brows, lighted as he read the message. He noted the engraved heading, "Markus & Epstein, Diamond Merchants." So Alec Markus was now a partner and wanted to see him—to offer him "a helping hand!" Williams smiled a bit grimly—a smile that had disillusionment and bitterness in it. The man whose testimony had sent him up; the man—so the evidence had said—he'd robbed, now wanted to help him. Well, he needed help. Only two dollars remained in the pocket of the cheap prison suit and jobs were hard to get—particularly for an ex-con. It could do no harm to see what Alec Markus had in mind.

Thoughts crowded into his brain as Williams looked round the small, dingy room for his hat. It was cheaper to share a room with some other fellow but Jack didn't know anyone and he'd never share his room with a stranger —he'd learned his lesson. "Hig" Sanders had taught him that. Hig who had seemed like a good sort. But now Sanders had disappeared—dropped from sight after a running gunfight with the police and Jack Williams had spent two years in jail after the same dicks had found the empty paper package in his top drawer. Alec Markus had identified the paper as having held the diamonds which had been stolen from him on the street. How the empty package had come into his bureau drawer Williams had never known though he didn't doubt that Sanders had put it there. This he couldn't prove for Sanders had vanished. What had happened to the diamonds no one ever knew.

And now, the man from whom he'd been accused of stealing, was offering him a job! Well, beggars couldn't be choosers. He'd see what Alec Markus had in mind. He wouldn't hold any grudge against Marcus for what he'd done. After all he had simply identified the wrapping paper which had contained the diamonds.

ALEC MARKUS rose heavily from behind his handsome glass-topped walnut desk, a broad smile of welcome beaming on his florid face. The paint on the door that Williams had just opened still showed its freshness in the narrow gold letters that pronounced this the office of Markus & Epstein, Diamond Merchants. The thick carpet that Jack's thin-soled shoes sank into deeply was new and rich. Alec Markus had risen to a partnership in the past two years. He had done well and he knew it.

Markus cordially stretched forth his well-kept hand to Williams who noticed it seemed soft and feminine when he shook it.

"Sit right down, Williams," said Markus not unkindly. His gaze was curiously intent on the ex-convict in his shabby clothes.

"Thanks," said Williams, briefly, his dark blue eyes glancing around the luxurious office, noting with appreciation the bright sporting prints on the walls. Marcus had certainly done well.

"Now, Williams, I want to try to help you. You know I hated to identify that empty package that sent you up, but it was the one the diamonds had been in." Markus' rather guttural voice sounded sincere. "The evidence against you was entirely circumstantial, though, of course, a jury agreed as to your guilt. Nevertheless I've always felt a little doubtful. If Sanders could only have been found it might have been different."

Williams' thin lips tightened. Alec Markus had had a change of heart. At the trial he'd seemed quite positive that Williams had been equally guilty with Sanders.

Markus continued smoothly, his glossy nails tapping gently on the glass top of his desk. "Now I am in a position to offer you a job here in the office— I've done well by myself in the past two years—and if you want it I'll put you on your honor. You probably think its funny for me to be willing to do this but I always try to help friends, my boy. That's one of my secrets of success." Markus' smooth, round face

was blandly important. "Your record up to the time of the—unfortunate incident—was very good, Williams. No bad marks at all. You're a young man not more than twenty-two—" Williams nodded—"and I want to give you another chance."

Williams felt as if he were in school. He cleared his throat and said, "thanks," in a low voice. After all this was pretty decent of the conceited ass.

"I can give you a job at—$15 a week." Markus glanced anxiously at Williams.

Jack started to shake his head—$15 a week—a mere pittance! He could just get by on it however, and jobs were hard to get. That would be like Markus, always trying to save a dollar even now when he was trying to play the big charitable business man.

"What do you want me to do?" said Jack.

"I want you to work in the outside office and find out what callers want. You'll find the work is very light. Mr. Epstein and I may have errands for you to do occasionally." Markus smiled confidentially and leaned across the desk toward Jack as he added, "Another thing, Williams, please don't tell Epstein, my partner, who you are. You see he might not appreciate your background!"

Jack Williams' hard jaw set itself for a brief second. Some day he wouldn't have to take such sarcastic remarks, but then again, perhaps Markus didn't mean to be nasty. And after all he was an ex-con!

"When do I start?" he said curtly.

"You can report Monday, Williams. And here is five dollars in advance." Markus held out a five spot in his fleshy hand.

"No, thanks," said Williams, a friendly smile crinkling his eyes. "I'll take it after I earn it. I'll be on deck Monday at nine.''

EPSTEIN, Markus' partner, paid no attention to him after a first meeting during which Jack could feel the bright keen eyes of the older man watching him closely. As days went on Jack noted that the stout little man wore a perpetual frown of worry etched deeply in his forehead as he flitted in and out of the office. He was a human dynamo. Williams, sitting quietly at his desk in the reception room often could hear Epstein's high-pitched voice raised in irritation as he and Markus discussed problems of the business. Epstein was the driving force of the firm without doubt.

One morning Markus came out to Jack's desk. ''I want you to deliver a valuable package to Fraser & Co. on Fifth Street,'' said Markus. He clutched the small envelope in his plump hand and looked at Williams hesitantly.

Jack pushed back his chair and stood up. ''Don't worry,'' he said with a smile, ''you can trust me.''

Markus' broad face seemed relieved. ''Of course I can, Williams,'' he said, patting Jack on the shoulder, ''but these are unusually valuable stones. Mr. Fraser wants them in a hurry. Deliver them to him personally. I've phoned him—you won't need a receipt. Remember these stones are very valuable, Williams—be extra careful.'' Markus seemed to hate to surrender the package.

Jack put on his hat and slipped the package into his inside coat pocket as he smiled confidently. ''I'll take good care of them, Mr. Markus,'' he said. ''You can rest assured of that.''

Jack closed the door of the office feeling a glow of well-being surge over him at the responsibility which Markus had placed on him. As he hurried down the hall toward the elevators he straightened his lean shoulders. Responsibility —confidence—those were what made life worth living. There was a new lightness in his step—a springiness which had been lacking for the past two years—ever since the day that crumpled paper had been found in his bureau drawer. Markus need not worry about the safety of the diamonds. He whistled softly as he swung down the hall.

As he turned the corner of the corridor near the elevator shaft, a bulky figure stepped directly into his path.

''Wait a minute, young fellow, I wanta speak to you.'' The big, hardvisaged man spoke curtly. ''Don't be in such a hurry.''

Jack's heart gave a great leap—his narrow face tightened. This was what had happened to Markus two years ago —a hold-up! No hold-up man, however bold, was going to take those diamonds, that pressed lumpily against his ribs, away without a struggle. If he lost that precious burden he would lose his chance to rehabilitate himself. He was an ex-con. No one would believe that he wasn't in league with the robber.

As Jack edged out to one side the big man reached for his hip pocket. Jack swung like lightning and caught his assailant on the point of the jaw. With a low grunt the heavier man acknowledged the blow that jerked his massive jaw up and back. For a moment he seemed dazed and Jack tried to slip past. Shaking his head the big man swung his huge arms toward his slender opponent and Jack felt a huge pawlike hand grab his arm and swing him in to a closer grip.

''Lissen, you, yuh can't get away with those diamonds!'' growled the man as he tightened his grasp around Jack's twisting figure.

Jack let his knees give away suddenly

and tried to slip down through the man's arms. If he could only get his arms around the other man's knees he'd have a chance to get him off his feet. Convulsively Jack grabbed down at the man's knees. They both fell in a struggling heap to the floor. The other's strength was far greater than Jack's, but Jack was fighting with a desperation born of the knowledge that if he lost this fight he lost the chance to make good. Again the thought flashed to his mind that his story would never be believed—he must keep possession of those precious diamonds even if it meant his life.

OVER and over the pair rolled on the tiled floor of the hall. The big man's hand was reaching slowly but surely for Jack's throat. Now it was at his collar and, struggle as he would, Jack could not force that hairy hand and wrist down. An inch more and that slowly lifting hand would have his throat in its clutch. Beads of perspiration broke out on Jack's face and his breath came in short gasps. His heavier opponent was now on top of him, his hard face gleaming down balefully triumphant. Suddenly Jack gave a twist engendered by all the muscle and will power at his command. As he did so he arched his lean form with an upward motion. Taken unaware his opponent was thrown to one side and the grasping fingers that had just reached Jack's throat were loosened. Jack's convulsive effort had thrown his assailant several feet to one side. Then the big man doggedly lunged in again. This time his hand caught Jack's throat. A stabbing pain shot through his tortured neck as the viselike fingers closed.

Suddenly a shot rang out and reverberated emptily along the bare corridor. A startled worried look came over the big man's face. "What the hell?" he said questioningly. His eyes swung down the corridor toward the office of Marcus and Epstein. His grasp loosened.

Then came the clang of a gong that echoed through the building and up the elevator shafts. Jack knew what that meant. Somewhere in the building a robbery had just been committed! The great edifice in which they were—the home of many world-famous firms of jewelers would be immediately sealed against entrance or exit till the robber was found. What a break of luck! With a sob of relief Jack laughed hoarsely. The diamonds were safe!

Even if the hold-up man got them from him he could never get out! Overcome by the emotion and the tax on his strength, Jack's head fell flat on the floor. The cold tiles felt good against his hot, sweaty face. Laughter, that was more like sobbing, shook his collapsed figure.

"Take 'em! Go on an' take 'em!" he said brokenly, gulping for breath. "Take 'em if you want 'em—an' try an' get out of the building with 'em!"

The big man released his grip and scrambled awkwardly to his feet. "What the hell?" he said again, looking anxiously in the direction from which the sound of the shot had come.

From his position on the floor Jack cried again, "Try an' get away with those diamonds now! Just try it!"

With a puzzled expresison on his rough-hewn face the big man gave him a surprised look. Then, to Jack's astonishment he ran heavily down the corridor toward the office of Markus & Epstein. Staggering weakly to his feet Jack followed him.

Toward them, down the long hall came a running figure. It was Markus. His face was white and he had beads of sweat on his wide forehead.

He looked at Jack, his surprised eyes

glaring like a crazy man's. "You murderer!" he screamed. Suddenly he pulled a gun from his pocket. Jack saw a gleam of ferocious intensity replace the first surprise that had been in the small eyes of the diamond merchant.

"There's something wrong," began Jack's erstwhile assailant hoarsely, reaching for Markus' arm. But as he spoke Markus' gun rang out. Jack felt a sharp searing pain in his side. Before Markus could fire again the big man grabbed him. At that same instant Jack dove in at Markus. Markus went down with a thump and the gun fell from his grasp.

Markus' soft muscles were no match for Jack and the big man who'd held him up and who now, incredibly, had turned out to be Jack's ally. A few seconds later a disarmed and trembling Markus was held by each arm by Jack and the hard-faced, burly stranger.

"Let me go!" shrieked Markus, his face convulsed with rage. "I tell you Epstein is murdered! Williams here murdered him and stole the diamonds——I saw him! He's got them on him." Markus struggled furiously to free himself.

At that moment the elevator doors opened and three of the uniformed guards of the building sprang from the car and advanced on the run.

"What's the matter, Mr. Markus?" one of them inquired deferentially, looking at the trio.

Markus spluttered excitedly. "It's murder, I tell you! My partner's been killed. This ex-convict here murdered him and stole a package of diamonds. He's got them on him. Search him and see!" Markus again struggled convulsively to break the grasp on his arms.

"Put up your hands!" sharply commanded the leader of the guards to Jack and to his former assailant.

With a grunt of either anger or contempt the big man slowly raised his arms, releasing Markus as he did so. Jack followed suit. Markus sprang away and reached eagerly for the gun on the floor.

LUCKILY one of the uniformed men got it first. For Markus' eyes were blazing with a demoniac gleam. He pointed an accusing, trembling finger at Jack who stood with his arms raised high above his head. Jack's right side had begun to feel strangely wet and hot. Slowly he felt a warm stickiness flow down across his thigh and down his leg. A curious faintness was creeping over him and the hall began to spin crazily before his eyes.

"Say, listen!" It was the big man who was speaking. "You damn hicks give me a fat pain. Take a look under my coat here. I'm a Bernard Agency man and if there ain't something rotten here I'm the Prince of Wales!"

Flipping back the big man's coat the leader of the guards revealed the badge of a private detective. "Say, what the hell——" he began. The big man interrupted.

"Don't say it——I agree," he said. He had assumed command of the situation. "One of you guys keep these two covered," he continued sharply pointing to Markus and Jack. "I wanna take a look in the office there."

The others hurried down the hall and a moment later a shout summoned the single guard who'd been left covering the irate Markus and the weakening Williams to bring his captives down to the office of Markus & Epstein. There on the new carpet lay the rotund figure of Henry Epstein, a neat hole bluing the center of his forehead. Upon Markus' request Jack was searched and the diamonds easily found. Markus started excitedly to state Jack's guilt.

"Wait a minute Markus, wait a minute," cut in the agency man curtly. "I was hired by your murdered partner there. Epstein was wise that you'd taken this guy Williams, an ex-convict, into the office—he had a lot more sense than you thought he had. Told me not to let this Williams fellow run any errands—didn't trust him —nor you either!

"Remember that guy Sanders?" he continued, eyeing Markus malevolently. "Well, last week we picked him up. We'd been after him for two years. Didn't know who he was for awhile —got him on another job but finally we made him spill. He told all about that frame-up you and him worked on Williams here an' how you sold the diamonds while he was beating it an' never did split with him. Epstein told me he wondered how you got the money to buy into the firm—though he didn't say much. Business was rotten, I guess, an' he needed some new capital. He was a real clever fellow."

Williams was swaying unsteadily on his feet though his eager mind was grasping every detail. The big man turned savagely on Markus. "Say, what was that shot I heard when I was battling this kid out in the hall?"

"Why—" stammered Markus, "why —that was when Williams shot Epstein and stole that package of diamonds you found on him!"

"Applesauce! That story don't come near fitting though it would have if I hadn't tried tuh collar the kid," stated the big man. "How in hell could the kid shoot Epstein when him and me was doin' a Gus Sonenberg out on the parquet? Answer that one, Markus!"

Markus subsided weakly. With difficulty Jack spoke. "Mr. Markus gave me a job—to help me," he said. "I thought you were a hold-up man an'

if you'd gotten those diamonds off me no one would ever have believed that I hadn't stole 'em myself."

"I know it, kid," said the big man kindly, "Markus had another sweet little set-up all arranged for you tuh fall into." He looked at the guards. "Do you get it?" He sounded enthusiastic. "He gives the kid here—an ex-con—a job, hands him some diamonds tuh deliver, then bumps off his own partner, rings the bell that keeps the kid from gettin' outa the building an' then says that the kid murdered the partner an' stole the diamonds!" He looked in admiration at Markus. "Boy, what a head!" he said. Then his glance swung toward the sprawled body on the floor. "An' yuh know, it might have worked, too," he said reflectively, "if the kid here hadn't put up such a battle with me. Yes, sir, it sure might have worked."

As he spoke Jack William's knees gave way from under him and he fell in a heap alongside the body of Henry Epstein. Without making a move to pick him up the big man looked down at his limp figure with the suspicion of a smile on his grim face.

"The lad's all right—just lost a little blood," he said. "He'll be one happy fella when he comes to. This little affair and Sanders' statement clears him."

The guards were busy putting the handcuffs on Alex Markus who seemed more dead than alive and offered no resistance. Jack Williams was stirring a bit on the floor.

The big man turned and gazed for a moment at a certificate hanging on the wall.

"Wouldn't yuh know it?" He turned to one of the guards and waved a hand at the neatly framed paper. "Life insurance for 100,000 berries made out to the missus. I said that little Epstein fella was damn clever."

SIGNS and PORTENTS

W E'RE not superstitious as a rule and signs and portents usually leave us cold and anything but quivering with excitement. However, we did have a premonition about three months ago, and now it seems that it's coming true with a vengeance. Our usual attitude of scepticism toward such forewarnings has consequently taken a serious beating and we're debating whether we ought not to take up fortune telling in a big way and capitalize on our oracular aptitudes.

All of which is just prelude to our confession that we had more than a bit of a suspicion that DIME DETECTIVE MAGAZINE was going to go over with a bang. Now it seems that suspicion has turned into reality. If the stack of letters which meet our eyes every morning from the pleased readers of the first two issues is any indication, our belief in the success of the new magazine has been amply justified.

Thanks for the interest you've shown. We appreciate it and hope that you won't cease to keep letting us know your reactions, preferences, taste in authors and type of stories. It's your magazine and we want to build it according to your specifications. If you'll keep on helping us as you have already we'll try to do our part. We liked it from the very beginning. We felt that you would and now you've told us so. That just about covers the ground so what do you mean——depression! It's a minus quantity where DIME DETECTIVE MAGAZINE is concerned and it's going to become more and more minus as the months go by.

With your help we're going to map out a program for this new year that won't be easy to beat. Our line-up of authors and artists is going to get better and better as the year advances and if you don't agree with us that DIME DETECTIVE MAGAZINE in 1932 is the most amazing value on the stands—— We were just on the verge of breaking out with another premonition so maybe we'd better not ride our qualities of second sight too hard. We'll let the forthcoming issues speak for themselves and you tell us if we've guessed wrong.

Now it's high time we changed the subject and turned to the real reason for this department, which is letting you in on the know about the personalities who make the magazine the thrillspecial it has become.

M YSTERY and detective fiction is a field that one usually thinks of as being the particular and special province of men writers. This is more often the case than not. However, there are a few authors of the opposite sex who have achieved eminent success with this type of yarn. Such names as Anna Katherine Green, Mary Roberts Rinehart and Mary Carolyn Davies naturally stand out alongside those of the foremost male exponents of the mystery story. And this month DIME DETECTIVE MAGAZINE opens the issue with a thrill-a-minute yarn by Madeleine Sharps Buchanan, a writer who ranks in the top row of detective fictioneers.

Mrs. Buchanan writes us from her home in Philadelphia that she started writing when she was seventeen. She began by doing work for the Philadelphia newspapers and has contributed to over thirty magazines since that time. She also writes for the movies and cited Dangerous Business, starring Constance Talmadge, as an example of her work in that field.

She began writing as a hobby but has lately devoted most of her time to it. Originally trained as a musician she turned to fiction writing and what was once her hobby has now become her profession while her music has become her avocation. Apart from her work she gets most of her pleasure and relaxation in driving her car. This summer, while on an automobile trip in Maine, she saw a lake like the one she has described so effectively in The White Diver of Death. She heard from one of the natives of the region a yarn about a ghost which was once supposed to have haunted the lake. It was a disconnected story, hardly more than a snatch of an idea, but it furnished the nucleus for the yarn you have just read.

If Mrs. Buchanan's automobile trips furnish the stimulus for her to do as thrilling yarns as the one woven around the murders at the lake let us insist that she go touring at least once a month.

I will train you at home to fill a BIG PAY Radio Job!

125

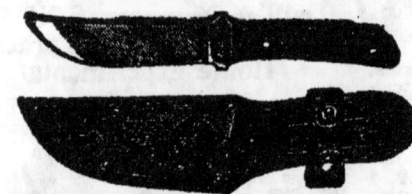

126

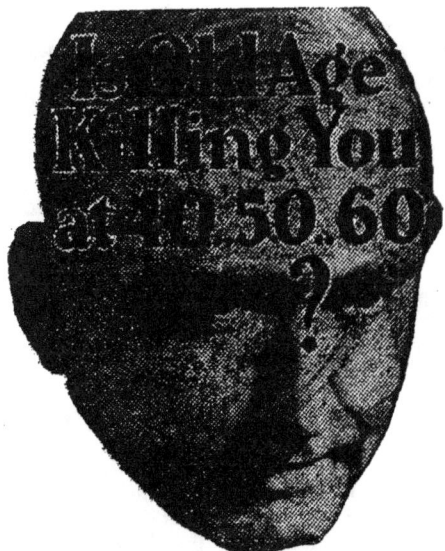

Are you aging too soon . . . getting up 5 to 10 times at night . . . is vitality ebbing steadily away . . . are you definitely on the down grade, half-living, blue, depressed, subject to chronic constipation, chronic fatigue, backache, foot and leg pains? Then look to the vital prostate gland.

New Facts About the Prostate Gland

In men past 40, do you know that these symptoms are often the direct result of prostate gland failure? Are you aware that these symptoms frequently warn of the most critical period of a man's life, and that prostate trouble unchecked usually goes from bad to worse . . . that it frequently leads to years of fruitless treatment and even surgery . . . that it even threatens life itself?

FREE to Men Past 40

No man past 40 should go on blindly blaming old age for these distressing conditions. Know the true meaning of these symptoms. Send for a new, illustrated booklet, "The Destroyer of Male Health," written by a well-known American Scientist, and see if these facts apply to you.

There is little or nothing that medicine can do for the prostate gland. Massage is annoying, expensive and not always effective. Now this scientist has perfected a totally different kind of treatment that you can use in your own home. It employs no drugs, medicine, or violet rays. It stimulates the vital prostate gland in a new natural way, and it is as harmless as brushing your hair. 100,000 men have used it with remarkable results.

Swift Natural Relief

Now physicians and surgeons in every part of the country are recommending this non-medical treatment. So directly does this new safe treatment go to the prostate gland that noticeable relief often follows overnight. So remarkable are the results that you can test it under a guarantee that unless you feel 10 years younger in 7 days you pay nothing.

Scientist's Book Free

Send now for this Scientist's free book and learn these new facts about the prostate gland and old age ailments. Simply mail the coupon to W. J. Kirk, president, 5549 Morris Ave., Steubenville, Ohio.